# THE GAME

*Also by A.K. Shevchenko*

Bequest

# THE GAME

### A.K. SHEVCHENKO

headline

First published in 2012 by HEADLINE PUBLISHING GROUP

1

Cataloguing in Publication Data is available from the British Library

ISBN 978 07553 5639 3 (Hardback)
ISBN 978 07553 5640 9 (Trade paperback)

Typeset in Garamond by Palimpsest Book Production Limited,
Falkirk, Stirlingshire

Printed and bound by CPI Group (UK) Ltd, Croydon, CR0 4YY

Headline's policy is to use papers that are natural, renewable
and recyclable products and made from wood grown in sustainable forests.
The logging and manufacturing processes are expected to conform to
the environmental regulations of the country of origin.

HEADLINE PUBLISHING GROUP
An Hachette UK Company
338 Euston Road
London NW1 3BH

www.headline.co.uk
www.hachette.co.uk

To Dima, Masha and Tanya – always

They are playing Tony's
game again . . .

# PART 1

# T *for Tepee, Tube, Train and Taxi*
# O *for Odessa*
# NY *for New York*
# S *for Strasbourg*

*Only those who leave will return.*
*If you want to come back,*
*You have to leave first . . .*

Gypsy song

# T FOR TEPEE, TUBE, TRAIN AND TAXI

## T for Tepee

### Tony

*Parramatta, Sydney, Australia*

The evening sun flickers through mosquito screens, making the shadows fluid, the gestures incomplete.

I check everything again – tickets, passport, keys; hesitate for a moment, wondering whether to hide both photographs in the drawer, put them in my bag or let them wait for me here, on the side of the desk, still aspiring to freedom. Those images have been a part of my life for too long. In fact, they have become my life.

There is too much grass in the first photograph, too much sky, and the three boys looking into the camera seem smaller, younger than sixteen.

It is the last day of school. Their ties are loose, their jackets are off, but they are not relaxed. There is something in the way one has put his hand on another one's shoulder, gripping it tightly; something in the expression of the third boy's brown eyes, in his raised eyebrows – as if he is trying to ask a question – that makes them look anxious and uneasy.

I am not in the photograph. I am taking a picture of the day that divides our lives into 'before and after'. The day that they might have buried deeply into the boxes somewhere in the attic, might have torn, crumpled, shredded a long time ago, but which is engraved into their memories just as it is into mine.

The second photograph is one of my most treasured possessions.

It is not an official version, not one of the many published on the front page of the newspapers, in textbooks and academic volumes, not the one my father has on his desk – every nod, every glance scrutinised and interpreted by scholars worldwide.

It was taken over six decades ago by somebody short, snapping from behind the first row of official photographers – an amateur who has caught history slightly off guard, giving it a different perspective.

The backdrop is cluttered with dark suits and heads, with the odd face looking at the lenses of official cameras higher up. These are not the stern, concentrated expressions of advisers from the official versions: there is a lot of pipe-smoking, hair-adjusting, turning away . . . The image is framed by the white archways of the palace, lit by the chandeliers of the hall behind.

Three men sitting in the foreground form a separate group – like the schoolboys, waiting for their history lesson to begin, each one of them with his own expectations.

It is a warm day, and the winter sun over the bald head of one of the men makes his thinker's forehead even larger. He is clutching a heavy fur hat and smiling into the camera, ignoring his adviser, who has leaned over to whisper something crucial.

A pale man in the centre is looking beyond the camera lenses, as if he can see something on the horizon, in the future of the world he is going to leave in less than three months. His prominent chin and thin lips are the features of a man with huge willpower, diminishing fast.

The third man looks composed, in total control. His hands are firmly clasped, his legs in shiny army boots are tucked under the seat. The peak of his cap is covering his eyes, casting a dark shadow, but I can see that he is hiding a smile, though his lips underneath the moustache are not smiling. He knows why they are all here, and not in Constantinople or Athens.

The caption under the photograph reads: *Churchill, Roosevelt and Stalin. Crimea Conference, Yalta, 4 February 1945.* It is the beginning, the first of eight days that would divide the world.

I am the only one who knows what connects those two

photographs: the three great men who changed the course of history, and the three schoolboys who are about to change it again.

Long shadows are sliding down towards the stacks of books now, taking the light and the life with them, making the images static again. I realise that I have been stroking the photographs absent-mindedly, as if trying to iron out the past, with no avail – yet . . .

I have decided: I am taking the boys with me, but the three leaders can wait for my return here, on my desk, slipped under the files. If I ever get back to this clearing between the mountains of books, of course, to those summits of knowledge left unconquered. I have won over the rest of the house, though it is hardly a triumph. It has been a year since Ruth left, and my possessions are gradually capturing her space. They started tentatively at first – a shirt on her chair, a newspaper on her bedside table – before spreading over the sofa, seizing her side of the bed . . .

At the moment, my house does not live up to its official name, proudly displayed outside: it is more of a tip than a chief's tepee.

The name, which became such a permanent joke, is hardly a joke any more.

'*Tepee*? Why, Tony? You can't dismantle your house and take it with you, if you ever decide to move back . . .'

'Your garden is so overgrown, mate, this place should be called a tree house . . .'

'You're a Pom, whatever you try to pull! Wear moccasins, put on the war paint, but your accent and your blond hair will give you away!'

'Hey, Black Eagle, you should stop drinking KC – not a Chieftain's beer. Here, I brought you a bottle of Khan Superdry, that's the lager to go for . . .'

I am sticking with The Tepee, whatever they say – it's the only connection I have with my past and with the first photograph. With the game we played then and the one we are about to play now.

It has taken me months to plan it all. To visit locations, to set up the clues. I sent the letters over a month ago, and though I don't expect any response, I know they will come. Blackmail? No need. They will play, I am sure of it. They don't know what I am going to say, what I am going to do, so they will be there.

The game will not work without all three of them, and they know it as well as I do – I need Levi's analytical genius, Jonty's bravery. As for Max . . . How could we ever play any game without Max?

Will I recognise them? I wonder. Jonty will be looming over the crowd, still stooping slightly, aware of his height; Levi will be late, I am sure, and wearing old-fashioned glasses – I can't imagine him without them.

I can still see them now, at our last Tepee Council – Levi puffing, diving into the safe dark space inside the mulberry branches hanging all the way to the ground, crossing above us, creating a tepee-shaped haven; Jonty bouncing impatiently on one of the split trunks outside the tepee; Max spread on the grass, his eyes half closed, humming, sun playing on his face . . .

I get up and close the window, saying goodbye to my garden, to the path that leads past overgrown bushes, past a mango tree, to the old mulberry at the bottom.

This tree was the reason I bought the house in the first place. Mulberries are almost human – I thought it then, and I am sure of it now: their leaves are heart-shaped; their berries turn the colour of flesh and then of blood, before covering the grass with purple stains. And when the berries are gone, the autumn leaves curl, hiding their sharp edges in the final act of self-protection, as if they are in pain – just as I want to do sometimes . . .

I put the photograph into my travel wallet, lock the bag and stride out of the house, never looking back – it is only ahead from now on. It is going to be a long flight and a long game, but I cannot get on with my life without playing it again. It's time.

# T for Tube

## Levi

*London, Northern Line*

I am surprised it took him so long. I expected his letter earlier, maybe ten, fifteen years ago, not now. Twenty-five years, after all.

An envelope with a koala stamp was sandwiched between the invitation to yet another bar mitzvah (where do I find the gift money?) and a letter informing me that I am lucky prizewinner N7345 (maybe that's the answer to the bar mitzvah gift).

Koala equals Australia, I thought. I don't know anybody in Australia, except Tony – though what do I know about him now? That he lives in Sydney, managing his father's mining companies no doubt; what else?

It was only when I heard Sami banging on the bathroom

door, shouting 'Raya, get out, you've been in there for ages
– I'll be late for school! I'm bursting, honestly . . . Do something, Dad, tell her, she doesn't care!' that I realised I'd been
staring at the letter for a while. One line was dancing in
front of my eyes (were my hands really shaking?), in his
familiar, still so familiar handwriting, sharp and decisive:
*We haven't finished the game, gentlemen. The meeting is under
the clock at Waterloo on Sunday, 23 September, 10.30 a.m.* Just
like that – blue ink, bold letters, as if we stopped playing
yesterday. No contact number, no return address, no ifs or
buts. I don't need to ask why.

Of course I am going. It's so easy: Northern Line, thirteen
stops. Unlucky number – not that I am superstitious or
anything. I can't wait to see him, the boy who gave me my
first chance . . . my only chance so far to be special.

I loved everything about him. The way he would hide an
invitation to the Tepee Council in the most unexpected of
places – in a shoe, inside a maths book. The way he would
give me his broadest smile in front of all 'Tony's hangers-on',
stopping me in the corridor during break – 'Hey, Levi, got
a sec?' I had a lifetime for him.

I was always late for the Tepee Councils, panting across
the rugby field to the mulberry tree, my pulse racing, my
brain clicking: the scale of punishment if . . . the consequences of . . . the long-term effects when . . .

But then how could one calculate the blast of excitement
that swept over me when he said: 'Why don't we . . .' that

electrifying thrill of our first tasks, the fun of yet another game?

Tony's games made the world more manageable. They were proof that if you planned carefully and played smartly, you could get away with anything in life. And we always did, didn't we? Until that last game . . .

*Under the clock at Waterloo . . . 10.30 a.m. . . .* His choice of meeting place is spot on, I think – hardly original, but perfect for a blind date. And this is a true blind date, this meeting. What if I don't recognise him? More importantly, will he recognise the plump Jewish boy in the balding man in a slightly crumpled suit? True, I am still chubby, and I still wear glasses, and there is an eternal Jewish melancholy reflected in my eyes, as Dana keeps telling me.

It is a different type of sadness, Dana, I think but will never tell her. It is not the despair of an outsider, of an immigrant's son any more. Now it is the doomed expression of a permanently exhausted man with zero expectations.

'You are not just letting yourself down, Levi, you are letting all of us down . . .' Dana and my mother don't speak for weeks, but somehow they have both got the same phrases honed to perfection.

Will Tony ask me about my life now? I wonder. If he does, I'll tell him that I am a GP in a respectable north London area, a proud father of three teenagers, that my wife is a Sophia Loren lookalike, even though her nose is slightly longer and a touch more crooked.

I am not going to confess to him that after three births Dana's nose is the only reminder of that likeness to Sophia Loren. Her nose, and the arguments in true Neapolitan style. She always wins them, of course she does – her name means 'judge' in Hebrew after all.

Tony won't need to know about the interminable coughing children I see day in day out, about Mrs Rosenblum, who shuffles into my surgery at least twice a month for her life-saving one-to-ones. On the days of her appointments I dish out apologies to other patients, stay after hours filling in records, only to come home to Dana's 'Mrs Rosenblum again?'

I might, just might admit to him how much I am looking forward to playing, how I have already accepted his new plans, yet unknown . . .

'The next station is Waterloo . . .' The tube is surprisingly crowded for a Sunday. A weird bunch of people in my late-morning carriage: tourists lugging heavy suitcases with labels you can study geography by; builders, their scuffed heavy boots splashed with paint, talking to each other in languages made of consonants; pensioners with trolley bags, mums with prams . . . When was the last time I did Sunday tube travel? And on weekdays I am already somewhere by this time of the day – treating, visiting, striving, completing. Not enough, apparently, as I get home to the regular 'You are letting all of us down . . .'

I want to adjust my walk as I step off the escalator, so

that I look confident and relaxed, but my shoulders betray me and stiffen, my legs turn soft, and I end up dragging my feet – a successful family man of forty-two walking like a seventy year old. I am early, eight minutes early, and relieved – he probably won't see me walking. Or maybe he will – is that him, at a Costa coffee table, smiling? No, far too young, and his smile is not for me – a girl in a bright red jacket has just waved back.

I turn to look at the crowd around me, but none of them looks like Tony: a grey-haired oversized American arguing with his wife; a girl with panda eyes, her mobile glued to her ear; a taut, strained woman, studying the departure board; a tall man in a North Face jacket, absorbed in his copy of the *Guardian* . . .

I look up at the clock and start counting the minutes, trying to ignore the panicky thoughts hitting me now at the speed of a commuter train. What if it is going to be just me and him? *Gentlemen*, he wrote, but what if the others refuse to come? It happened such a lifetime ago that sometimes I wonder whether it happened at all.

'Put these events and your fears into this envelope, gentlemen, and we'll come back to the game when you are ready,' was what he said. What makes him think we are ready now?

I turn my head to look at the far entrance to the station, and I see Tony. He is walking straight at me, grinning, as if somebody has stretched his skin too much and it has cracked, leaving creases around his eyes. It is definitely an older, more tanned version of him: his open smile, his straw hair, just as unruly, bleached by the sun. But it is the way he walks that is so instantly recognisable – a nonchalant strut that drove all our teachers mad. I take in the way he is dressed – an open-necked shirt, jeans and a well-cut navy blazer – and wonder if it is Australian formal or British casual. But there is no time to decide, as he is only ten . . . seven . . . five steps away, and I don't know what to do – shake his hand or hug him.

But he saves me, because he nods and pats my shoulder, mine and the shoulder of the man who is standing next to me – the lean man absorbed in his newspaper. Yes, he nods to us both – to me and . . . to Jonty! – and says the words I have been waiting to hear for the last twenty-five years: 'Morning, gentlemen. Glad to see you both. It's time we finished our game.'

# T for Train

## Jonty

Ha, ha and ha. No way am I going. No way. Technically I am not even in Britain, I only come home for the weekends. OK, and for holidays and meetings, but he doesn't need to know that. I could offer dozens of excuses – can always say that I didn't receive the letter, or had a speech to make, or was travelling to . . . Anyway, why should I even justify myself? This whole story is so deep in the past that there is absolutely no point in reopening it again.

That's what I thought when Lucy handed me the letter three weekends ago.

'Australia . . . who is it from?' she asked.

What could I tell her? About the game and about our oath? About the secret from all those years ago, which would threaten our organised family life, rotating around Minnie's ballet classes and her pony club, weekend dinner parties and other mandatory, routine things?

I'm not surprised he has found my address after all these years. Not difficult, given my high profile. If he's trying to blackmail me . . . Totally laughable. What for? He doesn't need the money, surely – he has always been the wealthiest of us all.

Power? Lobbying for some European project, maybe? But then he doesn't realise my influence is pretty limited, and things tend to be decided without me – even at home, where the family reorganised itself to regard me as a 'weekend daddy'.

I was still searching for an answer when Minnie's squeaks saved me.

'Mummy, take that angry pepper away from me! I wanted to see how it gives "a bit of a kick", as you said, but it doesn't kick, it bites my tongue, it's really nasty!' She was banging a toothmarked chilli on the table, tears streaming down her face. What a relief it was when Lucy rushed to her rescue, leaving me with my thoughts.

Unless Tony sent this letter to all of us. Then it is even more laughable. He doesn't really expect us to play after all those years, does he?

We haven't kept in touch, and I had to dig out our school photograph just to remember the faces.

Here is Levi, a step away from me and Max. He was always

treading behind us, as if expecting to be shooed away any minute. His myopic eyes are made larger and sadder by thick lenses, his shirt ends are hanging out, a button in the middle is missing, revealing flabby whiteness to the world. Only his clenched fists, held tight against his trousers, betray the worry and the fear of that day. I wonder if he is still as scruffy now. I heard he had become a doctor – a profession too tidy for a mathematical genius.

I am frowning at the camera, looking fretful and forlorn. My fingers are locked on Max's shoulder, tighter than necessary, as if I am trying to support him. Max is the reason I did not invent any excuses when I received the letter. That's why I am going – to protect Max again from whatever Tony may come up with. How often have I thought of finding Max, contacting him? I was following his career for a while, read about his appearances at Ronnie Scott's, about his tours, even went to one of his concerts ten years ago and hid in the back rows with the cognoscenti, but then I stopped tracking him – what's the point? My Max is in the past, not in the present. In that sunny day when he played on the lawn, eyes closed, his saxophone shimmering in the sun, the day that changed our lives for ever.

*The meeting is under the clock at Waterloo . . .* Tony could have suggested something less clichéd, less predictable, but knowing him, there must be a hidden agenda, something along the lines of: 'Four clock faces showing the same time . . . and our four faces showing *at* the same time.'

That was a big part of the game's attraction then – his play on words, his ability to fascinate us. We never knew what he would come up with next. He would raise his brows, his piercing grey eyes looking for some end goal in the distance – something invisible to us but so obvious to him – before saying dreamily, unhurriedly: 'Why don't we . . .'

He would stop there, not raising his voice to get our attention, not interrupting our banter, just being silent for a moment before coming up with something mischievous, dangerous. Tony always managed to dress up the plan, cover it in layers of temptation, frothy like the skirts of a cancan dancer.

*Evil is always more fascinating than kindness.* Where have I read that?

I don't know why we called our meetings a council – it wasn't one really. Tony was slowly, skilfully dragging us into the net of his ideas. He would light up the plan with neon funfair signs (*come with me, boys, let's go for a ride!*), and leave us to step into the game.

Looking back, I was always the first one to take the bait. Levi would still be thinking, doing his usual analysis-conclusion thing, before saying: 'Yes, let's.' Max would be in his dream world, humming something, missing the whole idea, only to wake up and say: 'Great, I'm in.'

But I was the one who was already in, always first, body and soul. Was it because of my boundless energy then, only controlled on the rugby pitch? Or because I didn't want to be left out, didn't want to miss Tony's plotting, watching his plans developing in the darkness of our den, our mulberry tepee, like old photographs – a smile, a note, a hiding place – before the whole picture would almost reveal itself, still lacking lustre, waiting for its glossy finish?

Almost, as we never knew what the final goal was. It was up to Tony to focus the camera and shoot.

I often wondered why Tony started the Tepee Councils, why he invented our game. Now, looking back, I understand.

We all had our different worlds outside the tepee, worlds with clear rules, already set by others.

I had my rugby team, where it was enough to know who played as flanker, fly half or full back. You knew their positions and accepted that they would be there to support you, no conversation needed. Levi had his streamlined existence of maths formulae, Max was testing the laws of harmony with his jazz, but Tony . . . what world of rules outside the Tepee Councils did he have?

He was too small for rugby, not as smart as Levi, not as musical as Max. So he created his own world, with rules crafted by him alone, the reality reflected in his games as in a hall of magic mirrors, becoming ugly, twisted and funny.

What sort of psycho game has he invented this time? Will he punish us for the past by trying to change our future? Not that I am going to surrender to his powers now . . .

I have to come clean. I am not going just to see Max; I

am going to face Tony as well. I need to show him that I am a leader now, not a follower. I am out of that dark tunnel, just like the train is out of it now, swishing across the Kent fields, taking me to face my past. It would have been so easy a few years back – straight to Waterloo. I have to get the tube and change lines now. Still, I arrive so early that I end up marching round the perimeter of the station twice, and still have plenty of time to linger under the clock. The only escape from this absurd situation is to hide in a newspaper. I'm not really worried, am I? Apprehensive, maybe, about what he is going to tell us. I am trying to concentrate on an article in the *Guardian* about the pros and cons of the new waste-processing unit in Sheffield, but end up staring at the page, absorbing announcements, voices, accents in the surround sound system of the big station:

'Platform nineteen for the ten twenty-three Southwest Trains service to Richmond . . .'

'Unattended . . . removed without warning . . .'

'Mum, can you, like, pick me up from the station? I don't know what time yet, I'm not on the train, but can you pick me up? It will be today sometime, like in the next hour or maybe two, I don't know yet . . .'

'Honey, what do you mean, there is no train to Windsor? Check the board again. The guidebook said Waterloo. If you had found the Hertz parking lot at Heathrow, honey, we would've been on the freeway by now . . .'

My hiding place doesn't work, because when somebody

touches my shoulder, I know that it is not a rushing passenger, bumping into me in his desperate last-minute race for the train. It is a different sort of nudge: between a friendly pat and a steely grip, reminding me of that hold he always had over us.

I look up, and there he is, his grey eyes smiling. He is as detached and laid-back as ever, nodding to me and to the balding, round-shouldered older man who is standing right next to me (God, is this Levi?). And then he says the words I've been dreading to hear all these years, the words I convinced myself he would never say again: 'Morning, gentlemen. Glad to see you both. It's time we finished our game. Shall we wait for our last player? I am sure he will come.'

# T for Taxi

## Alex

It's not me they'll be waiting for, not me at all, so I can be invisible under that clock – watching their encounter, listening to their stories. I'll be a silent observer of their tense laughter, of their hugs and embarrassed silences. I'll have the luxury of making the decision – whether to step in or not.

'Where to, Alex?' Joyce turns to me.

'Waterloo, please.'

I could have easily taken the train – there is a direct one from Richmond – but I need these forty minutes in my secure, comfortable world, created by Joyce. She has been driving me for five years now, through traffic jams and everyday dramas, to presentations and clients' meetings, to dinners and the divorce proceedings. And to the funeral.

Her cab is my only refuge now; her cockney 'Orright?' has been my pick-up in the morning and my lullaby for months.

Joyce's courageous back absorbed all the shocks of the custody battle, as she listened to my stifled account of the proceedings ('not the best for the children, not a responsible parent . . . travels all the time . . .'). But I *am* a responsible parent, and I am paying for the schools, and finally, hopefully, we have found a lovely au pair. I am the best parent they have got, I am sure of it. And I have the court decision to prove it. The kids are *all* I have got after the divorce, and after the funeral . . .

'Nearly there,' Joyce shouts.

I have decided. I'm not going to join them. I'll watch them meet and then quietly slip away, unrecognised: I am the last person they will expect to be there. Only thanks to Joyce's skilled manoeuvring around a newly erected 'Road Closed' sign, I am *not* the last. I think I am the first one to arrive, actually, as I don't see anybody remotely familiar under the clock yet.

Sunday stations have a lingering rhythm, not the fast-moving flow of the weekly commute: American tourists, teenage girls geared for shopping crusades, roast lunch guests . . . So Jonty, marching past me waving his long arms, really does stand out. It is definitely Jonty, his rugby shoulders still broad, with a jacket and a rucksack to match. I watch him doing his second station tour, wondering whether he will at least give me a quick glance. When he eventually stops under the clock, I hear loud puffing in my left ear. Only one person I used to know produced those noisy whale sounds. Now they belong to an overweight man in a crumpled navy coat covered in dog hairs. Levi. I knew he would come. I glance at him, taking in the way he looks now – his black hair receding, brown eyes panicky behind the lenses, stepping nervously from one foot to the other – still clumsy, still lost.

Good peripheral vision is something I am blessed with. Though my eyes are glued to the departure board above me, I am watching Jonty and Levi, both of them refusing to recognise the teenage boy in each other, absorbed in their anxious waiting for Tony. As the screen changes to page three for the fifth time, a new sound joins Levi's puffing. I hear 'Morning, gentlemen', and it takes all my willpower not to turn my head and look straight at him. Because I hope, just for a fleeting moment, that Tony will notice me first, recognise me, and it will become a very different meeting then.

But I am still invisible, watching them and the departure board, taking in every detail. They are standing there, greetings and graces done, joined together by their waiting for the boy who was the heart of their gang, the soul of their game. They will not leave until he is here. I should really move away, buy myself a coffee, sit at a table and watch them from a distance, but I can't. They are the magnet for my grief. I have to share it with somebody who does not yet know. Because they were his friends, after all.

I cough – not to clear my throat or attract attention, but to stop myself from choking. I don't want them to see me crying.

They turn and look at the tall, blonde woman with revealing grey roots standing too close to them, already a part of their group. I am aware that I have probably swallowed most of my lipstick, licking my dry lips, that my hair is tousled and my black coat is hanging off me shapelessly, a couple of sizes too big for me now.

I had planned to be theatrically casual. 'Hello, boys,' I was going to say, but instead it all comes out in blurted, blunt blobs: 'Morning, guys. You must be waiting for Max. I'm Alex, his twin sister. Remember me? Max won't come. He died six months ago. I found Tony's letter in his post. If it's OK with you, I'll be playing instead of him.'

I am getting used to this now – people not knowing what to say, what questions to ask, what words to offer. I have lost count of how many times I have felt guilty over these last six months, as if I am the one putting everybody through this embarrassing situation.

'Let's talk somewhere else,' says Tony finally, turning and leading the way, as if he already knows where this 'somewhere else' is. We follow him in an uncomfortable, broken single line, not looking at each other. But as he struts down the stairs and out of the station, crosses the road, dives under the bridge and turns to look at us, as if checking that we are still there, we all know where we are going. When was the last time we came here – twenty-three . . . no, twenty-five years ago. It was Jonty's idea then, to try out this new jazz bar, where single women mixed after work with older concert-goers, where the younger student crowd was welcome too, with a free flow of alcoholic drinks. Jonty invited Max, and we all went along, the hangers-on, an addendum to their outing.

I remember that bright evening well – piano music in the background, a syncopated melody echoing in the arches, huge paper sunflowers hanging from the ceiling, the smell of sausages with foreign names – merguez, saucisson . . . and me sitting next to Tony. It was the first time he touched me. Not deliberately, I thought. His knee brushed past my knee once, then again, and then his leg just stayed there, slowly welding me to him joint by joint: the side of my shin, then my knee, the warmth of his thigh until we were fused at the hip. There was no rubbing, pushing or leaning, just a comfortable sense of well-being, and neither the flimsy cotton of my summer dress nor the rough denim of his jeans could stop this feeling, so natural and so inevitable.

I am quietly relieved, as we walk in today, that the bar has a different energy now – it would have been wrong to lead us somewhere jovial. It is modern and trendy, with tall hotel-style flowers, not the place of vibrant primary colours it used to be.

Today Tony is sitting opposite me, slightly sideways, on the edge of a leather chair, hiding in his intangible bastion, fortified by all those years, by our marriages, by the distance between London and Sydney. We are divided by an invisible barrier, cemented by grief, by my news about Max. The marble-topped table is too narrow, making our togetherness incongruous.

We sit in silence, listening to the trains clattering above us. We don't know what to say to each other. Four strangers, connected by a too remote past. What can we talk about – work, children? Where do we start?

'So, how is life in Sydney?' Levi asks finally, to break the silence.

'Great,' is all Tony says, then he leans over and pulls his bag on to his lap. It is a battered leather satchel, the kind you see in old war films, or that a seasoned teacher would carry. I am expecting Tony to take out a family photograph: on the beach, or on the balcony of a white penthouse flat overlooking the harbour, or in the garden having a barbie. Most likely with a Barbie wife.

But instead he pulls out a bunch of envelopes and says: 'Just to remind you, as we haven't played for a while.' He is matter-of-fact and methodical, as if this 'while' was a couple of months and not twenty-five years. Classic Tony: economy of words, economy of gestures.

'You are getting two envelopes each,' he continues. 'The first you can open now. It sets the location. The letter inside the second envelope sets the task. It is for your eyes only – if you share the task, you'll ruin the game. I suggest you

open that envelope after the meeting, somewhere else . . .'
He stops, as if unsure about what to say next, then adds:
'. . . somewhere safe.'

What does he mean by safe? I wonder. Behind a locked
bedroom door so that nobody can see, or with people around
and safety in numbers?

'I can tell you, that the first stage has to be completed in
two weeks and that we'll finish the whole game on the
twenty-fourth of October.'

'What do you mean, the twenty-fourth of October?' interrupts Levi. 'I thought it would be just today, for old times'
sake.'

But Tony carries on, undeterred, as if he hasn't heard Levi's
question.

'We will meet twice more. The next meeting is in a fortnight, same time, same place. You remember, I'm sure, how
the stages of the game used to be assigned: fact-finding –
Levi; distraction – Max; and action – Jonty.

'However, as the stakes are higher than in our previous
games, stage one – fact-finding – has to be played by everybody. When we come back here in a fortnight, the next task
will depend on the results of the first stage.'

I look at the boys – Levi is too stunned to comment,
Jonty just purses his thin lips tighter. Or maybe they don't
want to talk in my presence. I remember their coded
messages, phrases unfinished, knowing smiles exchanged
when I was around – an unwelcome intruder from a female

world, from a different school, trying to break into their club.

Nobody speaks while Tony hands out the envelopes. Levi is the first to open his location one. The envelope is sealed and I notice that Levi is tearing it hurriedly. Curiosity or nervousness, or both?

I can't read the text in the envelope, but it is not difficult to read Levi's face: he doesn't understand it. It takes a whole long minute before he confirms: 'I just don't get it. What does it mean?' He shows us the note.

*Enough water – in French. Say it backwards.*

'*Assez d'eau*,' says Jonty glumly. He is obviously annoyed by the childishness of the note.

'What do you mean?' Levi looks at him.

'*Assez d'eau* means "enough water" in French,' says Jonty. 'I have been working in Strasbourg for years; I'm supposed to speak French by now.'

Levi whispers: 'Au . . . dess . . . ah,' and suddenly his face glows with the delight of discovery. 'Odessa! I should have known it, of course. That's a standing joke: a city built on the beach, but where there is never enough drinking water.'

There is another piece of paper in the envelope, full of columns of dates and places – I guess it is a travel itinerary. Levi pouts like a capricious toddler about to cry. His glasses have slipped from the bridge of his nose, but he does not seem to notice.

'I thought we would have a day of the game in London,

just to see each other again, but this . . . this is unreasonable, absurd even, and . . .' He stops, searching for the right words.

'You don't expect me to drop everything and travel there, surely,' he continues. 'I am a very busy man with a tight schedule. I save lives, by the way.' He fidgets under Jonty's scowl. 'OK, maybe not always, but I make people feel better. I have a bar mitzvah to attend on those dates you are suggesting, I have family duties . . . We are not sixteen any more! And by the way, if you are thinking of playing abroad, there are some of us, who work for international organisations, who would be better suited to . . .'

'Why are you looking at me?' Jonty's thin lips become a tight thread. He drums his fingers on his crumpled copy of the *Guardian*, studying the copy of the 1920s poster on the wall. He hasn't opened the envelope Tony has given him yet. 'I'm not playing at all,' he says finally. 'Silly and childish after all these years, you said it yourself.'

Tony remains silent, looking not at Jonty but at the bar behind him, waiting. I am studying Tony's face – following the shape of his eyebrows, counting every wrinkle around his eyes, noting the sharpness of his nose. As I get to his lips, he suddenly looks at me and smiles, as if reading my thoughts.

'I am playing,' I say hastily. I have already opened Max's envelope and read the first page: *The city of clear answers.*

That's easy; I work it out straight away: clear answers can only be 'yes' and 'no' – 'Y' and 'N', or NY. New York – the city I am so familiar with. I wonder what sort of challenge will be given in the second envelope, but remember that I should not open it now. At least I am learning their rules quickly. I look at Tony, and for an instant I wish I had kept that hairdresser's appointment to colour my grey roots, that my nails were not so schoolgirl-bitten and my coat was a touch more fitting. I want him to see me as a woman, not just as Max's sister. But this moment passes and I remember why I am here.

'Is the ticket paid for, then?' asks Levi. I notice that his pout has disappeared. He has adjusted his glasses as well.

'Non-refundable.' Tony looks straight at Levi now.

'I wish you had asked me first,' says Levi grumpily, but I can see that he is getting used to the idea. 'Maybe I'll play just this bit, for three days, to check it out . . . I always wanted to go to Odessa – and with a free ticket now,' he adds.

'I'm not getting involved in this,' snaps Jonty. He has not touched his envelope. I notice that he has not touched his coffee either.

Tony looks at him and asks: 'Then why are you here?'

Jonty opens his pursed lips but says nothing. Instead, he stretches, throws the *Guardian* on the table next to ours and starts on his envelope.

'A city that unites.' He reads the first line, then snaps: 'Christ, it's like going back to school! Whatever you want me to find out, I am not going to do anything beyond my remit! I am a high-profile politician, after all.'

In a skiing jacket and a yellow tie dotted with elephants, he looks it, too.

'And then? What's next? What are we playing for?' asks Levi.

Tony smiles – no, his eyes smile just a little – and turns to me, ignoring Levi. 'Thank you for stepping in, Alex. It's as if Max is playing with us again.'

That's it. I'm hooked, held prisoner by his chilled charm and that quiet, inscrutable confidence. We all are.

I remember how he does it – he has already worked out the whole game plan, even though he gives out single tasks. We won't know the purpose of the game, the final outcome, until he decides to tell us. Or rather, *if* he decides. That's what made it such fun for them in the first place, all those years ago.

I have no time to comment, because Tony is already fastening his satchel and getting up, scalding us with the sudden open smile I remember so well.

'So, what do you say . . .' He nearly says 'gentlemen', but remembers that I am here and stops. 'Why don't we have another quick coffee before we all go?'

Then he looks at us and repeats slowly, adding a totally different meaning without changing a single word: 'So, what do you say . . .' and pauses, giving us our last chance to opt out. 'Shall we?'

# O FOR ODESSA

**Levi**

Of course I said yes – to another coffee and to the five-day trip. When I opened the location envelope at Waterloo, saw the tickets and worked out that the route would take between a hundred and nine and a hundred and twelve hours to complete, moving across three countries (flight to Romanian Constanta, three days on the Black Sea cruise, a day in Odessa, on to Yalta in Crimea, and another day at sea before flying home from Istanbul), I had to think fast, think of something dull and unpleasant (Mrs Rosenblum describing her haemorrhoid troubles for twenty minutes?) to hide the joy I was not expected to feel.

'So, you just assumed that I would take five days out of my busy schedule for this?' I asked Tony then. I had to; that's what a responsible adult is supposed to say, isn't it? What I was thinking was: What great duties in your life, Levi, can stop you from taking your well-deserved five days of holiday remaining from last year? A free cruise? Without Dana? All she needs to know is that you're away at some medical conference . . .

I felt the same thrill an intrepid adventurer might feel sailing into unknown waters: neither storms nor the hardships of the voyage would stop my discoveries.

Levi, I said to myself three days later, walking into my cabin on the cruise ship, you could get used to living like this. A balcony with a moving sea view, a wardrobe far too spacious for my single bobbled pullover, a bed for two? You could accommodate four here!

I went out to dinner in anticipation. I'm on my own, I thought. The bed is vast; who knows . . .

It took me ten seconds to realise that I *will* sleep alone for these three nights, as I am easily the youngest here by at least two decades.

It is a small ship, with passenger numbers running into a couple of hundred, not thousands, and the appearance of a new man was noticed by everybody, especially as I am the only one who does not fall into the two categories here – grey hair or no hair at all.

I made a silly mistake at dinner, admitting to my table of immaculately dressed, powdered and cologned OAPs that I am a doctor. So now my sweet and curious ladies are pursuing me with the same questions again and again – about the new treatments for hair loss, and whether rheumatoid arthritis can be treated with antibiotics.

They are all on the explorer deck now, my doddering Marco Polos and Columbuses, looking at the unknown shores on the horizon, listening to the loudspeaker roaring in bursts, scaring the seagulls:

'. . . approaching the port of Odessa . . . plorer deck, where you can see the panorama of this ex . . . ry city. Stretching along the coast . . . port, one of the largest on the Black Sea, straight . . . ront of you . . .' The loudspeaker coughs, pauses for a moment and continues again, roaring louder but clearer:

'The city was founded by Catherine the Great in 1794, when the Russian empress decided to create a southern port to develop European trade. She granted the new port great privileges: Odessa basked in the tax-free regime of "porto franco" for forty years. The possibility of quick money at the "Russian El Dorado" attracted thousands of opportunists from all over Europe: Italian merchants and French chefs, British engineers and Greek sailors. As a result, Odessa, the youngest European city, also became the fastest-growing. Over fifty languages were spoken here in the nineteenth century. People settling here craved their big adventure . . .'

I am up for my big adventure too. I followed all the precautions when I opened the second envelope at home last Sunday – slipped it inside a newspaper, which I took to the bathroom, waving it demonstratively, buying myself some reading time and some privacy. The task was very short, like a military order, two lines only:

*Find out the best way for retrieval and secure delivery of Exhibit X to the UK.*

Big deal, I thought, reading the description of Exhibit X below.

Not 'big deal' the way my Sami or Raya or Nathan would say, shrugging their shoulders – everything is either 'whatever' or 'big deal' for them. I sometimes wonder if they have English lessons at school at all.

This is a genuinely big deal, a weighty piece of history, though I wouldn't know where to start guessing why war documents signed by three world leaders more than six decades ago are so important for our game. I have no doubt that this is a key task, though. I wonder if Tony chose me for it because I can speak the language, or because he believes that my fact-finding skills are still the best, if a little rusty after twenty-five years.

I was always the FF man – the fact-finder, in charge of logistics and research. 'Good Jewish brain,' Tony used to say. Jonty, with his 'dive-in', Action Man approach was an obvious AA, 'act alone', while Max . . . who could do DD, 'do and distract', better than Max? In fact he didn't even have to do anything – his smile turned everybody to warm wax, letting him mould any shape he wanted.

The loudspeaker bursts into life again: '. . . As a result of attracting traders from all over the world, Odessa built its own Babel tower of languages, its own unique dialect, with Russian, Yiddish, Greek and Italian words mixed together. The spirit of traders, sailors and smugglers created the city's unique attitude to life as a big game of chance – playing to win and laughing, singing and eating through the dark times. Odessa's carefree mentality is so distinct that there is even an international club of Odessites.'

I am a member of that club, I think.

Smart play, Tony, as usual. You knew that I would not say no to a stopover in Odessa, the city of my childhood, before my task destination. The only thing you misjudged was how I would stand out in this Saga crowd – unless that was your reminder that I always was and always will be the odd one out.

At school, I wasn't the outcast at all. More in a caste of my own. Not one of the untouchables, rather one of the unnoticeables. The invisible poor Jewish boy from north London on a maths scholarship to a top school.

I wasn't pushed in the corridors or elbowed in the canteen. Nobody noticed me, that's all.

'Going into town tonight?' somebody would say – through me, to a boy behind me or beside me.

I tried at first – stretching out my hand, saying hello. But after shaking my hand, after a second of hesitation they would go back to their conversations, to their plans and games, and I would become invisible again.

So I devised ways to deal with that. I would wander along the corridors looking busy, get to the classroom a minute late, as if I had been doing something crucial, far more important than lessons.

After all, this was better than being pinched and pushed and teased for being top of the class. I had had enough of that in my previous school. Here nobody laughed at me, but nobody noticed me either.

Until one day. 'Hey, Levi, got a sec?'

The loudspeaker coughs again, interrupting my thoughts: 'A sec . . . a second reminder today. The bars will be open for the next thirty minutes. Don't forget that twenty loyalty points will get you a complimentary drink . . .'

Twenty loyalty points for a free drink . . . And who said loyalty cannot be bought?

Mine was bought with one smile, one question: 'Hey, Levi, got a sec?'

I didn't even realise he was talking to me at first. A boy who was picked up from school at the end of term by a uniformed driver in a Rolls-Royce, while I was sent back on a bus; whose tennis racket was signed by a Wimbledon champion; whose holiday trips were the ultimate explorer's journeys, avidly discussed by everybody.

Tony was popular, but so was his money – he was always generous with tuck shop treats for friends and 'guests', as he called the hangers-on. And this boy was now standing there smiling broadly – was his smile really for me?

'Your logical reasoning is pretty impressive, Levi,' he said. 'We could do with some of that. Could we have the honour of your presence at our Tepee Council tomorrow at five? Maybe you could give me a hand – we'll go via the tuck shop first, to pick up supplies for the chiefs. What do you say?'

And so I became a member of the Tepee Council.

The others never really accepted me in the same way. Max didn't even notice me at first, but then he often wouldn't notice the world outside his music; you wanted to shake him occasionally to wake him up. Jonty was . . . no, he wasn't disapproving, we just existed on opposite fringes of the same universe, satellite planets on different orbits. Both of us lived in north London, often the last two left on the end-of-term school bus on the way home, Tony's spell diminishing with every mile further away from Oxfordshire. By the time we reached the North Circular, the spell would lift and we would take a sober look at each other – were we really friends?

Jonty's parents were well-known left-wing journalists, and I imagined him coming home to great debates over some relaxed shared stew, to his mother's 'This is exactly what the government should be doing to solve . . .', while I was returning to the world of after-hours leftovers at the disinfectant-smelling tables of my parents' café, to my father's silent presence in his broom-cupboard-sized office, doing the accounts. He was always around, my father – moving, smoking, eating, watching TV – but his energy wasn't there. It was as if somebody had switched him off, unplugged him when he left Odessa, and another charger was never found.

I was so excited to call him on Sunday: 'I am going to be in Odessa next week, Dad!'

I was hoping that I could swap my secret ('. . . only for a day, Dad, but can you please keep it to yourself, don't tell Dana') for his stories about about his . . . about *our* life in Odessa, but all he said was: 'Not many friends left there to see. Bring me a couple of photographs of our old courtyard at least, if you can.'

The loudspeaker bursts into life again: '. . . As you . . . taking in the . . . norama of Odessa, stretching . . . the coast, its green boulevards and gardens, you will be surprised to know that Odessa had no trees at all and the buildings were covered in sand and dust from the steppes for the first ten years. It was the Duke de Richelieu, the governor of the city – yes, the same Richelieu who fled the French Revolution and later became the prime minister of France – who created the oasis here. Odessa owes its splendid French boulevards to his vision. Though Richelieu was considered a romantic figure by many of his contemporaries, and Lord Byron even chose him as a prototype of Don Juan in his drama, the real-life governor was hard-working and practical. He ordered all the ships coming into the port to bring ten saplings each, and was often seen watering the gardens himself. Every afternoon he walked around his Odessa, saying that it was his job to look at the buildings, to listen to the citizens and to get the feel of the city.

'Today we would like to invite you to follow the steps of the great Frenchman. During our excursion on shore, we are going to stroll along the Primorsky Boulevard, founded by the duke, and will see the monument to Richelieu, who is watching the port below. Other highlights of the tour include the opulent Opera House, the Potemkin Steps and the world-famous "genius factory" – the Stolyarsky violin school, where the pupils have prepared a short concert for you. The tour buses will be waiting on the quayside. The ship will be moored at number nineteen. We are leaving for Yalta at . . . thirty. I repeat, at three . . . ty.'

The Odessa of the loudspeaker is not the city of my childhood.

Our courtyard in Moldavanka was a poor relation to the city of regal boulevards. I remember our green veranda, which gave us a ringside view of the talented if not lavish productions beneath: communal dramas, scandals and romances unfolding, framed by the screens of drying sheets. What else do I remember?

The dovecote in the corner, and Uncle Vasya in his perennial red vest, showing us his prize pigeons.

The only time my dad smacked me, when a passer-by dragged me, then five years old, from the street back into the courtyard and shouted up at the veranda:

'Whose boy is this? He was begging on the street, asking me for some ice cream money. Shame on you all, parents and neighbours – can't any of you feed the child?'

And the day we left, of course; I remember that day well. It was the first of September, and I was seven, looking forward to my first day of school, but instead I was woken up in the middle of the night by my father. I was not allowed to ask any questions about where we were going and why, but I knew that we were leaving for good.

I can still see it – a milky dawn, the deserted courtyard, two women on a green bench, the younger one – my mother – sniffing loudly, wiping her tears; the older one, my aunt, staring into space, her heavy hand on my kippa. It was too early for the spectators to shout to my mother from their verandas: 'Rimma, where are you dragging the boy so early? Banya is still closed!' Only two of Uncle Vasya's pigeons were watching us, from the top of the rickety ladder.

My aunt died last year, but some of those dramas might still be re-enacted by the same actors. I wonder if I will recognise them when I get to see my old courtyard today – it is only a short ride from the port.

The Saga explorers are already making a beeline for the bus, armed with guidebooks and cameras. I'll skip the tour; the violin geniuses of the Stolyarsky school will have to perform to a group without me.

The taxi is taking me back to my childhood, through cobbled streets, past baroque buildings and fancy boutiques.

'We are on Deribasovskaya now,' announces the driver.

'Why is it so important?' I ask, teasing him.

'You don't know Deribasovskaya?' He abandons the steering wheel for a second and turns to look at me in shock. I decide against further questions – I want to get to my courtyard in one piece.

'You speak with an accent,' continues the taxi driver. 'What backwoods do you come from that you don't know the most famous street in the world? How far away from Odessa do you live?' he asks.

I calculate quickly, converting miles into kilometres:

'Two thousand three hundred kilometres, give or take.'

'No wonder,' replies the taxi driver. 'Only somebody from so far away, from some deep provincial, rural place, would not know Deribasovskaya.'

I keep a dignified silence – my limited Russian vocabulary does not extend to an explanation that Deribasovskaya Street, together with Primorsky Boulevard and Pushkinskaya, was an integral part of 'Going to Town' operations when I was a child. In preparation, my mother dragged me away from my street pals and forced me into a chequered shirt, clean shorts and scuffed sandals, not forgetting to wash my neck and ears. That was the down side. But 'Going to Town' also meant a trip on the tram, crossing the invisible line from poverty to white cruise ships in the port, ice cream in the town park, the world of sailors, uniforms – students from the naval college – and short skirts, tanned legs and giggles on Deribasovskaya . . .

Now we are crossing this invisible border again, only in reverse. The houses here are reduced in size and grandeur; they are two- or single-storeyed, with archways leading into the wells of courtyards. The taxi driver zigzags to avoid the potholes.

'Here is your number twenty-four,' he says as he finally stops by the arch, 'but I can't drive into the courtyard, will have to wait for you here – look, somebody has blocked the entrance with an old fridge. And as you walk under the arch, look at your feet – the sewer manhole might be open.'

Where are those sceptics who say you cannot turn the clock back? Here I am, walking through the passage, past rows of rusty mailboxes, ducking under the low-hanging pipes, avoiding the manhole and the old fridge blocking half the entrance, into the space criss-crossed by the washing lines, into my childhood . . .

The dovecote where Uncle Vasya showed us his prize pigeons is still there, looming over the courtyard, with its perches and holes; there is a proper window underneath in a tiny box of a room – maybe this is Uncle Vasya's Rapunzel tower, his retirement escape from his witch of a wife?

Two trees in the middle of the courtyard – did we have those trees when I was a boy here? – growing by themselves, just like we did, occasionally watered and fed, but rarely noticed.

A car is parked next to the trees. How on earth does he drive out if there is a fridge blocking the entrance? He doesn't have to, I guess, judging by the lack of two wheels and the rusty bonnet.

My eyes are scanning the ground-floor level, not approving of its geometry – not a single straight line, just a hotchpotch of mismatched, patched corrugated fences of different colours.

I nod to a man painting his door sky blue in a vain attempt to hide his poverty, stumble over a communal table propped against one of the tilted fences.

Did I really live here? How would my life have turned out if we hadn't left?

This is my staircase. Second step from the top – that is where my friend Kostya fell and smashed his head while his parents were at work. Who was it who took him to hospital to have stitches, which neighbour? I remember his mother's shouting match with Sonya, our courtyard scandalmonger – Sonya complained that Kostya's blood had splashed all over her sheets and she couldn't wash it off. I look up at the once-green verandas of the first floor, and my eyes register with relief that at least there is some uniformity there – all the verandas are glassed and partitioned now. But how can the modern-day kids hide, play, race along the perimeter of the verandas?! Do they have to go up and down, negotiate dozens of those dubious metal stairs, without banisters, with bolts sticking out? I bet more than one head has needed stitches after a game here.

Which flat was ours? Here is number five. I remember that Lora, a sweet six-year-old first love of mine, lived here, so I should be going up the stairs to number four . . .

I open the veranda door straight into the back of an armchair with a fluffy pink gown on it. There is something in the gown – or rather somebody, as the dandelion remains of somebody's hair are sticking out and the sleeves reveal the parchment skin of hands covered in age spots.

'Are you from the council?' asks the woman in a voice surprisingly loud for such a feeble frame. 'When are you going to demolish all this at last?'

'No, I . . . I am just visiting,' I say, trying to find a doorbell.

That brings another memory: a doorbell was the first thing I made with my father, my first experiment in electricity. We bought a cable at Kirovsky flea market, found a very cheap bell there too, probably stolen, and I built it all by myself, my father watching me proudly, giving me occasional advice. Three months later, somebody cut my bell off – probably the same person who sold it to us in the first place.

We never replaced it, but who needed a bell anyway when you had the neighbours' telegraph warning you who was coming to see you? No bell could compete with: 'Hey, Levi, go and tell your mother that there is an urgent telegram for her – don't worry, nobody died, you have relatives from Kiev coming to stay, though I don't know which is worse . . .' Or: 'Levi, tell your father that Uncle Sasha and Uncle Nyuma are waiting for him in Mitzkevich Park, cold beer, crayfish and playing cards ready. But if your mother is at home, say that there is an emergency at the shipyard and he has to leave immediately. Don't mix those two messages up, boy, or you'll get a smack from both your mum and your dad!'

Where have these voices, these stories been hidden until today? So, no doorbell. Does this mean that whoever lives here now *still* has not replaced it thirty-three . . . no, thirty-five years on? I knock on the door.

'Knock louder,' suggests the woman in the pink gown. 'She is probably still asleep.'

I do what she suggests, but nobody opens it, and I just stand there, by the door to my childhood, knowing that it has closed for ever.

Well, at least I can take a photograph of the courtyard for my father.

As I go down the stairs, carefully balancing on every step, I am followed by stories about the council visiting and never doing anything, about the food prices nobody can swallow.

I am crossing the courtyard, trying to find the best spot for the picture, when the door of my old flat suddenly opens and a head full of dishevelled curls peers out. I turn back reluctantly and go up the stairs again.

The curls belong to a girl in her early twenties in a flimsy nightgown.

'And who are you?' she asks irritably. It is almost midday, but I have obviously interrupted her sleep.

'I used to live here,' I offer as explanation, only to get 'So what? *I* live here now' in return.

The girl tosses her crow-black curls, yawns and stretches

like an overgrown kitten. And I am smitten, totally. I have never experienced anything like this. Not a stir of desire, not a thought in my head about how pretty she is. I am caught in a tide, and walking away now means swimming against the current.

'Are you Jewish?' I ask her suddenly, as if this will bring us closer.

She laughs. 'Not everybody in Odessa is Jewish, you know. I am Greek,' she replies, and then adds pensively, 'I think I am Greek. Most of the Jewish families from this courtyard emigrated, thank God – snotty children, a stench of herring . . . I wasn't living here then; the neighbours told me.

'There was a Jewish granny in a flat downstairs, but she died last year. She was OK, though – very quiet, very sad. Everybody either laughs or argues in Moldavanka – that's the way it is here, it is as natural as sea air – but she was really unhappy. I tried to make her laugh more than once, but it didn't work, so I gave up.'

'I know,' I say.

'What do you mean, you know?' The girl is waking up.

'That sad Jewish granny was my aunt.'

The awakening is complete. It takes her a couple of seconds to put two and two together. 'So you are from the Shapiro family then? Why didn't you say so? OK, come in, walk around if you like.'

I want to tell her that my name is Freiman, Levi Freiman, but she has already wandered into the depths of the room to find her gown. She wraps it around her nightdress, only to pull the fabric down to reveal pert suntanned breasts.

I follow her into the dark corridor, like a dog pursuing an unusual, beguiling scent.

Did we really live here? How on earth could we all have fitted into this flat? One room, with a window overlooking the veranda, and a tiny windowless nook for my trestle bed – even the most dishonest estate agent would not have dared to call it a second bedroom.

'Coffee?' the girl offers, eyeing me with curiosity. 'I was about to make myself one.

'Your accent . . .' she continues, putting a Turkish coffee pot on a tiny cooker. 'You are from that emigré bunch, aren't you? The ones who come to Odessa on cruise ships, visiting their childhood and all that. So where do you live now? Brighton Beach in New York?'

Her knowledge of the history of Jewish immigration does not extend beyond America's 'little Odessa'.

'No, I live in London,' I reply.

I have never seen one word transform somebody so much, unless you count my daily professional destiny-changing words: 'operation', 'urgent X-ray', 'complications'.

'London?' She leaps away from the sink as if the water she is filling the kettle with has scalded her. 'London, England, you mean? My ex lives there.' She stops and smiles at me, for the first time, and the smile is bold and inviting.

Not inviting conversation, but leading me into temptation.

She leans over me – you couldn't get closer if you tried here, in a flat of this size.

'Would you like something stronger than coffee, maybe? How long are you in Odessa for? I am free today, so I could show you around if you like. We could go to the City Gardens, or to see our famous Opera House, or, better still, I'll take you to see our Monument to the Bribe. Just tell me,' she laughs and pats my hand, sending an electric shock down my spine, 'where else in the world can you find a monument to bribes, set in bronze? We had an official inauguration, all the papers wrote about it . . .'

Half a day with this girl . . . I would really love that. Or rather, I would love to spend time with her scent, her laugh.

'My taxi is here,' I sigh. 'But I'll be back soon, I am sure.' (Am I really?)

She looks at me seriously. 'Come back from your London, then. I'll be waiting.'

We sip strong coffee on the veranda, crouched over a tiny rickety table covered with oilcloth. The pink-gowned granny is sitting in her torn armchair, with her back to the table – this is her observation post, placed in a strategic position to oversee the doves flying into the dovecote and the bosomy matron downstairs who is shifting sheets drying on the ropes so that she can hang up her generously sized knickers.

'Lora!' Granny suddenly stands up from her armchair, shaking her dry fists indignantly. 'This is not your day to hang out the washing!'

Lora . . . did she say Lora? Is this puffy-faced mountain of flesh with greasy hair my childhood love?

The matron abandons the rope for a second and shouts back:

'It *is* my day, Nina Solomonovna, it's Wednesday. The Mogilevskys left for the beach early and didn't have time to take their sheets off, so I am moving them. What's the problem?'

'What on earth are you doing, Lora – you'll crease their sheets!' Granny does not give up.

'So,' says Lora defiantly. 'Mogilevskaya will come back from the beach well rested; she'll have enough strength to iron them!'

Granny catches the phrase and sends it back, continuing their shouting match: 'I know you have a mouth that never closes and you've got ten words ready when somebody offers you one, but can't you show some respect for a change? Mogilevskaya has three children by different fathers. She deserves a break occasionally! Stop scrunching her sheets!'

Lora stops for a moment only to take another pair of huge once-pink knickers out of the basket, then starts again: 'We know . . . we all know why there are different fathers – who would put up with Mogilevskaya for longer than one week? And we have had to live here with her for years . . .'

It could be somewhere in a back street of Naples, this scene: sheets and tongues flapping in the sun, the heady cocktail mix of the sea breeze and the stale smells of the courtyard. Except this is Odessa, and the melody of my childhood.

'Look, Mr Shapiro, look at this.' The girl pats my hand again. 'Our local attraction, this wall of art . . .'

She points at the grey wall of a shed, half covered with pieces of broken tiles, all different sizes and colours, arranged in an order my logical brain is struggling to understand.

'My neighbour is a tiler,' the girl explains. 'He brings those bits home and just sticks them to the wall. This is his mosaic vision of the world, he says – grey life with occasional bright glossy squares. "We should see beauty everywhere," he says. Can you see any beauty here?'

And she nods towards the corrugated fences, the rusty pipes and the pile of empty beer bottles by the dirty barbecue stand in the centre of the courtyard. I glance at her profile furtively and take it all in – the freckles on her cheekbones, the sleep line still running across her cheek, her black curls stroking her neck, that captivating divide in the décolletage of her gown . . .

'So', the girl turns to me, 'can you see any beauty here?'

'Yes,' I say firmly, tearing myself away from the chair – the taxi driver is already in the courtyard, scanning the verandas, ready to catch his non-paying passenger. 'Yes, I can see beauty.'

Only in the taxi do I realise that I didn't take a photograph for my father, nor did I ask the girl for her name or her telephone number. Never mind, I know her address – my childhood address – so when I am here next time . . .

It isn't until we get to the port that I remember that this is not the place I came to visit. Odessa is just a stopover on my way to locate Exhibit X. I wonder whether the word 'Odessa' is going to be there when I open the envelope with my next task. I try not to think about the Greek goddess stretching and yawning in her flimsy nightgown. Surely I would not accept the next stage of the game plan just to see her again?

# NY FOR NEW YORK

**Alex**

I tried to do it without him, honestly, tried to be a big girl. Started early, as well – too early, maybe that was the problem . . .

I couldn't sleep, because NY never does, all the guide-books will tell you that, its midnight melody punctuated by the staccato of sirens. So I took a taxi to Smalls club in the early hours – just to see Max's favourite place for a jam session. Iron door, narrow stairs, tiny hall with subdued lighting and mismatched chairs. The brick walls and the younger crowd both a sophisticated shade of green. Not a lot of space, nothing impressive, I thought.

I missed the first session of the evening – the solo guitar – and walked straight into a quartet with alto saxophone, just like Max's, and stayed to the end.

The audience here didn't just listen to jazz, they *were* jazz. The stage and the spectators blended together in this small

New York basement, making laughter, the clinking of glasses, scraps of conversations part of the music. In this tiny space you had to be in tune with every sound, and trust the music to lead you. No wonder Max loved it.

I read about this place in Max's last interview. And about his favourite city to visit, too. 'Music travels better across the water in Sydney,' he told the journalist. I would never have discovered my brother's favourite club, his favourite city otherwise. When did we really start growing apart? When did this cord that twisted us together snap? Or did it disintegrate slowly, day by day, thread by thread? I read somewhere that in rope bridges the construction is based on the strength of a single steel thread – if one thread snaps, the whole rope will break in thirty minutes. And then?

It was almost morning when I left the club after the jam session. I decided to wander, but you can't circle in this city, you can only march, manoeuvring around garbage bags left on the sidewalks for the morning collection. The grid of streets is lined and numbered for you, to keep your confused world under control.

After an hour of marching, my body clock whispered suggestively: 'Nearly lunchtime in London ... Look – Greengrass ... fresh orange juice and salad, maybe?'

Never trust the signs of New York ... Boy, I have been in this city so many times, I should know that by now. What made me think the 'Greengrass' over the deli referred to freshness?

# The Game

I trusted my eyes more than my nose, and my eyes let me down; they should have read the whole sign: 'Barry Greengrass, sturgeon king.'

That's why I am now stuck at this white Formica table, glassy-eyed trout staring from the counter at my breakfast in disbelief.

It is a true masterpiece, I must admit. I could easily enter my plate for the Turner Prize under the title 'Volcano': a yellow mountain of an omelette, dripping with the crusts of fried onions, erupting in slivers of salmon . . . Another plate with a cream cheese and lox bagel, and a huge mug of brown decaffeinated liquid of unknown taste and origin next to the plates. All this at six a.m., only because I said one word – 'Yes' – to a waiter's question: 'Full New Yorker breakfast for you?'

The air is filled with unusual words – *blintzes, mini babka, novie* – and the pungent odours of smoked fish and garlic pickles.

Good morning, New York, the city of clear answers. Tony was right, as usual. I wonder what his . . . what our game is about this time?

How many times did I watch them, envious, while they were plotting, trying to read into their tasks, waiting for them to finish their sentences, hung in mid-air . . . How I hoped they would include me, but it only happened once, in that last practical joke on Norman – and even then all they did was ask me to lend them my longest, loosest dress for a day.

And now here I am, finally playing and wishing that Max could play instead of me, just this once.

Looking back, they were totally incompatible: a music escapologist, an immigrant Einstein and a goofy giant with a perfect rugby tackle. But there was one Magnet they all had in common – Tony.

I don't know anything about his life now – the name of his wife, the age of his kids. How does he cope with the carefree Sydney 'B's: Bondi Beach and barbecues? Does he miss London at all?

Well, I can't ask now, it will have to wait for the next meeting. Tony wants his answers loud and clear, about something completely unexpected.

*Obtain a <u>full</u> copy of the Crimea Conference (4–11 February 1945) Protocol of Proceedings from the UN archives*, says my task.

Why? The heck would he tell me. I'll have to wait until the end of the game. Is Tony into changing history now?

*Obtain a full copy of . . .* How much easier can it get? I thought. Don't they have internet search engines in Australia? Unless his secretary does it for him and he hasn't got a clue.

Only the internet search came back with the result: *The matching records are prevented from being displayed for security reasons.*

Of course. 'Alex speaks fast but thinks slow,' as my ex would say. Tony must have known that already. I know why he chose Max for this task, too: because of the person in our lives – Max's and mine – for whom it would be easy, easy . . . but whom I am so reluctant to ask.

'My wife speaks fast but thinks slow' . . . What were Simon's other sayings?

'Money makes the world go round, so Alex runs after the money and everybody runs around her' was another one.

'Alex and her Alexythimia. . .' I'm so glad I can't remember many. But maybe with Alexythimia he was right, sort of.

'Alexythimia,' my ex-husband would wink to whoever was listening at the time, 'is a condition named after my wife.' He found a definition in a dictionary somewhere, and could cite it by heart any time, anywhere – it gave him real joy to nail those words into my promotion ladder: 'A person with Alexythimia has difficulty identifying the feelings of others and demonstrates a lack of understanding of those feelings. Typical responses are concrete and logical, often to the exclusion of emotional reactions to problems . . .'

Maybe he was right – I have no emotions left. No pain or grief or regret. But I do feel guilty.

Guilty that I am here and will be flying home on Sunday, when I really should be taking Luke swimming and Emma to her friend's birthday party this weekend. Christina will manage, bless her, she is a responsible and kind kid, though I wonder sometimes who is looking after whom – is it twenty-year-old Christina looking after my children, or my seven-year-old son and nine-year-old daughter looking after her?

They have grown up so much in these two years, my kids – and not just out of their old primary school sweaters. They have grown out of their old questions too: 'Why is Daddy talking so loudly?' 'Why is he not living with us any more?' and 'Why are you crying in the bathroom, Mummy?' We have a new set of brighter, bigger questions now: about another sleepover for Luke, and a swimming gala; about a spelling competition and a present for Emma's friend. And I won't be there on Saturday to answer them.

I feel guilty that I haven't told anybody in the office about the trip. Robbie knows, of course he does, he is my right hand, but for everybody else it's 'family circumstances' – pronounced in a grave and measured way. Otherwise, at our bank, the marketing director who jumped ship, leaving the cargo of sales projections, key accounts, profit margins and performance indicators unattended for a whole two days for a reason that is not life-threatening, would certainly be called to the dock.

And then there is the most overwhelming guilt of all, the guilt that catches me by surprise every day, and calls out to me, whispering: Max, Max, Max . . .

I should have tried to tie up that last thread, to hold on to that last hope, but I didn't. I thought my brother was coping after splitting up with Richard – performing, drug-free for months.

I was too caught up in my career, in my divorce, to understand what it meant when Max rang me a week before his overdose: 'I'm not going to the States, you know. Too busy here . . .' I should have realised that for Max not to go to New York, not to go on a tour he had been preparing for a year, it had to be something major, something worth not going for, the ultimate journey . . .

Did he have to stand with a billboard under my bedroom window so that I could see how unhappy he was?

I remember how he tried to do that once – raise a poster in a silent protest, in a desperate attempt to be noticed.

We were ten, back at Orchard Cottage for Christmas from our respective boarding schools. It was the first Christmas without Dad, and Mother decided to throw a showy 'we are fine on our own' party. She *was* fine, come to think of it – flying around, gifting her smile and charm. I was standing by the wall, absorbing the party atmosphere – pearls and perfume, conversations and canapés – but Max emerged from his bedroom with the poster, written in lopsided red letters, and walked around the room, holding it up for all the grown-ups to read. *I am Max* was all the poster said, and everybody found it really amusing – apart from our mother, of course.

Thank you, Tony – at least your envelope has made my world two-dimensional now: guilt plus the need for clear answers, and I am ready to start asking the questions, fuelled by the volcano breakfast.

There must have been extra magnesium in the raw salmon and gherkins, because the walk along the waterfront to the flagpoles of the UN glass building is quick and painless. Until I get there, that is. The building looms over me, reducing me with every step. The giant bronze muzzle of the gun outside is twisted into a knot, but still looks ominous enough to deter me from going any further.

'No entry,' confirms the security guard, and adds, just as I am about to turn back, defeated: 'The Visitors' Centre entrance is on First Avenue at Forty-Sixth Street.' He points at the sign above him saying just that. Yes, ignoring New York signs is becoming my new tradition.

I wish my children, whose complaints about my lack of navigation skills have become the refrain to our lives, were here to witness my morning – here I am, finding the Visitors' Centre entrance, passing through security, discovering the Enquiries Desk on the lower level of the Visitors' Lobby, right across from the coffee shop, all by myself, asking for directions only once . . . OK, twice, maybe.

I am too early – the Visitors' Centre is still closed, so I end up with another mug of brown liquid and study the posters: *Greetings from New York City, UN convoy peacefully sailing, The UN goes where others cannot or will not go* . . .

The girl who welcomes me half an hour later, at eight thirty on the dot, would make a great air hostess – her duty smile is perfect, her navy suit, blue blouse and stripy scarf impeccable.

'Welcome to the UN, an international territory,' she starts cheerfully. 'Our site belongs not to one country, but to all one hundred and ninety-two member states. If you would like to book a tour, you need to proceed upstairs; all the tours start on the main level at the Visitors' Lobby.

'I hope you'll have a chance to visit the Exhibitions Hall and to look around the artwork in the Plaza. Each piece of art has been donated to the United Nations by a member state.'

How many times a day does she chant that? I wonder.

'I am here to enquire about access to documents kept in the UN archives,' I say. 'The full copy of the Crimea Conference Protocol of Proceedings, February 1945.'

The girl pauses for a moment, struggling with a new, unrehearsed notion, frantically searching the database in her head, her smile never leaving her face.

Finally she regains her composure: 'Have you got your ID with you?'

She studies my passport, checking every letter before returning it to me.

'Those wishing to conduct research should first review the relevant printed UN official documents available at United Nations information centres, depository libraries or the United Nations Official Document System. UN documentation provides the context for the Archive Centre's records and could reduce the time necessary for research,' she says.

I turn around to check if she is reading an invisible autocue. Is it really possible for a human being to speak like that?

'You have to fill in a registration form,' the girl continues. 'When you get confirmation that your registration has been received, only then can you make an appointment with an archivist.'

I try a shortcut: 'I am from the UK, I'm in New York only for a day . . .' but she is back into her programmed responses.

'I can see this from your passport, madam. The registration process is mandatory if you would like to gain access to United Nations documents and declassified secretariat records. You have to fill in the registration form . . .'

'What about classified information?' I venture. 'How do I get access to those documents?'

There is so much strain in her smile that I fear she will burst. Finally she processes the information, and delivers another recorded message. I swear I can hear her click.

'You will have to check this with the archivist. To do that, you need to make an appointment, as visits are by appointment and pre-registration only. You should contact the Archive Centre to ensure that your registration form has been received before you can make an appointment . . .'

I am glad that, according to Simon and his definition of Alexythimia, I can't relate to my emotions, otherwise my response would be far too emotional. I would be arrested for grievous bodily harm, trying to find the button to fast-forward this girl.

Instead, I manage a neutral 'thank you' and am about to

leave, bidding farewell to the poster, *The UN goes where others cannot or will not go*, when the chirrupy girl takes pity on me.

'Madam', she leans over to me and lowers her voice, 'the documents you requested . . . I can see on the computer that they are on a third thirty-year security ban. Just to spare you the application process – you still won't get access.'

She *is* human, I think, studying the blue circles under her eyes, covered less thoroughly than she intended. I am relieved to find a crease on her jacket, too.

I give her a genuine smile and retreat to the taxi stand. I admit defeat; I cannot do it without him. But at least I have tried.

'Where to?' asks the taxi driver with a strong eastern European accent. I give his home address, but panic and change my mind by the next traffic lights, asking the driver to take me back to my hotel instead. He says something harsh, unintelligible in his language – about passengers like me, middle-aged, impulsive, scatterbrained women, no doubt.

I miss Joyce, the comfort of her cab, her cockney accent. How I need her no-nonsense comments to pull me together now!

But at least I can get to the comfort and familiarity of the hotel to celebrate my failed attempt to complete this task alone.

This hotel is my safe haven – I don't need to collect loyalty points to be a devoted customer; I am long converted. It is close to everything I want to see and never have time to – Broadway shows, Carnegie Hall, the shops on Fifth Avenue. But I have also chosen it for its proximity to another address – it will only take me twenty minutes to walk from here to his apartment.

A shower and a real coffee at last – I think I am ready for attempt number two. As I come out of the hotel, however, I decide on a brisk stroll through Central Park first, and turn right instead of left, 'because the mood is on me', as Joyce would say.

Central Park's September air is filled with non-city noises: the whoosh of frisbees and the splash of oars, the clink of glasses at the Boathouse terrace. Aren't they all supposed to be at work? But then, so am I.

I decide to sit down for a second, but don't move for a good ten minutes. How pathetic – a strong, independent woman who has survived and weathered many storms cannot persuade herself to walk to a meeting with a man who is already waiting for her!

Urban architecture has always been my saving grace: if you look up, not only do you discover a different world, you protect your eyes too – tears dry up. Tried, tested, guaranteed. So as I finally follow the street grid, getting closer and closer to his address, I keep looking up.

I have never noticed the tower on the apartment block opposite, its cupola and the balcony looming above the

Upper West Side. This could be a perfect place for him to live, as he has always escaped into his intellectual ivory tower, just like Max used to escape into his music. I wonder what his apartment is like . . . is it also in some sort of tower? Nearly there.

On the corner of 73rd and 74th Streets, I check a printout given to me by the concierge. *Upper West Side. A liberal area, popular with families, intellectuals and older people.* The man I am about to see ticks all three boxes. I have no doubt that he can help me. He knows everybody and everybody loves him, wherever he goes. I still do, too. It's not about the asking. It is the first hello that won't be easy.

The doorman of the red-brick building greets me with a smile, not asking any questions – he must have been warned that I am expected. I press the lift button . . . and here I am, outside his door, telling myself that I am here only because no one else can help me to complete this task, to move on to the next stage of the game.

I ring the bell, and he opens the door almost instantly, saying:

'Alex, what a lovely surprise!' It is not a surprise at all; he knows I am supposed to be here. I emailed him and he answered with a single line: *Great, can't wait to see you* – but maybe this is all he can say to me at the moment.

He stands there, his clever grey eyes watching me carefully – he does not know if he should make the first move. I lean against the door frame, wincing – not because the hard edge is sinking into my skull, but because I want to hug him so much that it hurts. Because I realise how much I have missed him and how much time we have both wasted.

Because all I want to do now is blank out my age, my dignity, my strong career woman mask, and throw my arms around him. Hold on tight, nuzzle into his chest – I had forgotten how tall he is, even stooped slightly – and just stand there, in a different time dimension.

I saw him at Max's funeral, but we hardly talked, though ironically it seemed the most obvious place to start again. But I am here now, and I so, so want to tell him that he is the man I have loved for as long as I can remember; that this is our chance, that . . .

Instead I give him my professional marketing smile and say, in the tone reserved for our top clients, aloof and inter-ested, yet not too familiar: 'Hi, Dad. Glad you could see me. There is something I need to talk to you about. Can I come in?'

He hugs me awkwardly and leads me into his apartment – all tidy and proper, the walls the right shade of stylish, a neat row of frames on the sideboard, all sorts of photo-graphs: Grandpa Jack, me and Max aged seven on a beach in Cornwall, Luke and Emma . . . How come? I have never sent him any photos of my children! I get closer and see Max in the background, a happy uncle hugging two happy kids on a zoo outing.

God, I am furious, ashamed of my own feelings, but

furious – Max sent images of my children to Dad, leaving me out of the equation again.

They first excluded me ages ago, when they discovered the bond I could not share. When Max came out and moved in with Richard, I didn't mind, but what really hurt me was that by doing that, he was now one step closer to Dad.

Dad left when we were nine. In my mother's circle, divorce was rare then – change of status was a costly exercise. Divorce because your husband, a leading American lawyer, had fallen for an Englishman, was unheard of and only whispered about. Dad moved back to the States and was banned from visiting us – it was done to protect us, apparently, but for years I could not forgive him for not trying harder. Until I went through the custody battle myself.

'Coffee?' he asks.

'Just water, Dad,' I say. Shame it is too early for something stronger; water might not give me the courage for what I am about to ask of him.

He gets me a glass and sits opposite me on the sofa, not sure what to say or do next. There is a quiet, elegant sadness around him, the understated assurance of a man who has lived and achieved a lot. I am getting used to the fact that this grey-haired gay widower (were they actually married?) in a cashmere polo neck is also my father.

We have to start somewhere. 'How are things?' will not cut it, so I get straight to my task.

'Dad,' I begin, 'I know you are a member of the Committee

on Historical Diplomatic Documentation.' (How on earth did Tony find this out? I never knew; I discovered it from Tony's second envelope – no suggestions, just a fact, a reminder. But there are many things I have yet to discover about my father.)

He nods, surprised. He was prepared for anything – me shouting abuse or hanging off his neck, sobbing; he was probably ready for a muffled request for a large sum of money – but not this.

'There are these files . . . the Yalta ones, from the Crimea Conference of 1945. Your committee classified them as secret again several years ago, for a third thirty-year period,' I say in one breath. 'Could you tell me why?'

It takes him a while to answer.

'How did *you* find out?' he says finally, studying my face, and I have to give him the unforgivable answer, use the one person he cannot check it with.

'Max told me.' I try to sound firm. Am I betraying my brother by saying that, or helping him by playing his part of the game? My father is still looking at me, waiting for a longer explanation.

I think how unconvincing and bizarre my true answer would sound – 'I am just a participant in a bigger game, a piece in a larger jigsaw' – and say instead: 'It's too complicated, Dad. Tell me for Max's sake, would you?'

He doesn't say anything for a while, but when he speaks, his every word is measured, as if he is delivering a speech in court.

'Too much knowledge can be dangerous, Alex,' he starts. 'We actually had quite a debate on the committee deciding how to classify those documents, as the classification directly reflects the level of *how* dangerous "too much knowledge" can be. Technically, those undisclosed Yalta records would not "cause grave damage to national security if publicly available", as per classification of secret documents, and therefore fall into the criteria of "confidential": "prejudicial to national security, causing undesirable effects if publicly available".

'I personally insisted on "secret" classification, however. Not only is the public not ready for the revelations contained in those documents, but I think the undesirable ripple effects could be significant and cause damage. Huge waves from the Black Sea!'

He tries to laugh the story off, and I pick it up and smile; I actually smile at my father for the first time in years. When was the last time I heard him laugh? I don't remember his laughter at all.

He pauses, and I shift in the armchair, in my expectation of the story – just as I did when I was a child, when Dad would read to me and Max. I even remember the stories – the Bakery Bear tongue-twister, *The Adventures of Huckleberry Finn* . . .

'Crimea is an interesting place,' he begins, 'fascinating history, really important strategically as the gateway to all continents by sea and by land. Historically it offered access to maritime civilisations for horsemen from the steppes of

73

Central Eurasia. Whoever you take – Greeks, Romans, Arabs, Crusaders, Genoese, Tartars or Russians – they all knew that possession of the Crimean peninsula would open up excellent trade prospects and make them the strongest power on the Black Sea. The Golden Horde conquered it; the Russians built the Sebastopol anchorage; and this port was fought for in the siege of Sebastopol during the Crimean War, and then again in the second siege of 1941–42. No wonder that Crimea, with its strategic routes, was chosen for the meeting of the three leaders at the end of the Second World War. The issues discussed at that meeting in February 1945 were key for the world order: rebuilding post-war Germany, Japan, Poland, in fact the division of the whole world after the war. It's all well documented in thousands of articles, textbooks and memoirs, as most of the documents relating to the conference are now accessible. Most, but not all. There are three documents still classified as secret, because, in theory, the issues reflected in those agreements could still be raised.'

'What agreements, Dad?' I try not to sound impatient.

He is still a lawyer, my father – his answer reveals only a part of the story, a taster of the truth: 'One of the documents, for example, includes the minutes of discussions about the California in Crimea project.

'When Roosevelt asked Stalin if he could buy the Livadiya Palace and its park in Crimea after the war, as he loved the place so much, Stalin laughed and agreed – you can read this in many textbooks as a funny detail, softening the enormity of the Crimea Conference, but not many people know what is behind that joke.'

'What do you mean by "California in Crimea", Dad?' I ask him, baffled.

He continues reluctantly: 'The Crimean climate is very similar to that of California, and with appropriate invest- ment – American investment, as it happens – it could have become a paradise. Certain families – too well known to disclose – put money into that project and never—'

'What about the other two documents?' I interrupt him, afraid that he will become too engrossed in the details and might decide not to reveal the whole picture.

He looks at me as if pleading with me not to probe any further and to abandon the whole idea.

'There are the minutes of the meeting on creating an independent Jewish republic in Crimea after the war – just think how different modern history would be if Israel . . .' he says, and stops.

'And the third?' I prompt.

'The third document is a codicil to the Protocol of Proceedings of 11 February 1945, which deals with matters of the UN . . .' he answers half-heartedly.

I decide against pushing him. It will all become clear when I read the copies he gets for me – *if* he gets them . . .

'Dad,' I say, looking straight at him, 'would it be possible to obtain the originals of those three documents? With your connections it wouldn't be that difficult, would it?'

What I am asking now probably translates into a breach of the Official Secrets Act, or whatever they call it here. Why am I doing this – not to impress Tony, surely? Is the end game worth such an effort?

'Luke has Max's eyes, doesn't he?' my father says instead of an answer, pointing at the photograph on the sideboard. He is gaining time, I guess.

'He's got some of Max's mannerisms too, amazingly,' I say and add something that might, just might nudge Dad towards a decision:

'I'm thinking of taking Luke and Emma to Orlando over the Christmas holidays – maybe, if you're free, you could join us for a weekend. I'll let you know the dates once I book the flights.'

My father is still looking at the photograph of my children, not at me. He is struggling with a dilemma, which is not really a dilemma any more – he would do anything to keep our relationship going, and if getting the secret documents from the Crimea Conference is what it takes to meet his grandchildren for the first time . . .

'I'll see what I can do,' he manages finally, but I know it's a yes.

'Are you planning to go to Crimea as well?' he asks.

'I don't think so,' I say carefully (no idea where Tony wants me to play next), 'but my friend . . . (since when is Levi my friend?), 'my . . .' (I struggle: business partner, participant in the project – what on earth do I call him?), 'my . . .

colleague,' I decide finally, 'is there now. He has gone to Odessa and then to Crimea as far as I know. He speaks fluent Russian, so . . .'

Dad gets up to open a drawer. 'Guess what? I have only recently discovered that we have a direct family connection with that part of the world and that period of history. How's that for a coincidence?'

He sounds excited, and I can't help noticing the inclusive 'we'. He pulls something out of the drawer. 'I found this in Grandpa Jack's papers when he died four months ago, eight weeks after Max.' (Grandpa Jack died?! I was seven the last time I saw my American grandfather, and I remember that he had huge hands and talked very loudly – I was a little scared of him.)

My father shows me a piece of paper: 'It was in his passport, so it must be something important. And confidential. Just look at the date – May 1945. In Russian! I guessed one word here – *Одесса* Odessa. Haven't had the chance to get the rest translated yet, so I've no idea what it's about. Maybe your . . . your colleague who speaks Russian and has travelled to Odessa could look at it.'

He's asking me to help him! A favour for a favour – fair enough; a business relationship I orchestrated myself. Only he breaks the pattern – sits opposite me and takes my hands, covers them with his, as if trying to shield me.

'Alex,' he says, 'I can't stop you from doing whatever you have to do, especially as you are not telling me why you need to do it.' He looks at me, hoping for an answer, but gives up after a minute of silence.

'Telling you that something is risky won't work – you were always such a daredevil as a child'. (Was I?) 'Just remember that you, Luke and Emma are the only people who matter to me now. Take care. I mean it – really take care.'

I nod, my hands still resting in his. I have nothing to worry about, I have so many men to protect me: Tony, Jonty, Levi (though I have my doubts about Levi). I also have my memory of Max. And now I have my father.

# S FOR STRASBOURG

**Jonty**

The location clue was easy. I come to this city so often that I am practically a resident – I am here again today for the plenary session. *A place UNI-ting a German poet and a French emperor* – of course I know the answer. My tram passes this building now: Strasbourg University, where both Napoleon and Goethe studied.

I am cursing myself for agreeing to do this. I did *not* agree, come to think of it. I was so numb after the news about Max at our Waterloo meeting that I didn't really listen to what was going on. Until Tony handed me the envelope with the location: *A place, UNI-ting a German poet and a French emperor . . .* I mean, how much more childish can it get?

I was walking past the university bookshop yesterday, and they had dozens of quotations hanging on bright ribbons in the shop window – some deep, some trite, but I stopped to read them because one of the quotations was labelled, unexpectedly, 'Odessa humour', under the joke: 'Life is not a referee. It will never give you extra time to score.'

Levi is in Odessa now – does he find it funny? I wonder. And Alex in New York – has she found her 'clear answers'? I could not really tell her at our meeting – or Levi or Tony – that I only came because I wanted to see Max. How could I? So I started opening the envelope just for something to do, and now I am stuck with my first task. *Find out how to invite the Governor of Crimea to speak at an open debate with press present*, said the note in my envelope. It should not be that difficult, actually, given my job.

My daughter is clearly impressed by what I do, even though she is only seven.

'Daddy works as a map, he gives directions to people. I think he is helping lots of people who get lost, because he is always travelling and never at home. But we are OK, Mummy says, because she knows her way to school and to Tesco without a map. I think she isn't sure about the directions to my ballet class, because she sometimes misses the turning when she is on the phone.'

Minnie's teacher told me this.

'So what *do* you do?' she asked, laughing, with benevolent curiosity. 'Are you really a map?'

'My daughter is right,' I said, trying to stand straighter, wishing that I was wearing a suit rather than old cords. 'I am a MEP, only it is pronounced differently: em ee pee . . .'

As I was saying it, I realised how ridiculous it sounded. I was about to explain this obvious abbreviation, to say that it meant 'Member of the European Parliament', to tell her that I was a politician legislating on important issues like mobile phone charges abroad, but then I saw her expression. She was still laughing, only now she was laughing at me.

'Perhaps,' she said hesitantly, just to round off the conversation, 'you should give a talk to the children in Minnie's class one day about what you do . . .'

I was saved by the bell, as I often am in the parliament.

And what *do* I do exactly? I thought then. What could I tell those children?

That when I was elected, seven years ago, I was the greenest MEP both in age and in political affiliation; that I was not fighting with windmills, but fighting for them, keen to vote for renewable energy, for my daughter's future?

My own energy seeped away slowly, through the cracks in the system, starting with the first email:

*Dear MEP, in view of new stringent rules, you have to register for your expenses and be allocated a personal fiscal number before getting access to the EPI portal. For further explanation please contact Madame Chasse at . . .*

Madame Chasse proved to have a very appropriate name – I chased her for a week, only to get the answer: *To receive your registration number, you have to contact Service Payments.*

Service Payments sent me to Service Derogations, who forwarded my email to Service Advances, who in turn had to get the authorisation from Madame Chasse . . . until finally, a fortnight later, I received an email: *Welcome to the web!*

By then I already understood that the web is created by thousands of invisible *fonctionnaires*, who weave it tirelessly with directives, orders, permits and rule changes. All that to make the MEP's life more structured, more comfortable . . . more entangled.

I caught myself on camera the other day. I was sipping coffee – you can't drink it here; it is too strong and too hot to drink (maybe that's deliberate, to encourage lobbying in the numerous bars?) – and watching the recorded plenary on the TV screen, when suddenly there it was, filmed from the top. My bald patch. The humiliation went further – the camera's close-up focused on the mismatching tie and shirt, my absent look. Not just absent – my lips were twisted in disdain. It was obvious that not only was I not listening, I resented being there!

When I go home for weekends, I board a train with a ticket into the small, comfortable world Lucy has created for herself and our daughter, a fantasy world of ponies, puppies and pink tutus. Even my daughter's name is Disney-cartooned – how did I ever agree to that?

At the end of the weekend, the train takes me back to the world that sets my tongue working, where the word 'conviction' sounds less and less like 'belief in your principles' and more and more like a prison sentence.

I manage my life by flipping the switch. Working in my world of fake beliefs, coming back to Lucy's make-believe one. Whatever the switch, isn't my world still the same? 'Daddy helps people who get lost,' says my naive daughter. No way, Minnie, I am lost myself.

Lucy and I protect our self-constructed worlds from each other, bridging them by unnecessary conversations: me repeating parliamentary small talk, Lucy polishing school-gate gossip, adding, 'That's settled then' to any suggestion before I even answer.

'Minnie won't recognise you soon, you hardly see her,' she said last Friday. 'You spend less and less time at home, and now you've decided to go to London on Sunday.'

'I have to work to fund your lifestyle' wouldn't go down well, I thought; there isn't much of a lifestyle and Sunday's hardly my working day, so I resorted to bribery: 'Why don't we all go to Strasbourg again for Easter, Minnie loved the bateaux-mouches last time . . .'

'The only thing she remembers from that visit is that pancakes in French are called *crêpes*,' said Lucy. 'She told the whole class about it, with the wrong pronunciation and the right attitude, and I had to go and discuss it with the teacher. What words are you planning to teach her this time?' She sounded menacingly calm.

'Talk of the sweet girl,' I said, relieved that Minnie had rolled into the kitchen – literally, balancing on her roller skates.

'Look what Poppy did to Mr Smith!' she announced, holding high the remains of my old teddy bear. Her ponytails bounced and she sounded jubilant – as if Mr Smith had been punished for competing with her for my attention.

'Why couldn't you stop Poppy?' I screamed, holding the salvaged remains of my shredded childhood – ear gone, one arm torn away, stuffing sticking out. 'You know what Mr Smith means to me! He was a present from my mother, he is so, so special . . . Or were you standing there watching her doing it?'

'Jonty,' intervened Lucy. She always deals with everything with the calm, get-on-with it manner of the professional nurse, which drives me mad. 'Minnie doesn't know what Mr Smith means to you, so stop shouting. Listen, there's a place where they can restore and mend old toys, apparently, called the Toy Surgery. Minnie's friend Debbie had her rabbit mended there, she couldn't sleep without it. Would you like *me* to find out where this place is?' This emphasis on 'me' is usually followed by 'I do everything anyway'.

'No,' I said hastily, pre-empting the strike. 'I can deal with it myself.'

I called the Toy Surgery: 'Our dog has mauled our daughter's teddy bear, is there anything you can do?'

I wasn't expecting this as an answer: 'We have a six-month waiting list, but if you are in a desperate situation, we can give your toy emergency treatment. Bring it in and leave it with us for three hours, and we'll see what we can do.'

So I spent my weekend driving to a little town in Essex, leaving Mr Smith at the mercy of a woman in a shed with a sign saying 'Toy Surgery', then going off in search of something to eat.

'No salads today, mate' in every café; a gang of ten-year-olds surrounding me – 'Oi, got a light?' – the girls all dressed as if they were ready for a hen party starting at lunchtime. Is this unknown world the Britain I represent?

When I came to collect Mr Smith two hours later, he looked much perkier and slightly overstuffed, with a stretched smile, as if he was back from cosmetic surgery, but he was *my* Mr Smith.

'Thank you,' I said. 'My daughter will be very pleased.'

The toy surgeon, a hippie woman in her sixties, looked at me with a perceptive smile. 'I bet you will be even happier,' she answered. 'This is your teddy bear, isn't it?'

'How do you know?' There was no point denying it.

'I have many men of your type coming to me with their childhood toys – accountants, bankers, politicians,' she started.

How did she know that I was a politician? I wondered.

'So what *is* my type?' I asked calmly. I should have walked away, but morose curiosity pinned me down.

'Well,' she said, 'you know – the type who goes through life without emotions, who says the right things and does what is expected, and whose only emotional attachment is to their childhood toy. I've seen men who cling to their teddy bear as if it is their core, their soul, the memory of the emotions they once had . . .'

She was a real psychologist, this toy doctor. I glanced over her shoulder at the neatly labelled boxes of stuffed dogs and rabbits, headless Action Men and even a plastic octopus. At least I wasn't alone. Maybe she was right, and I am the type that goes through life saying the right things and doing what is expected.

Everybody lives like this, I keep telling myself. I am luckier than most – I have my escapes and can justify them; I am lucky to have Magda. Why then the occasional bout of anguish in the middle of the night, after the pee trip? Why, standing by the upstairs window looking at the lawn that needs mowing, the car that needs servicing, the gate that needs repairing, at my packed bags, do I yearn for the utopian world of 'doing something you love'? Actually, 'doing something'. Not that my parliamentary life isn't busy – I'm always travelling or attending one debate or another, I speak to visitors' groups, lobbyists and the press, sit through intergroup meetings, committee meetings . . . My work includes many verbs – scrutinise, propose, amend, develop – but no action.

So when Alex said: 'I am playing for Max,' I thought that perhaps I should play too, just for the first stage, to help them out. I have always been up for AA – acting alone – tasks in the game, and I suspect that this first task of mine is more than just a fact-finding mission . . .

'Parlement Européen!' A kid's voice, brimming with hope, shouts into my ear. Whose idea was it to record children's voices to read the stop announcements? Maybe some marketing genius thought that the voices of the future would be a perfect match for those gliding futuristic trams. 'Parlement Européen' is my stop.

All that remains now is to cross the road and change direction. Can I do the same with my life?

I walk along the canal embankment to the parliament building, following the straggling teenage groups, changing their fluid dynamics, flowing from one attraction to another, oblivious to the glass construction in front of them.

Cells and tiers, that's what this building is about. Hundreds, thousands of glass cells. Whichever way you look at it ('the functional basic unit of life' in biology or 'part of a higher-dimensional object' in geometry), I am still a cell here in this massive tower, lost in transparent corridors without clear directions.

Most of the time the building is empty, occupied by security guards, school parties and cleaners. A chess game of big egos is played on the black and white tiled floor of the parliament courtyard only four days a month. Every time I move across those squares, I find it difficult to breathe, and look up to where, by the bizarre whim of an architect, real life is hidden.

The windows above me turn into a glass wall with nothing behind it but sky – offices vanish into thin air, and instead of computers and faces there is just the zigzag of the glass façade with the clouds and trees of the roof gardens.

Today the building is alive and buzzing – security guards, interns, assistants, journalists. It is the first day of the plenary session, the red highlight of my parliamentary calendar.

My life is divided into four bright colours: red and blue, turquoise and pink – as if Minnie has coloured in my month with her felt-tip pens.

Blue is the week for political group discussions, when MEPs, divided into alliances by their political views, are supposed to decide on their votes and formulate their positions before the plenary. (When was the last time I disagreed with the group position? Probably in my first year, when I was still fighting for windmills.) These are my favourite Brussels weeks – it is easy to hide in a big group, to follow the party line and then, at the end of discussions, escape into my secret world that nobody knows about, not even Magda.

Lucy always checks my calendar for the turquoise weeks, and not only because it is her favourite colour. These are the days when I am at home, coming to deal with 'local matters', and not only in my professional capacity. The weeks when I am a school-gate father, driver, ball player, dog walker – the weeks I could actually enjoy if not for Lucy's 'that's settled, then' discussion style.

Then there is pink, Minnie's colour – the Brussels committee weeks, when I am supposed to act as an expert, and can, in theory, express myself, be a rapporteur on the committee reports, come up with 'own-initiative proposals'. Only in practice, in my committee the initiative is mostly owned by others.

And that's how I colour in my month, until I get to the red week, to the climax of the Strasbourg plenary sitting – where we all gather to debate, vote, take positions and make final decisions. That's why I am in Strasbourg now.

I cross the black and white chess courtyard to the security queue. The guards are putting all their energy into these four days of plenary, stretching the queues longer and longer as a result. I nod to familiar faces, exchange smiles, until I finally step on to the carpet, covered in synthetic poppies and meadow flowers, into the world of my first task: *Find out how to invite the Governor of Crimea to speak at an open debate with press present.* I should start by checking the schedule of debates, perhaps; it is easy to get access to the programme from any public computer – only I need to find one first. The poppy-field carpet leads to the coffee shop, so I step on the flowers and follow my nose – there should be computer stations dotted around the main communal area.

Shame that Monique is not here today – she would have done the research for me, and much quicker, too. My assistant is attending her sister's wedding in Italy, which, she informed me with her charming pout, is a week-long affair. I would not be surprised, though, if a newsflash – 'MEP's assistant kidnapped by young Italian count blinded by her beauty' – appears in *Voici* this week.

Come back safely, Monique, I could use your charm today. I am the only one, it seems, not yet to be seduced by it – by the way you wear your blouse unbuttoned just a touch lower than needed, by the scent of your perfume when you lean close to talk to me sotto voce, by the way you pout when you introduce yourself, lingering on the first syllable of your name, your lips in a perfect, orgasmic 'O': '*Mo*nique . . .'

'You are so lucky with your researcher,' Franz Liebenz, a seasoned MEP, keeps telling me, clicking his tongue. His vices are firmly fastened under his green Tyrolean jacket, but his winks and smiles endorse my 'bit on the side'.

Yes, Franz Liebenz would approve if I had a crush on Monique, but Magda . . . Fifty at least, smokes like a chimney, heavy-set, with weighty opinions – full-on straight talking is what she is all about. Always dark-suited and high-heeled, not a hair out of place, her lipstick and nails signalling a red alert: don't mess with me! A schoolmistress of a more traditional type.

And yet I would be lost without Magda, without her husky laugh. She is my anchor and my safe haven at the same time. She takes me into her world, into her youth behind the Iron Curtain and the history of Poland, a country always going through trials and tribulations: 'Poland has been a source of trouble for over five hundred years . . .

that's what Roosevelt said to Stalin at the Yalta Conference – can you believe it, *hlopak*?'

She always calls me *hlopak* when we are together – 'little boy' in Polish, she explained to me. Sometimes, in the way she talks, the way she looks at me, there is a glimpse, a reminder of another woman. The same wit and strong opinions, the same smoky voice. There, I've admitted it for the first time. My lover reminds me of my dead mother – how sad is that?

Magda is one of the first people introduced to new MEPs, with a respectful whisper: 'the most powerful and influential lady . . .' She is the head of our press office. 'You would like your question to be added to the presss release? Meet me downstairs for a coffee in twenty minutes, we'll discuss this.' No 'maybes' or 'can yous', no prepositions either. That's how it all started for me: 'I heard you were interested in new green policies in Poland? Come to my apartment tonight, I have information for you . . .'

I wish I could ask Magda what to do about this Governor of Crimea thing; she would know, she always does. But then I would need to justify and explain the whole situation I have got myself into.

Somebody must have heard my prayers – I stumble across the portal, blinking at me, inviting me to check what's on the agenda for debates in October. 'Welcome to the web . . .'

I scroll down the topics of the debates – *The role of social media in the European educational programmes; Liberalising procedures for transnational inheritance; Silicone implants – the need for stricter legislation?* – until I find the perfect one: *The Black Sea region. What's next? Open house debate.* (Great, this one ticks both boxes: the topic fits and the press will be there.) *The debate will take place in two sessions as follows. . . Key discussions are led by the Committee of Regions.* (My committee!) *Date: 24 October.*

I am drawn in by the date. Did Tony know that the debate was taking place on 24 October when he gave us the end date for the game? Did he expect that I would be in my diary's 'red week' in Strasbourg for the fact-finding task? Of course he did. There are no coincidences with him.

Not as impressive as twenty-five years ago, Tony – all this information is easily accessible. All you needed to do was to find out the dates of the Strasbourg plenary sessions.

The details of MEPs' shunting back and forth between Strasbourg and Brussels are always in the papers; it's a favourite subject for many journalists and a vibrant topic for our own debates – we politicians are good at sticking on bright labels.

This constant travelling has been called 'a charade', 'haste and waste trips', the 'travelling circus'. I love the last one, because if you look closer, that's just what we are.

We have our old elephants here, cumbersome and slow, like Franz Liebenz; we have mimicking parrots, jumping monkeys and acrobats, somersaulting from one political group to another with great verbal agility. We have jugglers of ideas, who vary in dexterity – some juggle risky, sharp or heavy subjects, the others stick to familiar balls.

We have our own ringmaster, of course. He does not actually possess any other circus skill, but he is brilliant at attracting attention, looking important and announcing the next act.

I love watching them all from where I am sitting. My seat at the Hemicycle – the plenary hall – sums it up, really. I've moved up – not in our group hierarchy, but in the centre of the hall. I am neither the right wing nor the left wing, not ultra, or conservative. I have become a backbencher, a balding observer.

There are two people in the ring now, working the circle, waiting for the plenary sitting to start: Stephanie and Xavier. Both of them I know quite well, as they are members of my committee; both are keen rapporteurs, both are ready for the position of vice-chair – and neither of them is hiding this ambition.

Stephanie, who always impresses with the elegance of her dressage, is precise, pointed, controlled. Her questions are always thought-provoking, her proposals well considered, and I, for once, have an opinion – I'll definitely support her when it comes to electing a new committee vice-chair . . .

And there is Xavier. There is always Xavier, our polished, well-dressed demagogue. He is our fire-eater, only he has chosen hot air instead of fire. At least I've admitted that I would rather support anybody else's views than express my own, but Xavier never will.

Coasting and using the ideas of others are his strongest skills; he has done that for a decade or so. Today he is in his element. He loves the no-substance talk of the plenaries – adjournments of votes and closures of debates, tabling of amendments and deadlines for roll-call votes. He has this great knack of making something trivial and banal sound heavy with meaning; this talent got him to where he is now – only now he is stuck, going nowhere, because to become vice-chair, he needs to find and propose something of significance.

Bingo! I've worked it all out – simple and political.

To get the Governor of Crime invited to the debate, all I need to do is mention Stephanie to Xavier. Mention that she will have the chance to move forward using some new information for the new debate. Or maybe Xavier would like that chance . . . Stephanie is Xavier's arch-rival – she already has something he cannot compete with. She was born with it; or rather, born into it. She grew up, *très Parisienne*, basking in great ideas. When other people were bouncing tennis balls, she was playing ideas matches with her father. A far cry from Xavier's childhood in Limousin, in a family of provincial accountants. Stephanie does not flaunt her upbringing, just says that her father is a *'sociologue très cultivé'*.

I join Xavier for a coffee during the break. I have nothing to lose; it is almost fun, tinged with envy for another of Xavier's talents: to always look effortlessly stylish – the cut of the suit, the way he picks up his espresso, revealing small but expensive gold cufflinks.

'Great tie, Xavier,' I say. (First hurdle: I need to hold his attention, as he only listens to himself usually.) 'Listen, Xavier, how is this for an idea?' (Careful, don't say '*I might have an idea*' – the idea has to be *his* and his only.) 'We often invite presidents and leaders of political parties to the open house debates – how about the governor of a region? A region that potentially could be the next hot spot, the next war zone – Kurdistan, Darfur, Crimea?

'The last one is quite interesting – in the light of our Black Sea initiative . . . Isn't our committee in charge of the Black Sea debate in October? I have read up about Crimea' (true), 'but still find it difficult to understand why this small peninsula attracted so many wars, so many historical events. Did you know' (he didn't, but from now on he will tell everybody that it was his analysis), 'Crimea is unique geographically, as one can reach any continent from it by either sea or land. A perilous strategic position, don't you think? Plus there are so many ethnic, religious, political interests there: Muslims, Tartars and Christians; the Russian Black Sea fleet based in Ukrainian waters . . . If a war ever erupts here, it will be the Balkans multiplied by . . .'

Xavier drinks his coffee, throwing his elbow up, revealing a well-ironed shirt cuff. He checks his tie and nods with satisfaction, but shows no interest whatsoever in anything I've just said.

I continue my attack. Wouldn't it be great to invite some-body like the Governor of Crimea to the debate? I have a friend who has just been made an adviser to the governor; he might help to organise his visit.' (Jonty, you are twisting Churchill's speech in the most cruel way: never before, in the history of humanity, have I lied so much to so few . . .) Xavier has already put his cup down and is adjusting his tie, ready to leave.

I turn to crude flattery: 'Xavier, you are brilliant at setting up debates. I thought this would be the perfect one for you, but if you are not interested, I could mention the idea to Stephanie; she would love to do it, I am sure.' (Not sure at all, but that is irrelevant at this stage.)

Xavier is very good at putting on the French polished charm, but hopeless at masking his hatred. As soon as I suggest that Stephanie might be interested, he leans forward and shoots questions at me – I am hit by the friendly fire, but escape almost unscathed ten minutes later. Almost, because we are already late for the plenary sitting, missing the key discussion on the tighter legislation on silicone implants.

And it was easy, wasn't it?

On the way back to my observation post, to my seat at the Hemicycle, I think: Tony has done it again!

'Find out if such an invitation is possible' was the task, really, but I've already set the ball rolling. Xavier might be dictating the invitation right now . . .

I will be smarter at the next Waterloo meeting. I won't even open the next envelope; I won't be tempted. I'll just go to support my old friends, that's all . . . but were we really friends?

Tony and I were pushed together into the same cubicle, the same dorm – too close to fight, too close to distance ourselves. Of course I liked him – who didn't? Rich, full of ideas, the invitation always open, be it to a chicken pie or a weekend at his stately home. And he was funny – dangerously, keeping-you-on-the-edge, tightrope-walking funny.

Tony's nickname, Jester, was given to him by the head-master, of all people.

'Careful, Jester, your jokes are getting too close to the bone. You are at the King's whim, don't forget,' he said at assembly one day. And the name stuck.

Tony's practical jokes always had an unexpected element; they needed aides, not just an audience, and that's where I was brought in. They call it 'peer pressure' now – only there was no pressure from Tony, no cold orders or blatant blackmail. Just fun – pure and cruel. Take that birthday bath tradition I started: lifting the birthday boy like a pharoah, carrying him along the corridors, cheering, only to throw him into a cold bath and cover him with salt and pepper, adding vinegar to the water for additional taste – great fun for everybody, agony for the birthday boy.

Cold baths are often used for bullying and initiation at boarding schools, so there was nothing new here, but Tony said: 'Wouldn't it be great to turn something nasty into a birthday celebration instead – comical yet special?' He suggested and described it clearly enough for me to kick-start it next day – carrying Nick, one of our props, to the first Birthday Bath on the crest of a spectacular rugby win. Now, looking back, I think it was Tony's way of singling somebody out.

The Birthday Bath tradition was the first test of my friendship with him – a year into the tradition, I was tackled, lifted and carried along the corridors, waving my useless arms. In a final attempt to twist my way out of the execution, I looked back and caught sight of Tony – a picture of calmness, framed by the wooden panels of the walls, his eyes smiling: a quiet victor.

And in that moment, when his stillness, his silence was more deafening than the dozens of adrenalin-fuelled screams around me, I understood. For Tony, the fun was about staging the fight and then watching it unfold from a distance with the discerning smile of a smart coach.

He enjoyed the excitement of pulling the strings, of making people behave the way he wanted. Is this why he pushed me to start the Birthday Bath tradition in the first place? And did he really push me?

I stopped wriggling, paralysed by his look, frozen in admiration at his skill of making people think that they were making the decisions themselves.

We never discussed it afterwards, lying in the thick,

sleepless darkness of the cubicle, but we both knew – his power over me was intangible and absolute.

Later that term, Tony invented the Tepee Council and brought Max in.

They had spent most of the holiday together at Tony's house, apparently, and Tony just said: 'Max will be joining us in the Tepee – he is such fun!'

I wouldn't have called Max 'fun' – you never knew where he really was when he was talking to you – but he was *our* Max from now on; we could say: 'This is our best friend performing' when we heard the applause.

I kept watching how Tony was tying Max to us with his invisible knot, tightening it with a half-phrase, with a gesture.

'All right, Max? See you later,' his hand on Max's shoulder translated into: 'Don't go far . . .'

'How are you, Max?' meaning: 'Can you really cope without us?'

I think Max *did* need us; he was too gentle, too vulnerable to face life alone. So I pretended not to notice what Tony was doing – looking after Max made me feel stronger myself, and that's all that mattered.

Levi . . . I would have never made friends with Levi.

I watched him moving around the school, pretending to be busy, interrupting conversations with his compendium of useless facts, deductions, assumptions. I was dying to tell him: 'I know you want to be in the crowd. Do your sums,

Levi – the crowd doesn't want you!' So when Tony brought him to the Tepee Council, I thought at first it was one of his jokes. I learned to tolerate Levi's brains eventually; it didn't really matter – for me, the Tepee Councils were about Max.

We were not like other groups in our year, built on a military hierarchy and a similar pattern: a top dog, two or three desperate copycats at the bottom and one or two in-betweeners.

We were all very different, and that's why our group func-tioned so well: Tony cracked jokes and developed strategy, Levi would share his intellectual prowess, I would test my bravery and taste the danger, and Max . . . Max was the soul, definitely our soul – volatile and nebulous.

I'll still go to Waterloo on Sunday – out of politeness . . . out of curiosity . . . for Max's memory . . . Oh, for fuck's sake, Jonty, stop finding excuses: just be there – if only to say goodbye to them all!

Only the Sunday meeting turns out to be anything but goodbye.

It starts quite well, with a changed energy in the greetings – we are almost glad to see each other again. Almost, as I still think it was ridiculous for Tony to restart the game; I am never sure if I am glad to see Levi; and Alex, who is looking fresher and smarter this time (a new haircut, or more make-up? I can't figure it out), is a poignant reminder that Max is not with us.

'So,' Tony smiles, turning to Alex. 'How was it?'

'Quite easy,' she replies with a shrug. 'No chase, only one dangerous encounter, with a girl from the UN Visitors' Centre. There were, and still are, secrets, though. The documents you asked me to check exist, but are classified as secret. There is a US Advisory Committee on Historical Diplomatic Documentation, which reviews records and makes recommendations to the Office of the Historian at the US Department of State. This committee's recommendation several years ago was to classify those documents as secret again, for the third thirty-year period running.'

'Is this because they could still be valid?' Levi's logical brain is not even working overtime. All we have to do is catch up with him and listen.

Alex nods.

'And how do *you* know about it?' His deductive powers can't extend that far.

'Because,' continues Alex, 'this advisory committee consists of historians, international lawyers and members at large. And one of those international lawyers . . .' for some reason she looks at Tony, not at Levi, when she says this, 'is our . . . is my father.

'He has promised to send me the copies of the documents next week,' she adds almost triumphantly, still looking at Tony.

'I might have seen Russian copies of those documents', says Levi. 'When I was in the museum in Crimea last week. If it is the same thing, and I assume it is, then—'

He is about to add something, but Tony interrupts, stops him somehow, without saying a word.

'I always admire the ability of men to communicate silently,' says Alex. 'Raising a brow, just giving each other a brief look – but can you at least include me while I am here?'

'So, it went well,' Tony turns back to her. 'That's great.'

'Is that all you can say: "That's great"?' Alex sounds quite tense. 'As if I went to Brighton for a day on the beach, not all the way to New York! Thank you for the business-class ticket, by the way.'

'Technically,' says Levi, 'you could do that.'

'Do what?' Alex is chewing the nail off her little finger.

'Go to Brighton while you were in New York. It's only an hour away from Manhattan. You take a Q line from Fifty-Seventh Street via Times Square to Brighton Beach; last time I was there it was only two dollars each way. All the signs there are in Russian, and everybody speaks Russian. Half of Odessa lives there now.'

Yes, nothing has changed in all these years – Levi has just confirmed once again that he is good at logical analysis. And rubbish at jokes.

Tony unclasps his satchel to get out the envelopes. They are all AAs – 'act alone', my favourite.

'Where is the DD, the "do and distract" second stage?' asks Levi.

'With the time limit and the scale of this game, we are

jumping straight to AAs,' explains Tony. He covers the envelopes with his palm, as if giving a final blessing, before pushing them towards us. He raises his brows slightly, and his eyes open wider for an instant, two piercing beams showing us the way.

The coffees are getting cold and the waitress is circling around, waiting for tips. We are an unlikely prey – she must find us a weird bunch, sitting there watching the envelopes on the table in total silence.

Levi is the first to open his location envelope: '*The name of the file Alex was looking for in New York is the next location you need to visit* . . . What is the name of the file, Alex?' he asks impatiently.

Alex shrugs her shoulders and writes on a napkin: *Crimea*.

I look at Levi, expecting him to throw a tantrum, to say 'Again? I have just been!' but instead he smiles and asks: 'When?'

Maybe he knows something I don't know yet, something so exciting that his daily job of saving lives, or at least making people feel better, as he puts it, doesn't matter. Maybe Alex has written something else, added another thrilling place.

I look at the napkin, at the word Alex has scribbled, and suddenly feel my palms getting clammy. The white noise exploding in my ears is probably something only I can hear, as nobody else moves or reacts.

I can see very clearly what Tony has done. Another one of his twisted game ideas is staring back at me from the napkin.

I pick up Alex's pen and my subconscious sums it up for me. I cross out the 'a' with short, sharp horizontal lines, then add three long, finite vertical ones. My drawing looks like bars on a prison window, and now the reason why we are all here stares back at us – unsaid then, harboured for twenty-five years to be finally written now.

Levi has got it already and is looking at me intently, his myopic eyes huge behind the lenses of his glasses.

'It is not about Crimea, Alex,' I say. 'It is about a crime. A crime we committed twenty-five years ago.'

I expect her to ask: 'What crime?' but instead she whispers: 'What do you mean – we? Was Max involved?'

And that's when I say it. I am looking at the piece of paper with its five fatal letters, not at Alex, Tony or Levi, but I know they are all listening. I am saying this word aloud for the first time, though I have wanted to do it for the last twenty-five years. This word is a taboo, and I know that by releasing it now, I'll break the seal and there will be no way back. From now on I'll have to play to the end; we all will have to. Until the twenty-fourth of October and beyond.

'There was a death twenty-five years ago, as a result of our game.' I breathe out. 'Our crime . . .' I say, and enjoy, for a split second, the way the word 'our' sounds, proving that I am not on my own in this.

'Our crime was murder, Alex. We committed murder.'

# PART 2

## *The Game*

*That's when your strength is tested.*
*That's when your heart is tested*
*That's when your honour is tested*
*And can be swept ashore*
*You can be threatened, burdened, arrested, but still*
*Every man fights his own war.*

Attributed to Veronika Tushnova, Russian poet

# TONY'S WAR

*Odessa*

It was a near miss, our last Waterloo meeting – I thought I had foreseen and planned everything, but Jonty almost killed the game with his unexpected outburst.

'Jonty, did you hear my question?' Alex almost shouted at him across the table, scaring off the waitress. 'What did you mean when you said "we"? How was Max involved?'

I could not give him any time to answer, I had to stop it immediately.

So I started speaking, slowly, deliberately, shaping every word. They must have thought I was pausing to add weight to what I said, but in fact my mind was racing as I searched for arguments.

'This is not the time to revisit what happened,' I said. 'Let's finish the game first; we'll have time to discuss the past at our last meeting.'

'What if we are not going to play any more?' whispered Alex.

'I think you should, I really do,' I continued. 'Listen, Alex, we hid something all those years ago, and it led to a death. Now we are trying to find something hidden again. That's all I can say for now, before we play the next task. It won't bring back that person, but many deaths will be averted. Same principle, different scale, and our chance of a replay.'

As they all listened, I felt I was back in the director's seat, giving out instructions and controlling the game again, thingking of possible eventualities and unplanned questions.

So here I am, preparing for another contingency. Levi playing the AA stage was already a disaster waiting to happen, but his sudden initiative to return from Crimea via Odessa means that disaster is already here, waiting to take him for a final spin. I had to fly to Odessa to save the day, if not his life, and now I am stuck here, waiting for Levi.

It is early October; the summer crowds are gone, the street cafés bring out rugs and heaters in the evenings, but the days are still mellow. 'How can anybody live without the sea, tell me?' a waitress asked me last night, handing me a chequered blanket with my coffee. 'I could move to Moscow tomorrow, but there is no sea there! However tired or upset I am, I always go to the beach – to Lanjeron, just around the corner, or stop at Luzanovka on my way home, walk on the warm sand and let the water wash away all my frustrations.'

So I've decided to try the beach too – if I ever get there

with this joyrider. I wish this cab driver knew where he was going. It looked like a straight line on the map, but I am not a great walker, so I opted for the taxi ride to Lanjeron beach – ten minutes, I thought. He has been zigzagging the cobbled streets for half an hour now, laughing loudly as he listens to a monotonous newsreader on the radio, leaving me on my own at the back. I just hope the meter will stop clicking eventually.

If only I could understand why he is laughing. He tried to explain it to me at the traffic lights: 'Jokes, no politics, jokes only,' pointing at the radio. I guess the listless mono-logue he's listening to is a local comedy channel.

Simple connection, really: if you don't laugh together, you stop relating to each other.

'You are too serious, Tony. I know it comes with your job description, but we don't find the same things funny any more,' Ruth said to me when she was leaving last year. 'I mean, when you said, "I understand why you don't want children, Ruth, you already have your hands full with me!" why is that supposed to be funny? Sorry, Tony, I am too busy to be your babysitter . . . And how can we call it an "amicable split" if we have stopped being friends?'

I tried to tell her that I'm not always serious, but couldn't remember the last time we had had a laugh together. Instead, I thought of other people I laugh with, aged from five to eighty-five. One of them is Jane. Boy, we've had our laughs!

I often forget Jane is my aunt. My father's much younger

sister, stuck almost two decades below my emotionally deprived father and a decade above me, bursts with perennial joy and eternal desire to save the world. She has even made it her job: she has been on UN deployments in more countries than I have seen in the alarming news bulletins – which is not difficult, as Australian news don't always catch up with the rest of the world.

When Jane suggested a trip to Crimea last year, I had a sneaking suspicion that she was trying to save me, fresh from divorce, as well as the world. For the first time in years I was on my own for two months in the summer, and I agreed to join her. I wanted to see the Livadiya Palace, where they held the Yalta Conference, the hall with the round table where all the decisions were made, the Italian courtyard where the famous photograph of the three leaders was taken.

Maybe that photograph was the real reason I agreed to go with Jane to Crimea. I've known those faces as long as I've known myself – framed on the table of my father's study.

We've always had an ancestor taking part in one military campaign or another, involved in the preparation of one treaty or another: leading his troops at the assault of the great redan at Sebastopol, or part of the 400-strong British delegation at the Crimea Conference. My father was particularly proud of his Yalta Conference photo – the original, inherited from his great-uncle.

'Shame Antony will not follow the family tradition – I

can't imagine him being invited to this level of event,' I overheard him saying one day through the half-open doors of the study, as he was showing the photograph of the three leaders to yet another visitor. Then he added:

'The boy isn't fit enough to serve his country or smart enough to save it.' In his eyes, I did not deserve to inherit the power of the Name.

I'd failed him, I knew I had, though I had never worked out which was the worse disappointment for him – me, or his marriage to my mother. The only passion my parents shared was the passion of hating each other, and I was a lone reminder of that non-starter marriage, riding my tricycle along the corridors of our stately house which never became a home, followed by a new nanny. My mother, suspicious of my father's wandering hands, renewed them annually, on the first of January, together with her subscription to *The Lady*.

So what if one of my legs was slightly shorter than the other – it wasn't a pronounced limp, and I learned to hide it, developing a slow strut; so what if I hated sports day and maths?

I was desperate to prove my father wrong, desperate for him at least to like me even if he chose not to love me, but how?

History . . . I thought one day, looking at the old maps on the walls of my father's study, at the Yalta photograph, at the model soldiers carefully placed on the side table, frozen in battle, 'not to be touched under any circumstances', according to my father's instructions.

Maybe if I learned more about history, if I understood those battles, those maps, if I could talk to my father about it, he would listen . . .

I started reading, choosing the biographies of great leaders first – stories of small, crippled men who were destined for greatness: Napoleon with his height, Stalin with his withered left arm . . . I remember looking at my father's 'three great leaders in Yalta' for a while, trying to work it out – the impulsive man with the 'black dog' of depression, the leader with a terminal illness and the marshal with so many dark psychological secrets – how did they all become so powerful?

It was the Veteran's behaviour when Levi fainted in class once that gave me the answer. The real name of our chemistry teacher was Mr Parfitt, but we all called him the Veteran, because he'd served as a Royal Navy reserve officer in the Falklands War. We all knew somehow, though he never spoke about it, that he had spent ten months in hospital with internal injuries after a blast on his ship.

It fascinated me how he commanded respect by his presence alone, never raising his voice or descending to threats. His calm power over us kept us on our toes – you never knew whether he was joking or not.

It was one of those 'stand-watch-repeat' lessons, where we would crowd around the Veteran, concentrating on him and his bottles, on liquids and powders exploding, evaporating, boiling. He had already started the experiment when we heard a heavy thud and turned to see Levi, who was on the third day of a self-imposed weight-loss hunger strike, slumped on the floor.

'Leave him, boys, he'll come round as the blood flows back to his head,' said the Veteran, not looking at Levi and carrying on with his explanation: 'To crystallise an impure solid compound, add just enough hot solvent to completely dissolve it . . .'

Nobody but nobody rushed to help Levi – and even if somebody more likeable had been lying there, we would still have remained standing around the table, watching the experiment in progress.

That's when I recognised the secret of the Veteran's power over us – it was not his patience or his aloof manner, it was his ability to raise the stakes, to keep us guessing. If he lets the boy lie motionless on the floor and doesn't take any action, how does he know he will be all right? What will he do next?

'. . . and finish by setting it in an ice bath to complete the crystallisation process,' concluded the Veteran just as Levi sat up, scratching his head in bewilderment.

'Welcome back, Freiman,' said the Veteran. 'You have missed all the fun. Care to come back for the revision session?'

The whole class exploded with laughter; not much sympathy for poor Levi.

I realised then what I needed to do. I had to create a game, built on anticipation. Where fun was mixed with danger, where the leader provided total control and reassurance, protecting and cushioning, covering up when necessary and keeping his players guessing to the end what the outcome would be.

I have watched many teenage boys since then – they always live in the moment, unwilling to plan; their fear of failure is often the reason for not even trying to do something extraordinary. I know all this now.

But back then it was only my intuition whispering to me that I was the one with the ability to see the bigger picture. I could become a great strategist whose decisions would be accepted without question; I would be moving my model soldiers into the heat of the battle. That's when I understood that to become powerful, you don't have to be the tallest or the strongest; to get people to listen to you, you have to have that extra something, that sprinkling of magic dust that is often called magnetism, and always be several steps ahead.

But to become that leader, to direct the game, I had to choose my group wisely.

Jonty, of course, was already part of my group, and what a perfect action man he was, with his number 8 attitude, always rushing ahead, ready to attack, just waiting for the ball, for the direction – from me, of course.

I thought of other people I could include. Admiration

would be of assistance, blind loyalty no matter what . . . And who would be better to provide that than Levi Freiman, so desperate to fit in?

I watched him for a month: he was getting more and more miserable, stretching out his sweaty palm that nobody wanted to shake, wandering the corridors looking lost but pretending to have a set purpose. Finally, one afternoon, I stopped him: 'Hey, Levi, got a sec?'

I also needed a magician's assistant, a charmer who could provide a diversion. That was not so easy. The only Prince Charming we had was Norman, whose feline French manners, copied from his groomed, petite, precious French mother, did not go down well in the cold British dorms. His nickname was '*ma chérie*', and besides, he loved himself too much to adore anybody else.

The epiphany came at the Christmas family concert, which was the headmaster's idea: the boys could bring their home-grown actors or musicians to participate. But show me a teenage boy who would want to give either his friends or enemies the pleasure of such embarrassment!

Max Chandler brought his twin sister, however. That's when I met Alex for the first time.

They were performing 'St Louis Blues' together: Max playing his saxophone, Mr Brown, our English teacher, on the piano, with Alex singing.

Amazing how twins can be so alike yet so different – they had the same unruly hair, the same turned-up nose, but she was definitely the stronger and more decisive of the two. She had briskness, sharpness around her, while Max's movements were soft, like the subdued sound of his saxophone, which followed his sister's voice.

I couldn't say 'I really like your sister, Max – any chance of getting to know her better?' but I could start 'hanging out' with him, as teenagers would say now, inviting him ('. . . and Alex can come too, if she has nothing else to do') to our grand house, which his snob of a mother was only too thrilled to let them visit.

And then I thought . . . a musician is exactly what I need for the game. Somebody who would impress without trying, who would thrust our group into the limelight – he would be our star, one of us, one of Tony's crowd . . . A musician like Max – gullible, vulnerable, talented – would be perfect.

We had to start somewhere, so in the beginning our games were innocent, almost nursery style – we set off with bubbles and butterflies.

Our school's pride and joy, the fountain by the main entrance, started welcoming visitors with a rainbow of Fairy Liquid-induced bubbles. The headmaster's mounted night watch was pointless – with Levi's attention to timing, Jonty's speed and Max's occasional decision to practise Gershwin's 'Summertime' by the fountain, there was no chance of us being caught. The fountain stopped producing bubbles after a month or so, when the novelty wore off for us.

Releasing the butterflies from the biology lab was a trickier exercise – it involved keys, glass cabinets, torches and a lot of sign language, broken by stifled bursts of laughter – we tried to keep this release operation silent. Max's reaction was the only thing that surprised me then – he looked incredibly serious and determined, making sure that every single butterfly flew out. 'I don't want them to die here – they are so beautiful,' he explained. I often thought about it afterwards – if I'd chosen somebody else instead of Max for our group, would we have ended up playing the last game? Would we?

Then we moved to more elaborate scenarios, starting with 'why don't we sneak some dining-room trays out at night to go for a ride?'

Levi calculated the best time to get into the dining hall, Max charmed the dinner lady – or rather a dinner girl from the neighbouring farm – and Jonty carried the trays out, hiding them in the bushes.

How I remember that anticipation of dawn, tossing in bed, counting the minutes turning into hours; then running to the top of the hill with our plastic 'sleighs'. The thrill of the speed, of sudden movement – and bursts of laughter when Levi's tray gained momentum and flew over the lip of the hill.

Last year's trip to Crimea reminded me of those first, uncomplicated games – the same joy, the same thrill of adventure, only this time Jane was the producer and I was more of an action man.

Who would have thought that a trip planned as an exercise in roots searching, with a bit of soul-searching thrown in, would end up in a race on mountain roads in balaclavas? That we would be drinking with a nineteenth-century general and finding our ancestors in derelict submarine pens?

We went to a battle re-enactment at Alma, but did not really understand what was going on, with all the running and shouting. A man in an old-style Russian uniform kept winking at us as he sipped from his flask: 'I am supposed to be the Russian general Kiryanov, who was always drunk,' he explained. 'Let's have a couple of shots,' he winked at us again, 'and I'm not talking gunpowder here . . .'

We hired a car to drive to Balaklava, but could not find the war museum, though we searched the Tavricheskaya Quay for an invisible number sixteen for an hour, until Jane finally surrendered: 'I am starving . . .'

'Looking for the museum?' the owner of the café asked, putting plates of Crimean sole in front of us. 'Everybody does. It is under the harbour.' And it was, literally – in the abandoned Cold War nuclear submarine pens.

As we walked into the underground world of 'the last gentlemen's war', cavalry charged ahead, shells exploded, until we found shelter in a British officer's bunker house. His helmet was still on top of his travel trunk, a map waiting open on his camp desk, full dress uniform with all his medals on the chair. Could be our ancestor . . . I thought.

'Nineteenth-century story in a nuclear submarine pen – what an original idea,' said Jane as we drove along the mountain roads to Livadiya.

'Stop the car – it has to be done,' she ordered sternly, handing me something black and woollen. 'Just for a couple of miles. I've wanted to do this since I was a child, since I heard that word for the first time. It is the place to do it, too, with nobody here: everybody takes the lower coastal road now.'

The local police stopped us five minutes later, and it took us an hour to explain why the head of the UN border-monitoring mission and her nephew, both well into the age of understanding the consequences, were driving along a deserted Crimean mountain road *below* the speed limit and wearing balaclavas.

When they finally let us go, what a joy it was to drive down to the sea, to a sign that my multilingual aunt could decipher easily: 'Ливадия'.

The Livadiya Palace, summer residence of the last Russian tsar, took us by surprise – it was modern and modest, with electricity, telephone, and not just hot and cold, but even seawater running from the taps. The airy, light rooms were decorated sparingly, so as not to distract from the stunning views of the sea and the park below.

The guide was surprising, too. 'Peter Bodrov,' he introduced himself, and added, laughing, 'They often call me "the Livadiya caretaker" . . .'

Instead of delivering the standard commentary ('The Yalta Conference between British prime minister Winston Churchill, US president Franklin Delano Roosevelt and Soviet leader Joseph Stalin took place in February 1945 in Livadiya. The agreements reached included the demand for Germany's unconditional surrender; the establishment of a "provisional government of national unity" in Poland; the USSR's commitment to enter the war against Japan; discussions on the United Nations structure and other matters including the repatriation of Soviet citizens . . .'), he painted the big picture with accurate, bright brush strokes:

*Blue*
'Though the British and Soviet delegations stayed in the Vorontsov and Koreiz palaces respectively, as President Roosevelt was in a wheelchair, he was allowed to stay in Livadiya, where the conference took place. His bedroom was decorated to match the colour of his eyes – the curtains, the bedcovers, even the telephone were blue, his favourite colour. He liked it so much that he asked his daughter to photograph the room to show Mrs Roosevelt on his return.'

*Black*
'Look at this photograph, where Winston Churchill is offered a massive bowl of caviar and a spoon . . . his face says it all. It is the final breakfast, right here, in this panelled dining room. Churchill loved caviar, so he was always served

first – he called it the best starter to go with vodka, and Stalin was really pleased to hear that.'

*White*

'And this is the White Hall, where the final communiqué was signed.

'When Roosevelt invited Stalin to be the first to sign it, Stalin refused.

'"The American press has got sharp teeth. I will be accused of leading the American president and the British prime minister astray," he said. "Why don't we sign in the order of the Russian alphabet?" he proposed.

'Churchill did not agree – "Does this mean I will be last?" – and suggested the English alphabet.

'"Even though my signature will be last . . . how do you say it?– last but not least," replied Stalin, accepting Churchill's proposal.'

*Brown*

'Churchill often smoked cigars outside, and had a funny habit of throwing them on the floor of his veranda after a couple of puffs. Thick brown cigars covered the landing of his veranda, and nobody was allowed to touch them – Churchill's daughter explained that the doctors had told her father to lose weight, and he was throwing them on the floor so that he could pick them up and do some exercise while smoking at the same time.'

*Red*

'At the end of the conference, officers and soldiers from the three countries started exchanging souvenirs. The Russian buttons with red stars were the most popular. The American soldiers could not explain to the Soviet guards what they wanted, so they ended up pointing and tearing the buttons away, saying: "Red star – present." Nobody ended up fighting, though.'

Peter Bodrov lived and breathed this place, every nook and cranny. He had been here all his life, he told us, in a small gardener's house in the palace park.

At first he had lived with his father, a senior doctor in the 'people's sanatorium' they had turned the palace into in the thirties. His father had come back from the front unscathed only to be arrested and shot a year before Stalin's death: as the chief doctor for the 'state dacha' here, he had suggested physiotherapy for Stalin's withered arm. The leader did not forgive anybody who mentioned his weakness.

First history taught Peter Bodrov lessons here, then he himself taught history and English at a Yalta school, becoming a guide in the museum when he retired.

I was so glad I had a voice recorder with me – the one Ruth left behind. She often recorded messages for me when she was away, and I never had the courage to delete the messages, so now I was recording the story of Peter Bodrov over numerous past 'I love you's:

'All the plenary meetings took place at four or five p.m as Stalin was a night owl and everybody worked to his schedule.'

'Thank you, Peter.' That's my voice on the recording. Do I really sound like that?

'Have you travelled outside Crimea much?' This is Jane's voice asking the question.

'What for?' Peter says. 'If you know your geography, we are on the forty-fifth parallel, exactly halfway between the North Pole and the Equator. Crimea is a planet within a planet. We have mountains and valleys here, canyons . . . even our own volcano, the Ayu Dag – it looks like a sleeping bear, have you noticed? It is dormant, it never erupts, so your journey to the airport should be safe.

'I love travelling in Crimea. I have an old army jeep, which I restored – not a great engine, but it will do. Great for the coast trips to Gurzuf or Alushta.

'So, you told me you live in Australia now?' he asks me. There is a pause in the recording, where I nod. I can hear Peter laughing.

'Well, Australia nearly missed its chance due to Crimea – I bet you didn't know that! When America refused to accept British convicts in the eighteenth century, and British prisons were overflowing, the Russian Count Potemkin came up with an idea to settle thousands of British convicts in the newly acquired southern lands of Crimea. Vorontsov, the Russian ambassador to London, persuaded Empress

Catherine to turn the project down at the last minute, when the wave of rumours about the warm and welcoming Crimean lands had already reached British shores and led to a surge of new prisoners, who were hoping they would be sent to Crimea. Just think, we could have had a little Australia here!'

'I never knew . . .' – that's me, being pensive, but sounding sleepy.

'Welcome,' he laughs, 'from a failed settlement for British convicts to one that succeeded and prospered . . . "Thus we hope to prosper" – wasn't that the first motto of the *Sydney Gazette*?'

There is long silence on the recording, Jane and I are stunned by his knowledge. Yes, I thought then, he is right – the world comes to him.

'Besides, they have all come to me, the world leaders,' confirms Peter Bodrov, as if reading my thoughts. 'Churchill, Stalin and Roosevelt, Nixon and Gorbachev . . . And I have recorded these moments. I love photography. Hobby fit for a tsar,' he adds. 'Do you know, it was Tsar Nicholas II's hobby? That's why we have so many photographs of the daily life of his family.'

There is silence, some footsteps as we move to a different hall, then Peter's commentary on the tsar's photographs and the royal family's life in Livadiya. Then there is the sound of running water – the fountain in the centre of the Italian court, so familiar from the photograph on my father's desk.

'Is this where they were sitting, with the arches of the big hall behind them?' I ask, almost resuming the role of the guide.

'Here, let me show you.' There is pride in Bodrov's voice. 'This is a copy of the photograph I took with my father's beloved camera. Can you see where it is taken and who is in it? And the date – the ninth of February 1945 . . .'

I remember Jane wandering off, exploring the courtyard, while I stood there firing questions at him:

'Was it really taken by you? How old were you then – eight? How did you, an eight-year-old boy, manage to get through the three hundred-strong security from three countries to take that photograph?'

Peter sighs – he must have heard these questions many times before.

'The photo call was the most disorganised element of the whole conference,' he explains, and adds, 'This is not my opinion; I am quoting your compatriot Field Marshal Lord Alanbrooke. Nobody took charge, it was quite chaotic, I remember that well. Besides, I have always been such a part of this place that people stopped noticing me after a while. Stalin saw me, though. As the leaders were sitting down for the photograph, he looked at me and winked – or I thought he did . . . No, I wasn't scared, I was proud – if somebody had asked me what I was doing there, I would have said that Comrade Stalin had allowed me, Peter Bodrov, to stay and take the picture.'

'Peter and the Wolf . . .' I heard Jane muttering in the background, and then the recording crackled – that's where I switched the tape off to look at the photograph, asking him to sell me that copy. I remember how embarrassed he was, saying he could not possibly, and me saying that these fifty . . . one hundred . . . two hundred dollars would be quite handy if he wanted to mend his old war jeep.

This photograph is one of my most treasured possessions now – yes, the focus is smudged, it's taken from a low angle, but it's real history in the making. On the back Peter had written in his teacher's handwriting: *To a hundred years of peace!*

Another click as he continues with the history of Crimea.

'Have you got time to visit Mangup? It was the capital of the enigmatic kingdom of Teodoro, interesting excavations there . . . and Khersonesos, of course, you must see the ruins of the old Greek city before Sebastopol swallows it, it's in the suburbs already . . . and if you are interested in the Crimean War . . .'

'Oh, we have just been to see the battlefields, thank you.' That's Jane, interrupting as always. 'You know what surprised me?' she continues. 'How small the area of the war was – the first landing, the charge of the Light Brigade, the siege of Sebastopol, it didn't even spread across Crimea. The ladies were picnicking under their umbrellas in the hills, watching the battles . . . What do *you* think of the Crimean War, by the way?'

He coughs. There is a long pause on the recording, but it is still going: somebody's mobile phone ringing in the background, the shuffling of many feet – a tourist group passing by – a tired child whining: 'Ma-ma, Maaa . . .' All these mundane, indifferent sounds, gradually dying away in the background, as if waiting for him to say:

'The Crimean War? I think it is imminent.'

'Jane meant the nineteenth-century war, eighteen fifty four to fifty six.' That's me again.

'I know,' he answers calmly. 'I know she meant that, but I didn't. I am only a small man, but I have been living in Crimea long enough to understand its strategic importance. Besides, it is such a boiler . . . sorry, I think the word in English is "cauldron"? This is such a cauldron, so many tensions are bubbling under the surface that one day, with one splash of overspill, it will all erupt. The Crimean War started on a religious pretext, if you remember, as though the large powers in Europe wanted a war at that time and found an excuse to have it. Now, with billions invested in various oil pipelines, with the interests of continents not just states at stake here . . . Of course, just like our volcano, the Ayu Dag, it may remain dormant and never erupt. Ah, who am I to discuss it! I am just a small man, a guide here.' He stops.

'So, what do you think the solution is?' That's Jane again, with her 'save the world' hat on.

'Here, let me show you,' he says calmly. 'It used to be

marked top secret, but after the sixty-year rule, we are allowed to keep these documents if not on display yet, at least not in the safes any more.'

He is taking us along the corridor to the research office, sharing his life story with us on the way.

'I knew about this when I was a child, funnily enough. I remember how my mother, who was a waitress at the conference, came home late after one of the dinners and whispered to me, "Petrusha, I am so happy – there will be no war for a hundred years. Churchill suggested the toast and they all raised their glasses to a hundred years of peace!"'

'But I thought fifty years was mentioned in all the discussions,' I say, revealing more knowledge than necessary and instantly regretting it.

'At least,' he answers. 'If you read the documents carefully, they all say "*at least* fifty years" . . .'

There is a crackling noise on the tape again – that's when the recorder ran out of power and I was fiddling with it, putting new batteries in while he took us to a research room, unlocked a cabinet and read the protocols to us, translating as he went. I remember that Jane and I just stood there listening to him, looking at each other in disbelief.

The next thing on the recording is Jane's voice again:

'So why does nobody do anything about it; why can't they use these protocols to avert the war you predict?'

'I am not the person you should ask,' he says. 'Too many people would not want to remember that these documents exist, I guess. At least they are here as a reminder of what the world can still do.'

What a perfect game it would be, I thought then. Suitable for a replay of our last game. Ideal as a chance for me to prove to my father that though you have to be a soldier to start a war, you don't have to be one to stop it . . .

What a perfect game we are playing now. Except that I am stuck here on a beach in Odessa, surrounded by girls in mini bikinis and boys in fake Burberry caps, listening to the voice of history and waiting for Levi. I switch off the recorder, bidding farewell to Peter Bodrov, farewell to the Livadiya Palace. Levi should be there today – I wonder how he is getting on . . .

# LEVI'S WAR

## Yalta-Odessa

Short and direct, military again: *Retrieve the protocols safely from Yalta and find the best secure way of delivery to the UK.*

The logistics are easy this time – fly to Istanbul, Simferopol, and then to Yalta – it is only two stops on the trolley bus from the airport, apparently. That will be half a day altogether. A day there for safe retrieval, and then back to London via Odessa and Istanbul. I am not sure if this is the most secure route home, but it is certainly the most desirable.

I am the action man at last, not the perpetual fact-finder.

Though fact-finding can be dangerous too – just think of our last game, the game called 'Norman' . . .

I thought about it earlier today for the first time after all these years, watching the white foam on the sea we were flying over, subconsciously counting the boats. Looking back, it was a cruel joke, a really cruel joke. How many times have I come back to that day? Not often enough, if I am honest with myself. Not until Jonty said: 'We committed murder,' with a clear emphasis on the 'we'. I blamed Tony, Max, Jonty, but really it was all my fault, wasn't it?

I was the one who said: 'Have you noticed how Norman looks at Max's sister when she comes to the socials? He is always glued to Alex and Max, from the moment she comes through the gate.'

How long was it before Tony's new idea? 'Why don't we call our next game "Norman"? Levi, you remain on fact-finding alert; Jonty, it's time you tried some "do and distract"; and Max, you will have the honour of the action.'

When I opened my envelope, I shrugged my shoulders. 'That's too easy! I can do it at seventeen fifteen today.

Jonty laughed, reading his: 'How cool is that?'

Max was silent at first, then mumbled: 'I guess I can do it – but what for?' I could hardly hear him.

So I went off to put a note in Norman's maths book: *Meet me by the gate Saturday at 6 – will be waiting*. No signature, as the task instructed.

I put two and two together, saw at least a bigger part of Tony's grand plan, when I overheard Jonty in the dining room: 'She is such a stunner, Norm, and the way she looks at you – how did you manage that?'

I could guess what Max's task was. To bring Alex in, no doubt.

I grazed my elbow trying to get to our observation post at the cricket pavilion. ('Perfect for birdwatching,' I said to Tony then – how can I still remember such a crappy joke?)

Alex was standing by the gate with her back to us, looking at the main road. I remember thinking: why doesn't she look at the school entrance? Isn't she expecting Norman?

We should have stopped when Norman was scurrying to the gate, but our curiosity was fuelled by Jonty's running commentary. ('Shall we call it a kissing gate from now on, Norm? Shame I won't be here to see the action; there's a Guinness Premiership match on, want to see Wasps thrash Leicester . . .')

Norman was quite close when Alex turned round. Only it wasn't Alex – it was Max in a wig, wearing bright fluorescent eyeshadow and pink lipstick.

'Can't do this any more! Run, Norman!' he shouted. 'You were set up, this is an ambush!'

Jonty doubled up with laughter, and so did I.

*Borrow Alex's dress, wear a wig and wait by the second tree at the side gate* was all Max's task said, I discovered later. He guessed what it was for, I am sure he did, but was afraid to admit it, to lose our friendship.

Yes, we should have left it there and then, but wiping away the tears of laughter, I noticed that Tony wasn't laughing at all. He was watching Max and Norman from our hideout with a weird expression. I thought he was angry, really angry: his plans had never gone wrong before.

So I said what I said just to please him: 'Tony, have you ever heard Norman shouting "Has anybody seen my bag?" I haven't and you haven't, and you know why? Because he is fused to his bag, as if he is guarding the royal treasures. I wonder why . . .'

That was all I said, just a silly observation, climbing over a pile of cricket bats; not even at a Tepee Council.

'Why don't we hide his bag, then?' said Tony. 'Just for a day, to see what happens.'

We didn't discuss it any further, but Tony was already working on the game, wasn't he?

He was three steps ahead of me, ahead of all of us; he always is. Take today's trip, for example.

Last week he nodded when I showed him my route plan, as if he knew all about it. But if he did, why didn't he warn me that 'two stops on the trolley bus' from the airport would take two and a half hours? I want to ask him, when I see him again: 'Have you ever tried to cross the mountains, Tony, a hundred kilometres, on a bloody trolley bus? Clambering past woodland restaurant lodges with Disney figures outside (the one with the giant Shrek looked particularly inviting), past rocks decorated with colossal election posters (not a single smiling face!).

The trolley bus stopped once, by the sign *Angarsky crossing 752 metres above sea level*, only to rush down, screeching with joy that it had made it to the top, past coastal resorts and fruit markets, past more unsmiling candidates, along the sea all the way to Yalta.

How pleased I was when I could finally check into my hotel, sarcastically named the Hotel Sea Breeze. The only breeze here comes from the car fumes when you open the balcony door – the hotel looms over the main coastal road, almost opposite the Livadiya Palace.

I am glad to get back to the palace at last – white and brittle, tiered like a porcelain wedding cake. I wander round the museum again, saying hello to the familiar faces in the photographs: Winston eating his caviar with a spoon, Tsarina Alexandra leaning over her homework upstairs, watched over by her governess.

'The Livadiya Palace was built from Inkerman stone, which turns yellow with time,' starts the guide as I join the tour for the second time this month. 'In order to keep the building white, Russian architect Krasnov decided to cover the stone with a secret solution, which has kept it immaculate for a century. There are many other fascinating secrets hidden in this palace, but a two-hour excursion does not give us enough time to discover them all,' he continues.

I don't want to discover them all; I am only interested in one, I think.

The tourist guide is strong, gnarled and withered, like the oak trees in the palace park. I recognise him – he is the same guide who led our cruise tour a fortnight ago. He must be in his late seventies, his skin parched by southern sun, dried by winter winds. His English is surprisingly good. He shows us around with pride and dignity, as if it is his own house, stopping from time to time to rest on his cane.

He remembers lots of interesting figures if you listen to him:

'. . . one hundred and sixteen rooms, built in sixteen months by two thousand workers, completed in 1911 . . . the plenaries took place in the White Hall: two hundred and eighteen metres square, seven metres high, with four hundred lamps hidden behind the frieze . . . two and a half thousand people attended the conference, both military and diplomats, from three countries . . .'

But I am on a different mission here. I need to find a way to retrieve my Exhibit X.

'Amazingly, though the palace suffered greatly during the war,' the guide continues, leading us into a light-oak-panelled hall, 'the most fragile pieces were not broken – this Venetian chandelier, the French mirror, two Meissen vases . . .'

He stops by the display cabinet under the mirror. 'We have recently opened our archives following the sixty-year secrecy rule, and soon we'll have the chance to display other previously hidden documents discussed during the Crimean conference here.'

I am trying not to show my excitement. I know all about those documents now – I did a bit of plotting, Tony style, last time I was here. My coiffed cruise companions, curious by definition, asked all the right questions, briefed by me, so I know that they are in the research room across the corridor.

# The Game

But how on earth did Tony know when he was giving me my first task – *Find out the best way for retrieval . . .*?

I take a close-up photo of the Meissen vase, while listening to the guide, then pretend to take another picture, studying the red velvet of the display cabinet through the camera lens but in fact checking the exits and the windows.

I feel like a spy in an old movie – only this is my game and it's for real. Just as I am about to ask for a map of the palace, which would show all one hundred and sixteen rooms, the guide announces:

'You are in for a treat – we started doing the roof excursions only last week. We could take an old staircase to the roof to see the solarium. The views from there are magnificent. Is anybody interested?'

'I am,' I say, a bit too hastily. The roof excursion might just be the entry ticket to my next task.

My plan is simple: at the end of the last tour of the day, I'll go back to the wrought-iron staircase and climb to the roof terrace, to watch evening Yalta flickering on the left, to listen to the scraps of music along the coast, to stargaze until the clock on the palace tower strikes midnight.

Who would have thought that my long-lost dream of becoming a surgeon would come true today? I need a scalpel to open the flimsy lock of the research room, and then it is just a glass cabinet, no wires attached, so all I have to do is cut the glass with my scalpel, take the documents out and then put the glass back. Not sure about this last bit yet, but it will work somehow. Then I'll return to the roof to welcome the dawn of the new day, lounging behind one of the solarium columns, waiting for the first tourists. I'll come down with the first morning group and retire to my hotel for a well deserved sleep. Easy.

I decide to build up some stamina by going up and down the paths of the royal park, studying Latin names on rare cedars and sequoias. I even contemplate for a couple of minutes the mountain ascent on the tsar's path, but after studying the map by the palace entrance decide that I need to save my energy and refuel – chicken soup and ice cream in the museum café are much more important at this stage, before my night shift. After that, I join the last (my third!) evening tour of the palace and stay on the roof to admire the sea views long enough to hide behind a white column and watch the sun go down, the first evening lights of Yalta twinkling on the left. Everything is going according to plan.

As soon as I start moving, however, I discover two things which will not make my task easy: I forgot to bring a torch, and the staircase rattles, waking up the bats and the ghosts. At least the oak-panelled hall is lit by the dull white glow from the lamp outside, giving me just enough light for my operation. I get the scalpel out and note with satisfaction that my hands aren't shaking. I'd have made an excellent surgeon, whatever my mother says.

'You'll damage the door,' says a voice with my mother's unmistakable Russian accent. It must be my conscience talking to me. 'Leave it alone,' continues the voice, and now I can see somebody's shadow on the chair by the door.

I am ready to say: 'You were right, Mama' – not about my surgical skills, but about me never living up to my name, which means 'lion' in Russian: not brave enough, not aggressive enough. I am certainly not living up to my name now, though my rational brain understands the urgency of escape. This is not my conscience or my mother speaking. It is somebody else, waiting for me in the dark corner.

I run along the corridor, towards the grand White Hall. But as I rush into the Hall, light dazzles me. The Hall is suddenly flooded by it and he is standing by the entrance, leaning on his cane, looking straight at me. He is talking calmly, as if he has invited me to a night tour. I recognise him now, the guide from this morning.

'We are in the White Hall now, one of five reception halls in Livadiya,' he says. 'It is two hundred and eighteen metres square and seven metres high, and is lit by four hundred lamps. If you are wondering where they are, they are hidden behind the frieze . . .

'Four columns are made from one slab of marble,' he continues as I rush past the columns towards another exit, 'and the sculpture of the Greek goddess Penelope you are now passing was a present from the Odessites to the tsar. Penelope is a symbol of loyalty – where do *your* loyalties lie, young man? Who do you work for – the Americans? Mossad, maybe?'

I take a sharp left, rushing along the dark corridor with his voice following me: 'There are one hundred and sixteen rooms in the palace . . .'

I run back up the staircase to the roof – he won't catch up with me, I am half his age. I block the door with a chair and turn, relieved, only to see him already standing in front of me, continuing monotonously, with an ominous smile: 'Livadiya was built as a modern palace, with hot and cold water in the taps, telephones and electricity, and a lift that leads straight to the roof . . .'

He is approaching me slowly, leaning on his cane, and in the dark I can see the light from outside reflected in his glasses. He is getting closer, closer . . . What has he got in his hand? I can't see – a gun? No way am I going to jump, it is too high. Besides, he is too old, too weak to kill me – though now, as he pokes me with his cane, I start having doubts.

'Your husband has died in Crimea, under the stars, beaten to death by a pensioner on the roof of the tsar's palace' – I can only imagine what Dana will say when the embassy calls, though I'm sure which will come first: 'What was he doing in Crimea? He was supposed to be attending the national conference on new bronchitis treatments in Milton Keynes!' or: 'He has so let us down with his death, Levi, so let us down again . . .'

'Are you a spy?' he demands, still poking me. 'You have to confess.'

I can't think of what to say, I am too busy trying to escape from his sharp jabs, and he interprets the pause as silent agreement.

'I knew it!' he exclaims triumphantly, waving his cane. 'I always knew it – from the moment you first came here! I saw you last month with the pensioners' group . . . the way you were snooping around, asking questions: "Were there any secret discussions at the conference that are not yet in the public domain?" I mean, who asks such questions on a whistle-stop cruise tour? When I saw you again today, I said to myself: "This man is after something – watch him, Peter!" And I was right! So, what *are* you after?'

Levi, your fact-finding skills need brushing up – you were too obvious, I think, looking at the old man. He is the vigilante and I am a criminal; nothing will change that. The only way to avoid the unfair battle (I am still not sure about the winner/loser balance here) and escape from more than fair arrest is to ask him to help me.

It is my last chance not to blow my game task, so I tell him what he wants to hear.

'You are right,' I begin. 'I work for a secret international organisation (leading yourself deeper into trouble, Levi), can't give you the name (because I can't think of one; I am a north London GP, I haven't watched a single James Bond film), and we need to borrow the documents you have in the cabinet in the research room. It is important for us, and,' I say, to add significance, 'for the world. Do you understand?'

(Or did I watch *Goldfinger* once? I think this is a quote from there.)

Surprisingly, my rubbish lie works.

'To borrow . . . for how long?' he asks, and I remember that he is from my father's Soviet generation, that thinks in black and white. In his eyes, I am now a lighter shade of grey.

I think of the final date of the game, the twenty-fourth of October, and say: 'For a month.'

'Which document are you after?' His glasses are gleaming ominously. 'The protocol on the California in Crimea project, the UN agreement annexe or the record of discussions on the creation of the autonomous Jewish republic in Crimea? The last one, most likely.' (He does think I'm from Mossad, doesn't he?)

I have no idea which document I need; all Tony's task said was *Retrieve the protocols safely . . .*

'I need all three,' I say with a new-found firmness in my voice. 'They are all important – for Crimea and for the world.'

He pokes me with his cane again, only this time it is a poke of approval.

'You are right, they are important,' he says. 'I have been thinking of doing something with them myself. For a month, you said? Come with me,' he orders, and pokes me towards the tsar's life. The ten second ride from the roof is the most uncomfortable lift journey of my life. At least we don't get stuck, and he leads me to the entrance of the research centre.

He opens the door of the research room and leads me to the glass cabinet. I stand there, my scalpel and my action-man skills surplus to requirements, watching him as he unlocks the cabinet with his keys and gets the papers out.

'Are these the documents you are after?' he asks. I nod, reading the titles and the names of the participants, thinking how lucky I am. Too soon, as the guide puts the documents back, locks the cabinet again and turns to me. 'I expect you to give me a signed note confirming that the documents are on loan and you will be bringing them back in a month.' (Am I really hearing this? What do I put in the note: *Borrowed for the use of a secret organisation that is going to save the world*?)

'Now, if you want to spend the night here, it's up to you,' he says. 'But I suggest you return to your room, N212, at the Hotel Sea Breeze.' (He did watch me, didn't he!) 'Meet me at the tsar's path at six tomorrow morning – by the Rotunda. Bring your receipt note – don't forget your address and telephone number – and I'll deliver the documents.'

'It is six thousand seven hundred and twenty metres long, that path,' I protest. 'Wouldn't it be easier to give me the documents now?'

'Don't look for easy ways in life, my boy.' He shares his wisdom gravely. He pokes me again, the last time today, hopefully. 'If the tsar could walk it, you'll be able to. The Rotunda is halfway, only three thousand metres for you to go. You could do with a new fitness regime . . .' and he marches towards the exit, shaking his wise head.

At least I won't be taking that mountain trolley bus back, is my last thought before I crash out on the hard Sea Breeze pillow. I dream of Shrek from the roadside lodge force-feeding me while Snow White dances with the stern-faced election candidate – though after my surreal experience last night, nothing would surprise me. From tomorrow morning it will all be downhill, like the screeching joyful trolley bus: a pleasant three-hour boat trip to Odessa, then on to Istanbul . . . And with the documents in my suitcase.

Only it is not downhill all the way. It is two hours of dawn uphill struggle to meet my poking tormentor. At least every hundred metres they have signs carved on rocks, so I can concentrate on numbers and equations: 'three hundred metres' minus three stones out of my trainers; 'seven hundred' plus one fence blocking the path plus two short cuts; 'a thousand' minus one bottle of water finished, 'two thousand five hundred' plus eight columns of the Rotunda I can already see, which is not really round, only semicircular . . . until I reach my lucky number – 'three thousand metres' plus one wise guide, who must have got here in half the time, welcoming me in with his running commentary.

'Isn't it the best place to watch the sunrise?' he starts. 'Nicholas II thought so too. The Rotunda was built in 1843 for another palace, called the Oreanda. It survived the earthquake of 1927 and was restored in the 1970s. Have you brought the note, by the way?' he asks in one breath. I nod.

'Have you noticed that the Rotunda is built bang on the

cliff?' He continues his excursion. 'The steps below used to lead to another coastal path, but there is no access to it now.' He stands inside the rotunda, waving me to join him, and I suddenly realise that he has chosen a perfect location to deal with a 'Mossad agent' – one push, and with the rocks below, no access to the path and an eagle circling around, this is the best place to make somebody disappear . . .

I decide against entering, and start the dialogue from a distance. 'The world's press is already waiting for those documents – they will be the historic discoveries of the century!' I shout to him from the path. I'm not sure exactly what discoveries these will be – I have only seen the headings, after all. 'I expect that we will get the information published next . . . yes, next week, when I get back.'

He steps out of his comfort zone, away from the cliff-hanging colonnade, and approaches me, leaning on his cane. I am now facing him, my back propped against the rock, my feet steady – I am ready to fight when he drags me towards the cliff.

'The note!' he orders, and examines the piece of paper I hand him. I have put the surgery address and telephone number at the bottom, reasoning with myself that it is safer than giving the home address of our Golders Green semi. He nods solemnly, and instead of pushing me, hands me a package wrapped in yesterday's *Izvestiya*.

'Put them in your bag,' he instructs. 'Return them undamaged in a month's time.'

Our spy-like exchange takes two minutes and is witnessed by the lonely eagle and a couple of lost seagulls.

'How are you going to transport them to . . .' he checks the bottom of my note, 'to London?'

'Via Odessa and Istanbul.' For the first time in two days, I am actually telling him the truth.

He thinks about my route for a moment, then nods approvingly and adds:

'You can stay here and enjoy the views for a while – about twenty minutes would be enough, I think – then start your descent.'

And he is off, strong and firm, like a weathered Crimean rock. I sit in the Rotunda much longer than necessary, knowing that the weight of the documents is going to make my journey down even harder. Focus, Levi – a three-hour relaxed boat trip to Odessa is your next step . . . Only it does not get easier.

'. . . We did not have time to update the website.' The girl does not lift her head from her glossy magazine. 'Yes, I know it says "Yalta–Odessa shuttle, twelve forty" . . . The boat to Odessa is seasonal. The season finished two days ago. You can take an overnight bus,' she suggests, turning the page. 'It is only twelve hours . . .'

I rattle on an old Ikarus bus across the steppes, waking up at the bus stations that look like war bunkers, strange creatures of the night crowding the benches. It is a long ride and I am bursting, but refuse to leave the bus, still undecided: am I a superhero guarding the documents, or a coward with a lion's name, afraid of the bus stop zombies . . . Maybe this is the type of fun my kids will crave during their gap year, but I am too old for it.

Ah, Odessa at last, and the hotel should be comfortable and familiar, if only because of the name: the Londonskaya.

'I would like to inform you that I have a reservation,' I say in English, hoping that a well-spoken, old-fashioned request will compensate for the way I look.

'We are fully booked,' the receptionist retorts in perfect English. Her pretty face is blank – no smile, no acknowledgement for me. I am not in her system.

It is definitely the way I look after the night bus ride, I decide, catching my reflection in the gilded lobby mirror. Creased shirt, bloodshot eyes, and the hair, the hair!

The girl suddenly presents me with a smile, as if she has a nice surprise in store – and she does! 'We have another hotel in our group,' she says. 'It has just reopened after renovation, and we have upgraded you to a suite to compensate for your inconvenience. A car will take you to the Hotel Bristol now.'

'Bristol was my university town,' I sigh. My life there was far from comfortable, but it will do.

Odessa's Bristol, oozing refurbished grandeur, has a cool marbled lobby and velvet armchairs. My bedroom is as large as the entire top floor of our house in London, and the bed could accommodate four . . . five, yes, five people easily. This luxury is lost on me, though – I would rather spend my time in Moldavanka, in my old courtyard . . .

No more tiles have been added, the same knickers are on the ropes, the same man is cleaning the dovecote at the end – as if time has stopped here completely, frozen, waiting for my return.

I climb up the rusty iron staircase to the green veranda, walk into the tiny space with the oilcloth table and the empty granny's chair. Why am I disappointed that she isn't here? Isn't that what happens on this veranda at eleven o'clock – pink gown at her observation post and the girl behind the door of number five still asleep?

I am not panicking yet, but there is just the first cold trickle of fear: what if she is at work? What if it was her day off last time?

I knock, and she opens the door almost instantly, as if she was expecting me – already dressed this time, in jeans and a pink T-shirt. Her face lights up; she screams and hugs me, like a long-lost relative. I am standing there, disoriented and happy, with a young girl dangling off me, and all I can think about is her pert breasts pressing against my chest and her hair tickling my neck.

'I knew you would be back, Shapiro,' she exclaims. 'I knew it! How much time have you got this time? Half an hour again?'

'Today . . .' I stop, pretending to think. Need to sound important and not very excited. 'I have finished my business, leaving tomorrow morning. So if you are free . . .'

She waves me into the room. I try not to look at the ruffled bedding in the corner.

'You live here alone?' I start cautiously.

'Yes, the ultimate Moldavanka bride – with a dowry of a flat and without any relatives.' She laughs. 'So, if you are interested . . .' She winks at me.

I am lost for words. This is not what I had planned.

But she bails me out, carries on talking: 'My mum died from cancer seven years ago and my brother – he is two years older than me – is doing really well, has got his own flat now, cool car and all. So here I am, a proud bride-in-waiting.'

'And your father?' I ask.

'Oh, I never met him, but I think he was Greek. A handsome Greek sailor from a merchant ship, visiting Odessa. I'd like to think that, it's so romantic, isn't it? Otherwise why would my mother choose a Greek name for me – Zoya? It means "life", you know.'

I am not smitten any more; I am up to my neck in a feeling not known, not experienced by any man before – it cannot be analysed as 'chemical processes in the brain', or 'pheromones emitted', or . . . She is lighting me from within, this girl. In chemistry this would mean an explosion; in real life it is a feeling just short of a miracle.

So, her name is Zoya . . . She is very young, early twenties, I think.

'You were still at school when your mum died?' I ask. 'Who brought you up, then?'

149

'What do you mean?' She is looking at me as if I am totally dumb. 'The neighbours, of course – the courtyard in Moldavanka is like a family, don't you remember? Ah, you don't – you left ages ago. You know my neighbour in the pink gown, Auntie Klava, she used to be a teacher. Not my teacher, though – for me she has always been old, as long as I can remember. When social services wanted to take us to the orphanage, it was Auntie Klava, who insisted that she – and our courtyard – would look after us.

'And you know what? I am not scared of anything after Moldavanka School. We have all sorts here – remember the saying: Moldavanka will never be overpopulated, as half of the people are in prison, the other half bring them food parcels and then they swap. But we also have a tailor in our courtyard, Lora's husband is a mechanic on a big ship, and—'

Zoya hears loud voices at the end of the courtyard and jumps like a scared kitten. She rushes to the window and looks out, then drags me to the veranda, clutching my hand. There she opens the door of Auntie Klava's flat and pushes me in. Or rather squeezes me in, between the door frame and her neighbour, who is on her way to her observation post. Granny has no option but to shuffle aside so as not to be swept away by the tide of Zoya's energy. Zoya bulldozes me in and positions me in the centre of the room.

The whole insertion operation takes ten seconds.

'Auntie Klava, you know how much I respect you, I just

don't remember why,' starts Zoya. 'Listen, can you keep him here for five minutes, just five minutes, hey?'

Auntie Klava gives her a look that could reduce anyone to ashes.

'Why is he here, Zoya?' she shouts. I have forgotten that she has a real teacher's voice, this woman. She speaks fast, throwing question after question at Zoya, pushing me back to the door with her shockingly sharp knuckles.

I've had my fair share of senior attacks during this game, I think. First the cruise crowd, then the guide with his painful magic touch, and now this Klava . . .

But Zoya stands firm, her hands still on my shoulders, squeezing them – is that why I allowed her to push me in? Even though it is clear that she has something more important to do, or somebody more important to see, and I am now merely an object to be hidden away.

'You've come to kill me at last, Zoya!' shouts Klava. 'And you've brought a hit man with you to do it! Why am I not surprised? You have been killing me for years with your behaviour, all those sleepless nights I had because of you . . . I will only find rest when I shut my eyes for ever.'

'Auntie Klava, I don't want you to shut your eyes, just your mouth if at all possible,' laughs Zoya. 'Just for five minutes, pleeease? He is very quiet, I promise, doesn't talk much. You can ask him about London . . . or America – yes, you can talk to him about New York, he knows all about Brighton Beach.'

I turn to say that though I know a lot about Brighton Beach, I don't really want to talk to Klava about it, but Zoya has already gone.

I remain standing in the middle of the room while Klava examines me closely – I must be an unusual exhibit in the list of Zoya's suitors. Even if she invited me to sit down, there is nowhere to sit: she is in the one chair in the room; the couch is occupied by three cats. That explains the smell, I think. There are pieces of rags everywhere, half-empty jars on the table, saucers with crusty remains . . . The silence lasts for a whole minute and ten seconds – I count, as the only sound I can hear is the ticking of the clock on the wall.

'So,' she breaks the silence, 'are you Baby Shapiro, then?'

Nobody has ever called me Baby Shapiro – not now, not when I was small. I was always Levi Freiman, as far as I can remember. Or Lyova, as my parents call me. This is the second time I've been called Shapiro – Zoya thought I was from the Shapiro family last time I was here. It takes a moment for the question to sink in.

Granny continues, impatiently: 'You are Lyova, Rimma and Misha's son?' Not only does she remember my parents' names, she calls me Lyova. Only my parents call me that; for everybody else I am Levi.

'Well,' she says, in her teacher's voice, 'you *are* Misha's son, aren't you?'

If she was living here when we were, why don't I remember her? Was she always at school? But I do remember what my mother often says when she counts the money at the end of the day in the café: 'If only Klava could see us now . . .' Does she mean *this* Klava?

'I am Lyova,' I admit cautiously. 'Only my last name is Freiman . . .'

'Freiman, Shmeiman – you can choose whatever name you like now, but you will always be Baby Shapiro to me!' she shouts.

'I remember so well the day you left . . .' She shuffles to the window and looks out into the courtyard, as if we were still there. 'It was early, really early . . . Rimma thought everybody was still asleep, but I knew that dozens of eyes were watching you from behind the curtains. I was standing where you are standing now, crying, helpless. I knew you had to go, I heard your parents' discussion the night before – the walls are quite thin. The whole courtyard knew.'

'Why did we have to leave?' I ask her.

She looks past me, into that day thirty-five years ago.

'Because your father was an honest man, that's why. And it is not always a good profession to have. Why are you asking me? Ask him . . .'

There is a quick, impatient knock at the door.

'Your princess is here, come to collect you,' says Auntie Klava, and there is a note of warmth in her voice. 'What a girl she is. I couldn't cope without her.'

I think my grasp of the language is not good enough any

more – isn't it the same girl knocking who according to Klava has been trying to kill her for years?

'She drives me up the wall,' continues Klava. 'Sometimes literally, as my couch is next to her wall, and these youngsters can get quite noisy. But she's the only one who pops in from time to time with a bottle of milk or some sausage, enough for me and the cats, and refuses to take any money. The rest of the courtyard just keep saying hello – they are all waiting for me to die, I am telling you, to get hold of my flat, but what's the point, if the council are promising to knock us down any minute? I have lived here all my life, I don't mind the toilet in the courtyard and all this washing hanging around. It will be the death of me when they demolish this green veranda . . . Zoya is lovely, I am telling you. So sad that she—'

'Auntie Klava, open up! What are you doing there, both of you, canoodling? Why have you locked the door?'

Zoya looks in through the netted window, drums on the glass, tries the door handle again.

'Take your hit man back, Zoya, he failed this time!' Granny shouts, shuffling past me to the door.

I turn to ask her what she was about to say, but Zoya is already here, pumping my hand with the same energy as when she was shoving me in, offering no explanation whatsoever.

As she pulls me out into the courtyard, there is a loud splash right next to us – the dovecote hermit throws down a bucket of dirty water.

'Thank you!' Zoya shouts, looking up. 'Thank you for not pouring it on our heads!'

That's exactly what my mother used to shout! I stand in the middle of the courtyard, taking photographs for my dad: the dovecote, our veranda, the communal table in the middle . . . The trees have grown and my first love Lora has turned into a bosomy matron, but some things never change.

'Zoya,' I manage, as she drags me across the street, 'I wanted to ask you – this is not far, is it?' I show her the piece of paper with the address.

She looks at me, surprised. 'It is five minutes' walk away. But why? It is an ordinary street, tiny park at the end, hardly even a park, there is nothing there.'

'There is for me,' I say quietly. 'Please, Zoya. I'll explain later.'

She shrugs her shoulders, lets go of my hand and strides ahead, showing me the way.

So, this is the road. Nothing special, Zoya was right, dilapidated two-storey houses on both sides, timid birch trees protected by concrete rings and a small monument further away.

This is where it happened. Last week, in a rare moment we had together, my father asked me to come here, and told me why.

Told me in his usual distant manner, looking out of the window of his boxy office, sitting with his back to me, rocking slightly, as if he was reading a prayer. Not that he believes in any God. Though listening to his story, I would be prepared to accept the idea of divine intervention.

I can hear him talking now, as I walk along the same street, counting the steps he took. Only now there is no crowd on the pavement, nobody is watching. And no guard dogs. I close my eyes as I hear his voice . . .

*I was not scared, just sleepy. Why had Mama woken us up so early?*

*She said we were going for a long walk now, but I didn't understand why so early and why so many people were joining us. I also didn't understand why my mama said as we started walking:*

*'Misha, we are going to play hide and seek. When I push you out, you run and hide in the crowd. Don't call out for me, just be quiet. I'll find you, sooner or later, I know I'll find you.'*

*Aunt Isla was with us, and Grandma Elsa too. We never used to play hide and seek together. They were all looking at me, waiting for me to hide. They looked very serious, as if their life depended on this game.*

*And why were so many people watching us? As if they were queuing for kerosene or bread, but it was a thicker queue, a live corridor.*

*Mama leaned over to me and gave me a crumpled hand-kerchief. It was heavy; there was something in it. 'Hold on to it,' she said. 'It's magic. If you have it, I'll find you wherever you are. Just hold on to it.'*

## The Game

*She kissed my cheek with one long kiss and suddenly pushed me out, into the watching queue. 'Run, Misha,' she whispered into my ear. 'Run and hide. Just hold on to the magic hand-kerchief and I'll find you.'*

*She was smiling, but there were tears in her eyes. Why was she crying? It was such fun, the best game of hide and seek ever. My mama never played with me; she was always working or queuing for food or talking to Aunt Isla in loud whispers. I didn't know what they were talking about, I didn't under-stand it at all. The words were strange, foreign: evacuation, coupon, Tashkent, ghetto . . .*

*I held on to the magic handkerchief and ran, burrowed though the crowd, trying to hide behind the backs of the grown-ups. Suddenly somebody's strong hand touched my shoulder: 'Come with me, boy, let's hide.' The game became more inter-esting now, with this grown woman playing with me. She had a kind face, with wide cheekbones. She took me out of the crowd, fast, her hand still on my shoulder, and we walked and walked until I was tired.*

*'My mama will never find me if we go further,' I said.*

*'Oh, she will, don't worry, my* hlopchyk,*' she said, calling me 'boy' in her soft Ukrainian accent.*

*We went to the second floor of a house on Kanatnaya, two blocks away from where we lived, and by then I was tired, and I lay on her big bed and waited and waited until I fell asleep.*

*It was dark when I woke up. The woman with the kind face was sitting under a green lampshade, with my magic handkerchief untied on the table. Now I could see what was inside it: my grandmother's wedding ring, her large hoop earrings, Auntie Isla's bracelet and my mother's chain. I became scared. Why had this woman taken our jewellery? What if she was a wicked witch who stole children and precious things?*

*I ran to the table and pushed her away with all my strength. 'Get away from my magic handkerchief,' I shouted. 'My mama will never find me! Why did you do this?'*

*The woman pulled me in and unexpectedly kissed the back of my head. 'What is your name,* hlopchyk? *Misha . . . I always wanted a boy, but never had children. I will look after you. Don't cry, we'll wait for your mama here. My name is Auntie Oxona – will you remember?'*

*'This is my nephew Misha – his parents were killed by a bomb, so he's come to live with me,' she told the neighbours. They guessed, but nobody said anything. This was Odessa, remember, where somebody else's life was often more important than your own . . .*

*Years later Auntie Oxona explained what happened that day.*

*My mother pushed me away from death row, out of the column going to the Prohorovsky Park to be sent to the concentration camp in Bogdanovka. Our family disappeared in that column, together with a hundred thousand other Jews from Odessa – burned alive, machine-gunned through holes in warehouse walls, hanged, frozen to death in Slobodka. There is a small birch tree park in Prohorovsky Square now, Levi.*

# The Game

*Please go there for me, take a picture. If I cannot go back myself, at least I will have a photograph of that place. That's where I was pushed back into life . . . Will you do this for me?*

'Hey, Londoner, are you OK there?' Zoya is watching me with curiosity. 'He was three hundred and forty steps away,' I say, catching my breath after counting aloud.

Three hundred and forty steps from the bronze children trying to break out of the barbed wire, to the place where he started this walk, where Zoya, very real, very alive, is standing now, almost shouting at me.

'Maybe you could explain to me what is going on. Why are we here? And why have I just stood for ten minutes watching you meditate or whatever weird thing you were doing?'

She sounds like an impatient toddler, so I distract her, like I do with the children (and sometimes their mothers) in my morning surgeries, with my own question about something else: 'Is *this* the tram stop we need, Zoya? Or shall we get a taxi?'

'Taxi, taxi, of course,' she says confidently. 'If we are going to see Odessa's Monument to the Bribe, you might as well spend some money.'

Ten minutes later, Zoya is pointing at a bronze youngster in a wig, balancing on a giant orange. 'See this man? That's the emperor, Pavel I think his name was . . . The story goes that he was prescribed fruit when he was ill – you know, all that vitamin C, it's good for your immune system, my doctor keeps telling me that . . .'

'What doctor?' I ask, but Zoya has already continued with the story, slightly breathless. 'Some Odessa merchants heard about it and sent the emperor a gift of three thousand oranges straight from a Greek ship – in February! Oh, I forgot to add, they asked for a hefty loan to complete the port construction at the same time.

'Those oranges were served during a dinner the emperor had with his favourites, so there was bound to be a result,' laughs Zoya. 'The emperor gave the money to finish the port, the city grew, and now we have a monument to those oranges, to the bribe . . .'

We stop by a street café with a fence made of painted bicycles and piles of fake books supporting the tables.

Zoya smiles suggestively – 'Time for lunch?' – and shouts into the semi-darkness of the café: 'Is anybody alive here?'

'Not really,' answers a waiter lazily, not raising his eyes from the book he is reading.

'Then send somebody who is already dead – we are hungry here!' shouts Zoya, and in the same breath continues, turning to me: 'Hey, let me show you something . . .'

She writes her name in Cyrillic – *ЗОЯ* – and pushes the piece of paper towards me.

'Look,' she assumes the tone of a primary school teacher, 'just look at this carefully. What do you see?' She taps her fingers impatiently, then cups her hand over the last letter.

'Well?' she asks. 'Look carefully. 30 . . .' I can read in Cyrillic, just about, but why do I always see formulae everywhere?
'The number thirty?' I suggest.

'Exactly!' She approves of my answer and removes her hand. 'And now?'

'Thirty plus the letter Я,' I say, sounding and probably looking like the village idiot.

'Oh,' she sighs, giving up. 'Я means "me", right? This is my name code, thirty plus Я. It means that there are thirty "me"s in it; I can choose whoever I want to be, every day of the month! Great, isn't it?' she says, delighted.

I look at her, thinking: *whoever you are trying to be, Zoya, you are just a child really . . . What do I talk to you about? Lessons?*

Zoya shouts into the darkness of the cafe: 'WE ARE STARVING!' then turns back to me. 'I love this place. The service is hopeless, but it is all about books – just look around. I love reading. You know,' she adds enthusiastically, 'my favourite book is English, yes, yes: *Oliver Twist*. I read it three times! You remember in the film . . . in the book, I mean, when Nancy takes Oliver to the bridge? I always cry when I watch it . . .'

She makes a sad face and takes something out of her bag. 'Talking of books . . . I was going to ask you a favour. I am applying for your Open University correspondence course – English literature, what else? I've completed the application, was about to post it . . . no, I couldn't email, I don't

trust the internet in Odessa, nothing ever works here prop-
erly . . . Anyway, since you are here and going to London
tomorrow . . . Perfect timing, isn't it?' (That's why she was
so happy to see me!) 'The application is in here.'

She hands me an envelope with a telephone number and
a name – Λ Е Н Я – written neatly on it. (Not another
envelope! I think.)

'Could you give it to my ex, who lives in London now?
Here is the name and the telephone number. Please make
sure he gets it . . .'

'I can send your application myself,' I suggest.

'No,' she says hastily. 'Lenya promised. He will do it.' She
pats my hand. 'Thank you! See? I could have posted it, but
I was waiting for you, I knew you would come back!'

It is a lie, it must be; she could not have known I would
be back, she could not have been waiting for me, could she?
Come on, Freiman, why can't you be pragmatic when this
girl is smiling at you?

As we wait for the food to arrive, we talk, or rather, Zoya
talks. About her brother, who took her to the 'Twelve Steps'
programme to save her from drug addiction, about her
dream of a new flat closer to the centre of Odessa, and how
she would love to work with children but instead is stuck
in a boring shop . . .

'The shop!' She jumps up. 'I am supposed to be at work
by now! What time is it? Listen, I must go. Your hotel is
just around the corner. Turn left at the end of the street.

Please let me know when you come again, we'll have fun
. . . This is my number. Call me when you've given the letter
to Lenya, tell me what he says . . .'

She kisses me on both cheeks, gives me a hug and flies
out. I am sitting there dumbfounded, wondering whether
it was something I said or didn't say, or whether she was
genuinely late. At least I've got her telephone number now.

I look at her name, written in Russian: *ЗОЯ* – 30 + 'me'
– thinking: Who is this girl, really? And what number, what
lucky lottery number, does she mean for me?

I pay for the lunch we never had and drift out. Zoya was
right, the hotel is around the corner, but even crossing the
road is an adventure in this town.

I am shaken by a sharp, shrieking noise – a strange tram
is moving slowly towards me. It is all jazzed up, literally:
covered in balloons and flowers, with thirties Dixieland
music blaring out of its glassless windows. I just have enough
time to take a step back, as the music-box tram clatters past,
carrying the band and the passengers away. A tall woman
by the window on the far side is obviously enjoying this –
she is moving from side to side, laughing, clapping. I can't
see her face, but she looks just like Alex.

'I bet you're loving every minute of this, Levi,' says a voice.
Somebody is standing behind me, speaking with a hint of
an Australian accent. And the voice is rather familiar.

I have obviously been drugged in that bookworm café,
either by the waiter, who looked doped to me already, or

by Zoya. Maybe she did not rush back to work after all;
perhaps she is hiding behind the glass pyramid at the end
of Primorsky Boulevard, waiting to . . . to do what?

'You didn't really think I'd leave you on your own at a
moment of such importance, did you? I've been waiting in
the hotel for ages!'

Tony. I turn – and of course it is Tony. Why should I be
surprised? If he flew all the way from Australia to start this
game, he might as well watch us, wherever we are. Still, I
am annoyed, like a child given a bright toy only to have it
taken away. It was my act-alone task after all. It is pointless
to ask him what he is doing here. He won't say; besides, he
is already standing next to me. I just have to accept it.

'How are you getting on, Levi?' continues Tony, as if we
are picking up a conversation we started ten minutes ago.
'Any luck with the documents?'

'As a matter of fact, yes,' I tell him, 'and the whole
operation only took forty-eight hours – not counting the
overnight bus, that is.'

'Shall we have a look at them?' he asks, already walking
into the hotel lobby. It looks like my act-alone days are over.

'Was it challenging?' He sounds genuinely interested as
we carry on along the corridor to my room. I want to tell
him about me being a superhero with my scalpel, but I can't
lie and Tony knows that. So I have to tell him about the
guide instead. Tony listens, occasionally asking for clarifica-
tion: 'what time was it when he caught you? Did you check

the documents during the handover? Did he ask you about your route home?'

In the room, I lay the papers on the bed like a pack of cards – 'California in Crimea', the independent Jewish republic, the UN agreement codicil – and step back, waiting for Tony to examine them in silence.

'They are explosive,' I say finally. 'I read all of them. Would you like me to translate?'

'No need,' says Tony calmly. 'I know what they mean.'

Of course he does; why did I even ask? I try again, hoping to squeeze at least one answer out of him at this stage. 'Which one are we using for the game, Tony?'

Tony has already assembled the papers, spread on the bed, into a neat pile.

'It is irrelevant which one of the three protocols will be used,' he explains. 'They all mean one thing, crucially – a change of control over Crimean territory. Such a change would make many people unhappy. The Turks, for a start – they control the Dardanelles passage out of the Black Sea. The smugglers won't be thrilled, either – they have a free-trade zone in Odessa negotiated until 2025. And then there is the military issue, of the Black Sea fleet . . .'

Tony is not his usual ironic self, and his eyes are not smiling either.

'Tony,' I say, 'this is not a game any more, is it? This is for real. The scale, the dangers . . . Do you ever think about what happened during the last game? Don't you think we might end the same way again? This is really going too far; it's not about throwing the dice and waiting for the next move . . .'

'Monopoly . . .' says Tony pensively. 'Thanks for the prompt, Levi. I didn't think of this one before – the monopoly of the oil pipelines. Another group who don't want the protocols to become public. You know,' he continues, 'I was thinking about you going to Istanbul tomorrow . . . I'm not sure it is the best route, even though I booked you a first-class cabin. It is the most obvious route, you are right – but they will know that too.'

'Who are *they*?' I ask. 'What do you mean?'

'You didn't think that guide would just let you go with the documents, did you?' asks Tony. 'He watched you in Livadiya; why would he stop? He has alerted somebody to watch you now, no doubt.'

'Well, I left him a note with my address,' I am about to say, but stop – even I understand how ridiculous this sounds.

'Listen, Levi, I really think it would be safer to take a different route back tomorrow morning,' says Tony. 'I have got another idea – and it's going to be fun.' He winks. 'Have you ever travelled through a black hole? Well, tomorrow is your chance. We can travel through Transdnistria, a self-proclaimed republic with dodgy borders. 'It is only sixty kilometres from Odessa – and officially the black hole of Europe. There are watchtowers, thousands of border guards, a UN border-monitoring mission, but they are all struggling.

You know the properties of black holes: they are invisible to observers and equipment.'

'How are we going to get through this black hole?' I ask, trying not to sound doomed.

'You'll see.' Even Tony sounds excited. 'It will certainly be a journey to impress your kids with . . . I think you might need some sleep now – I'll knock on your door at five.' This is Tony to a T, persuasive and secretive.

Though what would my children think if they could see me now, wedged between wooden crates in stark darkness in the back of a Romanian fruit truck? If they asked me how I had ended up here, I could not give them a coherent answer. ('What's new? You mumble most of the time anyway,' my wife would comment.) It was all too quick – getting to the port at dawn, Tony negotiating with a driver who was supervising the loading of bananas from a ship, climbing into the back of the truck, the engine starting . . .

I could write down the black hole formulas, Tony, and discuss the Schwarzschild radius, but at the moment, all the properties of black holes are here in this truck: time has stopped, it's pitch black, and my whole being is filled with primeval, paralysing fear – as if I have already experienced it, lived through it. My head is throbbing, I am out of breath, and if we don't stop soon, I'll be sick all over the bananas.

Did my ancestors feel the same way all those years ago, hiding in their houses, caught in the tornado of the Jewish pogroms, which brought destruction, pillage and blood?

Is this the same fear that made the survivors lick their wounds, grab their children and escape from Odessa – from its leafy boulevards, its French patisseries . . . abandon all the beauty of the city because the air here now smelled of fear that made them run, and hide, and run and hide again? Only here, in this truck, there is nowhere to hide.

'Daddy, you have to think outside the box.' I remember my daughter's childhood joke. 'If you are in a metal box, no locks, no doors, nowhere to escape, just a table in the middle, how would you get out?'

Then she would laugh and tell me, ignoring all the rules and spellings and dangers: 'You run around the room until your feet get sore, use the saw to cut the table in half, two halves make a whole, jump through the hole, shout until your voice gets hoarse, jump on the horse and gallop away!'

My children are all I can think of now. Sami, Raya, Natan – will I ever see you again, will I get out of this truck alive?

The truck has stopped and there are angry voices outside, banging, shouting – and now a grinding sound . . . somebody is opening the back door.

In the darkness of the truck I forgot how bright the world could be. It is sunny outside, and we are parked on the road leading to the border control post in the distance, but there are no border guards and our truck driver is nowhere to be seen either. Did he do a runner or has he been killed already?

'Get out!' somebody shouts, only I can't – my legs won't let me. We must still be at the centre of the black hole, with no gravity – I am weightless, I can't move, so Tony half carries, half pushes me out. 'Don't do anything silly,' he whispers. You already have, Tony, I think. We should have taken the boat . . .

My eyes are adjusting to the bright light and I can now see them clearly. There are four men altogether – two waiting by the black Jeep Cherokee, the other two standing by the back door of the truck. All of them in leather jackets, hands in their pockets. Can't see the guns yet.

All of them are quite young, and the face of the gangster who is standing in front of me looks vaguely familiar. He has all the 'leader of the gang' status symbols: shaved head, the broadest shoulders and a broken nose. Perfect casting, perfect setting for an action movie about some eastern European mafia. Shame I can't take a photograph now – it would have earned me Brownie points with my Sami and Natan; even Raya might have noticed me after that.

The leader stands too close to us to shoot, but he would have no problem knocking me out with one sharp hook, I guess. 'Where is it?' he demands. 'Where is the document?' He does not sound too intimidating, surprisingly, and he shows no hatred – maybe because killing people is a routine job for him.

Tony is the picture of calmness; he has not uttered a word. Of course, he doesn't understand what they are saying. And I am not in the mood to interpret. I swallow hard and realise that my vocal cords are paralysed too; I can't answer.

'I am not here to play games,' continues the leader. 'Just give us the fucking document.'

He is now standing even closer, watching us, while his assistant lugs our bags out. I can't think, but my sixth sense whispers to me that if I move now, I'll lose a tooth in three seconds.

The search is surprisingly quick. They start with my bag, and within a minute the henchman calls out: 'Here it is!' He pulls out Zoya's letter and passes it to the guy with the broken nose: 'Look, it says "Lenya" and it has his telephone number.'

'This is my friend's application,' I protest. 'She is applying to the Open University, she loves English literature and *Oliver Twist . . .*' (Why am I telling him all this?)

The change in the gangsters is dramatic. They are laughing so much that one of them ends up wiping away tears, while another one rolls on the grass.

I nudge Tony – 'Should we escape now?' – but he makes a gesture to stay where we are. 'What if they are armed?' he whispers.

'This is . . . this is her best yet,' the gangster leader says finally, breathless from laughter. 'Really the best. The only university Zoya would ever attend is the Odessa poker school. She *would* say *Oliver Twist*, wouldn't she? We all know that story by heart – it's about us. We grew up playing thieves and smugglers like other children play soldiers and astronauts. We are from Moldavanka, remember. Zoya's nickname is Nancy – she has a heart of gold, that girl, she just mixes with the wrong company. At least she told you the truth when she said the letter was to Lenya.'

He tears away the edge of Zoya's envelope, scans the lined pages and shows them to his leather-clad assistant.

'And why am I not surprised? Look, she has described all our smuggling routes so that Lenya can use them too. Listen, we are decent people, we only smuggle vodka and tobacco. Now Lenya *is* a criminal. Smuggling vodka is one thing, but trafficking girls is another. I suspect he tried to sell Zoya too, when he offered her a weekend trip to Turkey. I intervened just in time, my friends had a quiet word with him, and now he is hiding in London. He was the one who started her on drugs, too, but she refuses to fucking forget the bastard! When I popped in to see her yesterday, I thought she was a bit quick to get rid of me, so I came back later and Klava mentioned that she had gone into town with an Englishman. It did not take me long to find you – there are only three or four places she would have taken you to – I found you quite quickly and was watching you from a distance. When I saw her handing you a letter . . . We are smarter here than we look!' He winks and pats me on the shoulder. His hand is heavy. Too heavy to imagine what it might do with one single blow.

I should really ask what is going to happen to us, but instead I blurt out: 'Zoya . . . what will happen to her now?'

'Are you worried about her?' Our chief puts his hand in

his pocket – I expect him to produce a gun, but instead he takes out a handkerchief, blows his broken nose and sighs. 'I am too . . . I managed to stop her this time, but I can't watch her twenty-four seven!'

'I wish I could get my hands on Lenya . . .' His twists his hands in a gesture that leaves me in no doubt what he would do to him. 'This bastard has killed her already, in a way, with his dirty needles – gave her Speed . . .'

'You mean LSD?' I ask.

'Oh, that as well,' he sighs.

'SPEED – you know, this immune disease where it is . . . called AIDS in English, I think. Get the difference?' he says glumly. 'SPEED versus AIDS? Here people die quickly, while where you are from there is hope and help . . .

'I sorted Zoya out with the "Twelve Steps" programme – she is not taking drugs now, and she works in my friend's shop when she is not too tired, but I don't know how long she has left.'

Why didn't my logical brain work it out earlier! Now I understand why his face looks familiar. He has Zoya's eyes. 'Are you Zoya's brother?' I ask.

'Do I look like her sister to you?' He laughs at his own joke and blows his nose again.

'*Spasibo*,' I suddenly say to him.

'What are you thanking me for?' He is genuinely surprised.

I can't tell him that he has helped me to solve Zoya's formula; it is so clear to me now. Her name does not have thirty 'me's – $30 + \text{Я}$; it's $3 + \text{O} + \text{Я}$. There are only three 'me's there: a child desperate for love and protection, a Nancy, and a very sick girl, covering her fear with bravado. Three 'me's with a zero in the middle; non-existence in the middle of a name that means 'life' . . . A mathematical nonsense.

The wind brings new voices and new steps – three men have left the border post and are running towards us. They are too far away for us to hear what they are saying or to see their faces, but I guess that these are the border guards, coming back with the truck driver.

'Sorry, guys, you are on your own now – we don't need publicity,' says Zoya's brother, and spits through his front teeth. The Jeep brigade read this as the signal to start the car.

'By the way, there are better ways to travel,' says Zoya's brother, putting the letter into the pocket of his jacket. 'You could have had a first-class cabin to Turkey with every luxury, no questions asked. Just had to speak to us . . . we know the right people.'

'Levi,' says Tony quickly, as I watch the black Jeep reversing on the grass, 'when the border guards ask what we are doing here, tell them that we are ramblers, researching routes for a tourist agency, walking the area . . . that we got lost here and stopped to ask for directions. The driver will deny that he knows us; it is illegal to transport people.'

What dumbo would believe that? Particularly as I greet

the border guards in Russian, hoping that it will help our dialogue.

'If you are an Englishman, with your profile and accent,' says one of the guards, interrupting my jumbled explanation, 'then I am the Roman emperor. You can kick the Jews out of Odessa, but not Odessa out of the Jews.' He laughs and hits me at the same time.

I double up in blinding pain, noting that the blow has located my solar plexus and my kidneys perfectly. This is the shortest answer to the question I once asked my father: 'Why did we leave Odessa?' Because of people like this border guard, that's why.

I am already on the ground, covering my face from further blows. I can hear Tony's calm voice saying something in English, and the beating stops as suddenly as it started.

'Victor, let's lock them up – this second guy does look like a foreigner. Let the boss deal with them,' says another of the guards.

'What do you think they meant by "Let the boss deal with them"?' I ask Tony, when we are locked in a window-less room at the border post.

'Could be anything,' says Tony. 'From prison to . . . anything, really. We are in a black hole, remember? The laws of physics don't apply here.'

I don't know why Tony's tone is so ironic. It *is* a black hole, and my family don't know where I am, and judging by developments, they might never find out . . . I sit on the floor, silent, nursing a twisted wrist and waiting for the boss . . .

The boss, the head of the UN border mission, turns out to be a small and very English woman.

'Did he hit you, tell me?' she demands, examining my bruises. 'Appalling. With all the training we are giving them here, all the funds . . .'

She turns her attention to Tony, who looks quite relaxed. He smiles and says: 'Hi, Jane.'

I can't believe what I am hearing. He says to the Head of the UN Mission in the Eastern European black hole 'Hi, Jane'?

It gets worse, because she frowns and says to him: 'When you said "see you soon", Tony, I didn't realise this is what you meant!'

She turns her attention to me. 'Tony I understand . . . not approve, but sort of understand – he has never grown up, he spends his time with children. But you? I've checked your ID – Levi Freiman, GP, married with three children . . . How could you let him lead you into this mess?'

Without giving me a chance to say anything, she adds: 'I have no time to discuss this. The last thing I need now is to have to deal with your paperwork, organise you a car . . .' and she disappears, leaving me with nothing but questions. What does all this mean? Why did she say that Tony spends his time with children? I thought he didn't have any children!

There is something bigger, far more important, that I need to ask Tony, who smiles at me reassuringly. How I want to wipe that smile off your face just for once! I think. Loyalty and belonging – is this my payment for that? I should have turned my back on you many years ago, after those brambles . . .

It was a great game at first – Tony's 'Why don't we sneak some dining room trays out at night to go for a ride?'

The thrill of sliding down the hill – and the sudden burning pain before the realisation of what had happened.

No wonder they nicknamed me the Fat Controller – I flew over the lip of the hill straight into the brambles. It took me a couple of minutes to realise that the yelping, puppylike sound was coming from me, and the laughter from Jonty and Max, standing at the top of the hill watching. Tony was right next to me, trying to help me – or so I thought. He was watching me waving my hands helplessly, but not offering to pull me out, as if he was curious to see how long it would take me to realise that the more I waved, the more painful it would be. He watched me getting up, trying not to scratch my bleeding arms and legs, only to say, just like the Veteran did when I fainted: 'Great effort, Freiman. Care to have another go?'

Years later, already a doctor, I understood that the Veteran didn't want his troops to panic; that was why he continued the lesson, keeping an eye on me. With Tony it was different. I'll never forget the way he looked at me, as if he enjoyed seeing me in pain. He came to me at breakfast the next day, however, and said, nodding at my cut, swollen wrists: 'I'm really sorry, Levi. Does it still hurt? Meet me at the tuck shop at four – I think you deserve an extra chicken pie for bravery.'

Wasn't that what Alex was singing at the Christmas concert? The 'St Louis Blues', if I remember . . . Yes, I loved that man, just as the schoolboy in the song loved his pies. And who says loyalty can't be bought?

I never told Jonty or Max. I pushed that incident to the back of my mind until today, until that burning slash of pain hit my kidneys . . .

Where do I get the strength to head-butt him, to push him against the wall? He is so surprised (I have never hit anybody) that at first he does not react. Then he pushes me back – his hands far too strong for such a small frame – and says: 'Levi, hey, calm down. Levi, listen, I didn't know we would end up here, I promise. I just thought it would be an adventure to have an hour-long ride in the lorry, that's all. Aunt Jane was a back-up plan – and it worked, see. It's nearly over . . . but you must admit, apart from the border guards, it was fun, wasn't it?'

'It's not about the lorry or your aunt Jane,' I say. 'It's about me being an action man. You haven't given me the AA task, have you?'

'What do you mean?' Tony tries to look surprised, but he knows exactly what I mean.

'Tony,' I say, 'I played this game hoping that for the first time in my life I'd be able to act alone. Not as a smart boy who lives in the world of formulae, not as a husband lost in a Jewish Bermuda Triangle of children-wife-mother, not as a failed surgeon, but as Levi. As myself. I was so proud that you chose me to do this – with the dangers and all. But the Odessa boys searched my bag, then the border guards kicked all my stuff out of it, and they still didn't find the papers I brought from Crimea. I haven't forgotten the rules: find out, do and distract . . . I was just a "distract", wasn't I?'

Tony is looking at the wall above me. 'You must be shattered . . . Let's talk later – the worst is over now. The car will take us to Chisinau, there is a flight to Vienna tonight, and then—'

'Tony,' I interrupt him, surprised how detached my voice sounds, though all I want to do is punch him, 'I need to know now. Yesterday, when we looked at the documents in the hotel, I saw you put them back into my bag. If they're not here, where the hell are they?'

# ALEX'S WAR

*Odessa*

The last three days did not happen. They couldn't and they didn't. I am in the cosiness of Joyce's cab on the way home, and everything that happened is not a memory, but the fantasy of a tired, overworked woman, crumpled like the piece of paper it started with; strange and unexpected like the words that unlocked it: *Festina Lente* . . .

'I don't understand,' I said when I opened my envelope at the Waterloo meeting. 'I have never heard of Festina Lente. Some Italian village . . . where is it?' The name had such a Mediterranean feel, made me think of song festivals and lazy days on the terrace, of ice creams in the harbour . . .

'It's a Latin phrase,' said Levi. '*Festina lente* means "You'll go faster by going slower", or "make haste slower" . . . I am a doctor, I am supposed to remember some Latin,' he added almost apologetically, when Jonty looked at him.

'This is your task for now – slow down and wait for the next step,' explained Tony.

Only I ended up waiting for the next step in Odessa – my second unplanned trip in a month. Odessa sums up *Festina Lente* perfectly – time slows down there, people breathe deeper, the sea follows you everywhere you go.

It could be Marseilles or Naples, with its blend of grandeur and shabbiness: griffins with peeling noses, one-armed caryatids, graffitied arches leading into grand squares . . .

There are weird street signs everywhere – at least those I could read, the ones that were in English:

*Odessa Gambling Club*. And below, '*Nobody judges the winners*' – *Catherine the Great*.

*You are not pregnant yet? Come and see us!* (What was inside? I wondered – an IVF clinic, a nightclub, a sex shop?)

A bearded man in a nineteenth-century lacy dress, and a sign: *Katya Hoffman*. What the hell . . . ? I am always disturbed by questions with no clear answers, so I walked in. Green lampshades, jacquard curtains, thick tablecloths and candles on the tables . . . A café!

'Are you on your own?' asked the waitress in perfect English. How did she guess I was a foreigner? 'What would you like to eat?' she continued before I sat down. 'I can tell you that unusual salads are our speciality: smoked duck, blue cheese and pear, spicy aubergine . . .'

'Could I see the menu first, please?'

'What do you need a menu for?' The waitress looked genuinely surprised. 'I can tell you all you need to know.'

'Could you tell me why your café is called Katya Hoffman?' I asked her, hoping for more success here. This was what I came in for, after all.

'That's easy,' replied the waitress with a bored expression; she probably answered this question twenty times a day. 'Catherine the Great founded our city, and Albert Hoffman was the chemist who invented LSD or some other drug, don't know for sure . . . Our name reflects the city's atmosphere: chilled and relaxed, yet with a strong female ego.'

I laughed.

'Is that funny?' She sounded surprised. 'I never noticed. Humour is everywhere in Odessa, on the radio, in the streets, even in the City Concert Hall – it has the worst acoustics in town, as it is in the building of the former stock exchange, totally soundproof.

'Humour is our daily bread, the way we live. My ninety-year-old grandmother told me this morning, as I was leaving: "Tanya, have you heard? Our neighbour Raisa has to change her last name! She has lived with her name for eighty-five years and now she has to change it! And you know why? Her husband, that tight-fisted bastard, bought her a second-hand tombstone!" Not that funny, hey? But then my granny winked at me and added: "Just as well I am a widow."

'I don't know how to explain it in English,' said Tanya. 'It's not just about jokes, it's our attitude to life – ironic, cynical almost: everything is defied, laughed at – death, danger . . .

'Find yourself a spare pair of ears to listen to what you want to eat – I am busy,' she shouted to a young American couple at the corner table.

'Your English is very good,' I commented. 'And I love the decor of your café. Who chose the paintings?' The walls were covered with an eclectic mix: Modigliani, Picasso, Rubens . . .

'The owner, Tamara,' answered the girl. 'They are all portraits of strong single women, like her.' (Of course! How come I did not notice?) The waitress leaned towards me and whispered: 'But they are all copies, not the originals, you know . . .'

'I would never have guessed,' I replied.

'I'm coming.' She waved at the couple at the corner table, who obviously hadn't found any 'spare ears' to listen to their order.

'So,' the girl chose for me, 'smoked duck salad and Turkish coffee?'

I sipped the strong coffee, savouring the faint unfamiliar aroma of the café (not pot, I hoped), thinking how the paintings here, chosen by the invisible Tamara, pretty much summed up my life: I am just like those portraits – a strong single woman, only a fake, a copy, not the original.

I have my posts to lean on: the kids at home, Joyce on the way to work, Robbie in the office. I am a sprinter, taking a deep breath and running from post to post, afraid to stop, gasping. And there they are, always, helping me to forget. Not Max's death, but my life with Simon.

From grin to grim. One letter makes all the difference. When and how did this happen? I can only remember the milestones.

Our first serious argument at the airport – about who left the bag with the baby paraphernalia on the carousel, with the car keys in a zipped pocket. I was holding nine-month-old Emma, jet-lagged from a long-haul flight, my back against the car – there was nowhere to hide as he shouted and spat, ignoring a gay couple passing by. As I leaned over to strap Emma into her pushchair – her only possession salvaged from the carousel so far – I overheard one of the guys saying to the other: 'I'll give them a year maximum. What do you think?'

It took five.

I try to forget that evening when I came back from the office party and ended up in a bed and breakfast across the road because he left his keys in the door: 'I was fast asleep, darling. Sorry, I didn't hear you . . .'

And that trip to Las Vegas. Of course I remember that. 'A surprise for my wonderful director wife – I'm whisking her to Las Vegas . . . What do you mean, you have a board presentation on Monday? This is my special treat.' Las Vegas was where he hit me for the first time. He was really drunk, and I refused . . . I tried to refuse to have sex with him.

'It was a bit of rough foreplay, darling,' he said next morning. 'I didn't know you liked that sort of thing.' He often called Luke, born eight and a half months later, his Lucky Strike.

When did he move from 'You are the smartest wife in the world' to 'Alex talks fast but thinks slow'?

From helping me to set up a new laptop – he is an IT consultant, after all – to my emails deleted, messages about meetings disappearing?

From carrying me all the way down the slope when I broke my leg skiing to breaking my arm pushing me against the door – 'Sorry, darling, did it hurt? I didn't mean to, you know that.'

It wasn't the pain that made me decide. Shame and fear were my allies in this silent war – invisible to others, I thought, with me being the only casualty.

It was at our Simon-free Sunday breakfast, when he was away at one of his countless weekend 'conferences', when Emma said matter-of-factly, licking yoghurt off the lid: 'Mum, you shouldn't cry when he hurts you. You only make it worse, he gets really angry.'

I looked at my daughter and thought: I don't want her to grow up thinking this is normal. And I don't want Luke to behave like his father. Ever.

That's what they all help me forget – Luke with his 'Mum, tell Emma to stop – she's tidying my room again, it's my mess'; Joyce with her 'Orright?'; and Robbie . . . good old Robbie, our department workhorse. Not everybody wants to be a leader, and Robbie thrives on the workload, quietly making projects happen. I can always rely on him. He saved me again with this trip . . .

'I'm taking a couple of days off, Robbie,' I said.

'Aren't you supposed to be leading a client presentation on those dates?' he asked.

'I need to go to Odessa, I really do.'

'Where's that? Why?' He sounded shocked.

I showed him the invitation: *The organising committee of the Odessa International Jazz festival is delighted to invite you to award our first memorial Max Chandler Prize this year. The prize is awarded to the most promising young jazz musician, together with a scholarship to further his education. The organisers will cover the air fares and the hotel expenses. We really hope you can come.*

Robbie was silent for a moment. 'Key account, Alex . . . it took you weeks to prepare . . .'

'I think it will be a perfect opportunity for you to do it, Robbie,' I said. I'll coach you, give you all the data – you know this account well, you can answer any questions. The invitation was quite unexpected and the timing is awful, but I'll only be away for two or three days, I promise. I have to go.'

'Go, Alex,' was all he said. 'Of course I'll do it for you. Good luck . . .'

So I did.

Nothing from Tony, no instructions or calls – really,

really disappointing. The boys were playing in their given locations – Jonty in Strasbourg, and Levi should be somewhere on the shores of the Black Sea, not that far away. I knew that he and Jonty were under strictest instructions not to talk to each other, but maybe I could track Levi down, just to find out what was happening? They were still leaving me out as they did when we were sixteen! Tony gave me the first envelope only because it was Max's – and that was it . . .

When I asked them at Waterloo: 'Was Max involved?' it was my futile attempt to hear: 'Of course not . . .' But I know he was, he told me that himself.

They think I don't know what they did, but I knew all along, from the day Max borrowed my long summer dress. 'It's in my task, Alex – could I have it for a day? Just for a joke.' He sounded flat.

'Then why are you so miserable? It's supposed to be fun,' I said, opening the wardrobe.

'Because if I don't do it, I'll betray my friendship. If I do, I'll betray . . .' He didn't say anything then, but maybe he meant 'my love'?

Norman *was* his first love, I understood it in August that year, when after spending most of the summer in his room, sharing it only with his music, he cracked one evening and told me what had happened: about the dress, the bag and that last day of term . . .

When I found Tony's letter in Max's mail, I knew I had to

go to that meeting at Waterloo – to see the boys who had pushed my brother towards betrayal. I wasn't sure exactly what I wanted to do – plot revenge against Tony the All-Powerful, or find another guilty party because I couldn't carry my guilt alone. Or pick up where I'd left it with Tony in the late spring, before the dress and before the bag incident.

Why do I keep coming back to our date by the lake in the gardens of their stately home, to its non-completeness? It is distinctly, painfully unfinished, like a line drawn halfway across the page in a geometry exam, or a song abandoned at the school concert before the final note. His kiss, his hand touching the silk of my blouse, gently stroking the fabric, stopping just before . . . I remember that he said something and I laughed, but the memory never offers me any prompts as to what exactly it was he said. Then he sat up, rubbed his forehead and stared at the lake, frowning, waiting for Max.

I never dared to ask him what had happened. Why didn't he want me? Was it something I did, or the way I looked or moved? We never discussed it, avoiding situations where we would be left alone together, but this yearning remained with me all my life, after dozens of drunken student nights when sex just happened, after a month in bed with my now ex, which was all lust, lust, lust . . .

Wagner's horns and trumpets carried me out of my memories. I didn't need to look at the mobile to see who was calling; the Ride of the Valkyries ringtone is assigned to one person only.

I hesitated whether to answer – it would mean awkward silences, explaining about Odessa, Max's prize . . . I'd already paid for my lunch, so I could leave the café and talk on the way to the hotel – or not . . .

The melody got louder, more impatient. I sighed, stood up and picked up the phone. 'How are you, Mum?'

'Alex? Where are you? I spoke to Christina, she said that you are travelling again . . .'

'I'm away on business – just for two days, Mum,' I said. 'I am fine.'

Of course I am fine. It took us years to hone our conversations to perfection: impersonal subjects, no probing questions, the balance of non-interfering preserved. We are experts now, my mother and me.

We worked hard on this truce.

'I've just checked with Christina – the kids are fine too,' I added, not waiting for her to ask the question.

'Oh, yes . . . that's why I'm calling – to remind you that I'm expecting them on Sunday, in three weeks' time,' she said. 'Would you drop them off around eleven? I'll give them lunch.' (Meaning she won't need to worry about cooking dinner, or making up beds in the spare room, or checking on Luke in the middle of the night if he has a nightmare . . .)

'And could you collect them around five?' she carried on.

This would translate into me wandering around Oxford staring at tourists and students, as it makes no sense at all to drive back to London only to return three hours later, while my mother enjoys the company of my kids, pencilled in her diary between her morning walk and tea with her friend Margo.

'I'm in New York, Mum,' I said, surprising myself, with a touch of guilty pleasure. I imagined her freezing, like a rabbit caught in the headlights – the same expression of desperation and instinctive fear.

'Doing anything nice?' she asked cautiously. That wasn't what she meant. 'Have you seen your father?' That was what she asked me, really.

I thought my next shot might endanger our truce, so I retreated. 'It is such a busy trip, Mum, no time for anything. . .'

'So will you bring Luke and Emma on that Sunday?' She sounded more relaxed.

I was saved by the horns, though they were a far cry from Wagner – the motorcade of wedding cars was trundling slowly along the street towards my hotel, honking loudly.

'Sorry, Mum, I can't hear you, will catch up later!' I shouted, hanging up. I'd negotiated peace, though probably a short-lasting one.

'You are from London . . . Then it must feel like home from home for you,' said the girl at the reception of the Londonskaya hotel, handing me my key.

It certainly didn't feel like home – my hall has three chipped tiles and two missing, and there is a plastic IKEA lampshade there, not a crystal chandelier. My bedroom in

London is a quarter of the size of this enormous room, and I don't have a memorial plaque outside it: *Robert Stevenson, the English novelist, stayed in this room during his visit to Odessa . . .*

'Mrs Robinson? There you are!' A girl was running towards me across the vast lobby. 'Welcome to our city!' She was full of energy, bouncing like a Labrador puppy and wearing a perfect seaside town outfit: striped Breton top with jeans.

I wanted to say: 'I am a "Ms", a definite "Ms" for some time now,' but the girl was still in bouncing mode: 'I am Galya,' she continued. 'I work for the festival committee, we have planned a tour of the city for you – we haven't got much time, but at least it will give you some idea about Odessa's rich history. Our time has already started, so we'd better go now, otherwise you'll be late for the tram.'

'What tram?' I asked.

'You'll see.' She winked at me.

Amazing, I thought. First the waitress, now the festival girl – the younger generation here still exercises the old Soviet command and control: impossible to protest, humiliation guaranteed . . .

'Oh, before I forget, here are your tickets,' added Galya. 'You are now flying to London via Brussels, as you requested.'

'I didn't re—' I started to protest, but Galya carried on undeterred. 'Shall we start with the Potemkin Steps?'

'Galya, can we start with the bench outside, on the

boulevard?' I suggested. 'There are a couple of pages I wanted to ask you to translate for me first.'

Galya looked genuinely offended. 'What about the Potemkin Steps? Everybody wants to see the steps! Japanese groups come just for them! And the monument to the duke . . .'

'Later, Galya, please.' I had to apply the same firmness I use with our graduate trainees when they arrive exploding with ideas.

Galya nodded, her lower lip protruding slightly. 'It's your time,' she said. 'I get paid anyway.'

We settled on the bench, and I handed her the Russian letter my father had taken from Grandpa Jack's passport – hoping, praying that she would not ask any questions, because if she did – where would I start?

But she had already written me off as a reluctant tourist.

She unfolded the letter, read the first line – *Odessa* – and the date: *7 May 1945*.

'Is it some family heirloom?' she asked, and started reading in a soft voice, not waiting for my answer, stopping every now and then to search for the right word, drawing me into the black and white chronicle of the wartime love story, into the melody of desperate happiness where imminent freedom means the end, not the beginning . . .

*So this is it, my love.*

*I have written this letter a hundred times in my mind, but never thought I would have the strength to put it down on paper.*

*But I have no choice – you are leaving tomorrow.*

*There are so many things you still don't know about me – so here I am, telling you about my life, in my language, my dearest, hoping you'll be able to read this letter one day.*

*I have only known you for a month, but have become ten years older and a thousand times richer since we met. Do you remember that evening?*

*I was returning from a violin lesson, humming with joy – what a treat! I had been paid with a fresh loaf, wrapped in a newspaper, and I was walking down Gogolya, past the ruins of our school, smelling warm bread, reading the headlines:* Soviet Army close to Berlin, Yalta Conference decision implemented: Odessa repatriation centre bidding farewell to French and Belgian officers.

*I heard your footsteps behind me, your heavy breathing too close. If I had known that my love was chasing me, I would have stopped immediately! I tried to run, but I had no strength, so I turned to face the enemy. You were looming over me in your unfamiliar ragged uniform, looking not at me, but at my loaf. When you took your officer's knife out, I thought: I have survived three cold years on my own, I need to stay alive to wait for my mother's return – so I gave you the loaf. Bread and my violin was all I had. And – a miracle! You sliced the crust, just the crust, the top of the loaf, and handed the rest back to me, saying: 'Spasibo.' Then you asked me in English, munching your crust – do you remember? You asked: 'What is your name?'*

*I understood then – you were from the repatriation centre, from the transit camp in Lutsdorf, waiting to be sent home on one of those huge British transport ships that were coming into the port every week now.*

*'Are you English?' I asked.*

*'No.' You smiled broadly. 'American.' And stretched out your huge hand – 'Jack.'*

*You are bigger than me, so you must be hungrier, I thought – and breaking the loaf, I gave you a larger piece and said, trying to remember my school English lessons: 'My name is Sasha.'*

*And that's how it started . . .*

*So, what do you know about me?*

*You know that I am a violin teacher; you carried my violin case many times, waiting for me outside the school at Sobornaya. It is not our violin school, I tried to explain to you, not the famous Stolyarsky, the 'me-named school' as Maestro Stolyarsky called it. The school where he told our parents that their children were 'ordinary geniuses', where he would say to us: 'Learn your laws of physics, children – if you don't practise for one day, there is no force that will allow you to catch up in two!' and shout at Fima: 'You are playing Mozart as if you are peeing into an empty bucket.' That school is gone – I showed you the ruins, but you didn't understand. Poor Maestro, our dear Stolyarsky, will never return to rebuild it. He died in Sverdlovsk last year, somebody told me.*

*You asked me why I lived alone, looking at the pre-war*

*photograph of my parents on the piano. You understood that my father was killed at the front, and you asked, pointing at my mother's photograph – did she die too? And I could not explain that I was still waiting for her, four years on . . .*

*Why did I let her go to Privoz market that day? She was hoping to exchange her rabbit fur jacket for bread and eggs – but she never came back.*

*I waited all night, then went to Privoz to look for her. A kind trader whispered to me that there had been a round-up there the day before, with people pushed into columns, documents checked and Jews sent to the ghetto in Bogdanovka. 'Terrible rumours about that ghetto; you should not go there, girl. So what that you have a Russian name in your passport – they will take one look at you, with your short black curls and your pale face, and they won't bother to check your documents. Here, take this egg, and go home and hide,' she whispered.*

*But I didn't believe her – how could I, when the whole of Odessa was covered in leaflets?* Decree N 35: To provide order and security in Odessa, all Jews are to be evacuated to the Ochakov area, where accommodation will be provided. They will be allowed to apply for any agricultural and industrial jobs in the area. Governor Aleksyanu.

*This sounded reassuring, didn't it?*

*I ignored the other leaflets, with the swastika and the words* Befehl *and* Jewish, *and the warning* will be shot immediately if not done in seven days *underlined, with something about exchanging Soviet documents for document N34 in the text in between.*

*I pushed my panic away, thinking that my mother would have been sent to Ochakov, that a nice farmer would have asked her to help him and she would be warm and fed. Only my mother has pianist's hands, and she is slim and weak, not farmer's stock. And she would not have left me; she would have found a way to get back to me if she was alive. But I still hope, I am still waiting. The war will be over soon, and she'll turn up on the doorstep and ask: 'Have you practised much when I was away? That passage in the third movement of the Tchaikovsky Concerto – that spiccato bowing – did it get any easier?'*

*And I'll tell her proudly that I am not just a pupil now – I am a teacher! That winter when she . . . when she decided to go away, it was the music that saved me – people still wanted to pay for violin lessons, can you believe that?*

*You asked me about the piece of rope on the piano.*

*'This is Rudik,' I said. You didn't understand, but how could you – it is impossible to explain what I felt when I saw my first love, my 'ordinary genius' Rudik, hanging off a tree in Alexandrovsky Street together with dozens of others, murdered in revenge when the governor's car was blown up. This piece of rope is my last memory of Rudik; it is the last thing that touched him.*

*I tried to explain to you that I am not betraying Rudik now, that my love for you is so different.*

*With Rudik, the harmony was made of simple, clear arpeggios. I had known him since I was ten, had played in the same orchestra, given performances together for years, but with you . . .*

*It is like the American music they play at the Londonskaya now (you took me dancing there once, remember?): unfamiliar, joyful and exciting at the same time.*

*I wish I could ask you what you saw in me: pale, thin, flat-chested, short-haired . . . You know, I once played Cherubino in the school's production of* The Marriage of Figaro. *'A perfect teenage boy,' our professor Zinger said then.*

*Did you love my music more than me? I played Bach's Adagio in A minor for you, and Wieniawski's Légende . . .*

*I didn't know I still had this charge of warmth and tender-ness in me after all the suffering. I crave you. I love your smile and your broad hands. The way your pupils get darker when you concentrate on something.*

*Funny how it is possible to be so happy and so scared at the same time. Fear mixed with love – what can be stronger? Only loss, I guess.*

*I was afraid from the moment I saw you. Afraid of you, then afraid for you, and now, as I write this letter, afraid of losing you.*

*When I don't see you for some time, I am terrified that this is all just a dream, a fantasy, and I won't feel the same way when I see you again. But then we meet and you smile, you cup me in your huge hands, and I know that love is there, always there.*

# The Game

*There is one thing I am not afraid of, though. When life separates us, which is inevitable, I know that it won't take away my love – you are so deep inside me, starting from the tips of my fingers, in my veins and blood cells, in my pulse . . .*

*On Sunday, when we met in Arcadia, you said something to me and I only understood two words – 'Churchill' and 'victory'.*

*It all became clear on Monday.* Clementine Churchill visits Odessa *was all over the newspapers; everybody was talking about it.* Lady Churchill opens a hospital for Soviet soldiers and visits British officers at the Odessa transit camp, *and below, a sentence so final that no appeal in the world could move it, no judge could overrule it:* American pilots and Italian soldiers will also leave on a British transport ship.

*I know that I am never going to see you again – the leaflets with the decree forbidding marriage with foreigners are posted all around the port, on every corner. It is as if they are shouting at me: never, never, never . . .*

*Tomorrow when you leave I will come home and pick up my violin. I cannot cry – I have forgotten how to – but the violin will do it for me. I will play Tchaikovsky's Violin Concerto in D. Because for me this is about us, this is our story. It is in D Major, with hope in the air and my heart pounding louder – the expectation of the end of the war and the welcoming of freedom.*

*I'll start with the Canzonetta, the second movement – to warm my fingers, to think, to remember our first evening . . .*

*Canzonetta means 'a little song', and that's what I was doing as I walked down the street with that loaf – singing quietly, listening to street sounds and footsteps that sounded just like the flutes and clarinets in the second movement, following each other.*

*And then I'll play the third movement, Allegro Vivacissimo. It is so difficult, I never thought I would be able to play it, but I can now, miraculously. I wish my old teacher, Vera Samoylovna, could hear it – but she is still in Tashkent.*

*The next passage, that's me running along the street away from you, faster, faster; and this A major section, heavy and low – this is you walking behind me. And again, my light steps in D major: I'm trying to run away . . .*

*As the melody returns, it's spring; only spring can sound like this, with these flute-like flageolets. I can hear the orchestra again – the oboe talking to the clarinet – and then my violin starts, tenderly, gently . . .*

*The next passages are all about joy and speed – how quickly all this happened, and the joy of going higher and higher together. And this is the sea, us swimming into the moonlight at Lanjeron beach, straight into the arpeggios, into the feeling of freedom with no borders, only the horizon.*

*The lower notes again, your steps . . . The melody is coming back, and you should be returning – only you're not; you are walking away from me.*

*And then the pain, a huge wave, and finally the coda – I am running down the steps to say farewell, and then it is not*

*me playing any more, but the orchestra again, taking you home
across the seas and the storms on a huge boat.*

*I don't know if I will have the strength to play the last bars
of the coda – so joyful, so D major – but I'll try, I promise.*

*Do remember, my dearest, that somewhere in this small
world, across the ocean, there is another part of you, cherished
and loved. All you have to do is whisper* lyublyu *and I'll hear
you.*

*I have your cap with me, and one of your buttons – I carry
it in my pocket as a keepsake to make you safe. Your smell is
already fading, but there is another smell that will always be
ours, just yours and mine, wherever we are – the smell of warm
bread.*

*I love you, Jack.*


'Alexandra . . .' Galya folded the letter carefully, 'what a
beautiful story.'

'Yes,' I agreed.

'No, the letter is signed *Alexandra*,' she explained.

'But I thought the girl was called Sasha?' I asked.

'Sasha is a diminutive for Alexandra in Russian.' Galya
resumed her teacher's tone. 'Alexandra is more formal, more
suitable for a final farewell.'

I needed to understand, immediately, to soothe my
confused world, so I called my father – I hadn't talked to
him for years; now it was the second time in a month. He
did not answer the phone for a while.

'Dad,' I shouted, as if it would help him to hear me better across the ocean, see my anguish. 'Why did it take you such a long time to pick up?'

'It is two in the morning in New York, Alex . . .' came the sleepy reply.

'Why am I called Alex, Dad?'

There was silence at the other end. Either my father thought I was on drugs, or he couldn't remember.

'Your mother said it was quite a regal name, and it was one of those rare occasions when I agreed with her,' he said finally. 'Why do you ask?'

'But who chose my name? Was it really Mum?' I continued shouting.

Galya was looking at me in amazement. 'And I've always thought that English ladies were very reserved . . .' she muttered.

'I suppose Grandpa Jack was the first to suggest it.' My father was waking up. 'He said it would be a lovely name for a girl, and we all agreed. As I said, your mother and I . . . Are you all right, kid? Where are you?'

'Dad,' I shouted again, 'Grandpa Jack's letter – the one you gave me when I said I had a friend . . . a colleague going to Odessa, remember? The letter you found in Grandpa Jack's passport but couldn't translate . . . It's . . . Oh, go back to bed, good night . . . No, don't go back to bed yet! One final question – what did Grandpa Jack do after the war? Was he a pilot or a musician?'

'You don't remember him at all, do you?' he said. 'Yes, the last time you saw him you were about ten . . . He was shell-shocked – quite deaf, in fact. How could he ever have become a musician? He owned a bakery in Iowa; it was your great-grandfather's bakery, and Grandpa Jack took over after the war. I sold it when he died. Good night, Alex. I hope you are safe, wherever you are.'

And he left me on the bench with two Odessa girls, Sasha and Galya, and this story that was now mine.

Of course Grandpa Jack owned a bakery! I thought. When Dad used to read us the Bakery Bear tongue-twister, he was always saying: 'This is about your grandfather. "Bill, there is a big brown bear in the bakery!"'

'Mrs Robinson,' suggested Galya timidly, 'you have an hour before they collect you to go to the festival. Maybe you would like to see the Stolyarsky school? It is just around the corner . . .'

'I would love to, Galya,' I said. 'I have one last request before we go, please.'

'Another letter?' surrendered Galya.

'No,' I smiled. 'Just call me by my first name, not Mrs Robinson. My first name is Alexandra.'

We walked along the boulevard, Galya talking quickly and clearly, throwing dates, names, events at me.

'We are all "water fowl" in Odessa, everybody is connected to the sea here – all the boys dream of becoming either sailors or smugglers, depending on which area they grew up in. Even the city founders were Black Sea fleet officers; we call them our three musketeers: De Ribas, De Volan and De Lanjeron, though our musketeers were in the same boat as Richelieu, not fighting him,' chuckled Galya. 'He left Odessa to rule France, unfortunately, our duke, Richelieu, but when he was leaving, he promised to come back, as Odessa had such a hold over him. So here he is,' she said proudly, stopping by the bronze monument.

'By the way, would you like some ice cream, Mrs Robins . . . Alexandra? We were the first city in the Russian empire where people were allowed to eat ice cream in the street – it was a terribly daring thing to do in those days.'

'No thank you, Galya,' I said. I was trying to drag myself back into Galya's story, told with such ardour, but all I could see was a thin, tired and blissfully happy violin teacher, who gave me her name.

I saw Odessa in a different light now. My hotel, Londonskaya – that was where they went dancing. As Galya recited: 'These are the famous Potemkin Steps, designed in such a way that they look wider at the bottom,' I could see Sasha running down all one hundred and ninety-two of them to the port, to watch his ship leaving. I peeped into a sunlit courtyard where grapes were covering the walls – maybe she had even lived here?

'Here we are,' chanted Galya. 'We have arrived at the stop of our famous jazz tram.'

The tram would be perfect for an Indian wedding – it

was decorated with garlands of flowers, balloons and signs in an unknown alphabet. The band was already inside, waiting for me to take my place as guest of honour.

'Galya, what do the signs say?' I asked.

'Oh . . .' She stopped. 'This is very Odessa, difficult to translate, but I'll try: "If you want to have an outlandish experience – get a boat, not a tram . . ." "If you think Duke Ellington was the best, then you haven't heard our Sanya play!"'

As if to confirm this, the band started playing something very familiar. I'd heard this somewhere before . . . yes, when we danced at my friend Tara's wedding. 'Galya,' I shouted in her ear, 'this is not jazz, this is "Seven Forty", a Jewish melody.'

'We always send off our jazz tram with this music,' explained Galya. 'Our first steam trams, leaving at seven forty, were seen off by a Klezmer musicians' band, hence the name of the melody. It is a tribute to tradition.'

Yes, I thought, tapping my feet. New Orleans it certainly ain't, but the joy is contagious. I was about to get on to the tram when Galya ran to me and hugged me.

'Have fun today. Goodbye, Alexandra,' was all she said.

I was caught in the tide of the festival, rattling along the streets in the tram, stopping to listen to various bands on the way, until the wave finally brought me to a concert hall with a peeling plaster ceiling and the most incongruous couple on stage – a bosomy matron in a long shiny dress and a young presenter in a snazzy mini outfit. There was no harmony in this couple, just like there was no harmony in the neo-jazz group they had just announced: a trio of stoned youths producing a cacophony of sounds.

I started questioning my decision to come here, to a city my brother had never visited. Riding around Odessa in a jazz tram was fun, but I had far more important things to do at home than worrying whether the peeling plaster above me was going to collapse now, or whether it would wait until I left the theatre.

The incongruous couple were back on stage. I was glad to see them, as they provided a welcome respite from the stoned trio.

'And now,' the bosomy presenter announced in both Russian and broken English, in a piercing soprano (probably a failed opera singer), 'the highlight of this year's festival. The Odessa Jazz Festival organisers have decided to establish a prize for a promising young musician in memory of the Golden Saxophone, Max Chandler.

'This year, to present the first prize, we have the honour to welcome the sister of Max Chandler, Alexandra Robinson.' She almost sang the last phrase triumphantly – definitely a failed soprano.

As I got up and made my way to the stage, the snazzy girl intervened, skipping impatiently with excitement: 'We have another surprise tonight. As the first winner of the Max Chandler memorial prize is a saxophone player, he will have the honour of performing for us on Max Chandler's alto saxophone!'

When was I last on a stage? I wondered. Probably when I sang with Max at his school concert. But then I had Max's melody as a prop, and I was standing on the edge of the stage, not moving across it.

I made my way to the centre of the stage, acutely aware that a tall Englishwoman on wooden legs clutching a saxophone was probably not the most graceful thing the audience had seen today. Though the stoned youths certainly weren't a pretty sight either. At least I was moving away from the danger of the peeling plaster.

Luckily, the attention shifted away from me as the young player about to receive the prize appeared from backstage. As I looked at him, I regretted for the umpteenth time making the decision to come here.

For moving towards me across the stage was a teenager who looked like a council estate yob just released after his tenth ASBO warning. He strutted on to the stage, his skinny tattooed shoulders dictating the rhythm of his walk. He wore trainers, jeans hanging off his bum and a loose vest. He did not look like a musician to me – but then in this city, nothing was what it seemed: a sweet-looking guide had the steely grip of a Soviet officer, a jazz tram departed with a Jewish folk melody, and a waitress refused to bring you a menu.

'Yasha is this year's festival find,' continued the snazzy

presenter. 'Igor Pavlotsky' (I guessed this was one of the organisers) 'heard him play by the Potemkin Steps one day. When asked what music meant for him, Yasha said' (she checked her notes): '"It is like the sea. I swim in it, it is deep and warm and carries me forward like a wave."'

The prize would allow Yasha to purchase his own saxophone and to start taking professional lessons. A Moldavanka orphan, he had taught himself to play, with sporadic tuition from his alcoholic neighbour, whose saxophone he had been using.

Probably punching the guy every time he wanted to get hold of it, I thought.

We stood in silence, measuring each other up, thousands of eyes on us. Eventually I did the unthinkable – I handed Max's saxophone to the yob, and muttered something in English – did I really say 'Well done'?

He grabbed it, actually grabbed it – I would rather he punched me than treated Max's saxophone this way.

It's only for ten minutes, I reassured myself. Our physics teacher's phrase, 'think of your oral exams as ten minutes of disgrace', came to mind for no reason.

Yasha clasped the saxophone and produced the first three unsure notes of Gershwin's 'Summertime': 'E-C-E . . .' Then he changed position, closed his eyes and he was off, swimming in the music, carrying the whole audience away, and in this Odessa orphan I suddenly saw my brother. The school summer jazz concert, and Max, his eyes closed, leading us all into the melody.

My cheeks grew hot and wet – I was crying, for the first time since Max had died. I couldn't cry when I heard the news, not at the funeral, not in the bathroom at home afterwards. This Odessa kid had unplugged me, unleashed my grief.

When he had finished, he handed me the saxophone and smiled. And I knew that it had been worth making the trip just for these few minutes, just for the look in his eyes when he said, '*Spasibo*.'

They looked after me really well, the organisers – sent Galya to do the city tour, gave me the tram ride, and took me to a restaurant called Jazzy-Buzzy (what else?) with dozens of photographs of jazz musicians on the walls. My brother looked out at me from one of them, and I felt complete and safe.

I drank a little bit too much, and laughed a little too loudly at the jokes in a language I didn't understand, and my head was spinning when I finally got back to my enormous room. Even the noise of the wedding downstairs, and some Phil Collins songs in a strong Russian accent, couldn't tarnish it. It had been quite a day. Good night, Odessa . . .

The knocking was not loud, but persistent – it must have been going on for a while.

'. . . In too deep . . .' – Odessa's answer to Phil Collins was still going strong with the songs of my youth.

I had fallen asleep propped against the pillows, still dressed, the festival programme in my hand.

'Who is this?' My voice betrayed me, too tired to shout. I got out of bed, my world still spinning, and came to the door to listen to heavy breathing outside. Heavy breathing, plus no reply.

'Are you going to Crimea? To Odessa? Be careful, Alex,' my father had said. What was he trying to warn me about? The knocking was close to banging now – or did it seem so loud because I had drunk too much?

'I'll call the police.' This time I do shout, but Phil Collins outside is really belting it out – nobody would hear me if they forced the door to come in now. What would they be after?

'It's me, Alex.' I heard a familiar voice. I was still dreaming – this could not be happening for real, and yet it was.

Back in London, in the darkness of Joyce's cab, I am reliving it again – my blurred fantasy, from the moment I heard him.

I open the door, he puts his finger to his lips and then to mine and comes in. What happens next is a silent dance. I pour all my anger and all my pain into it. He still has his finger against my lips as he enters the room, but I don't want my lips to be sealed. I open my mouth wide and take his fingers in, and bite them, holding him close to me. He should be wincing from pain, but he isn't – he props his thumb under my chin, pushes my head up and slides his lips down to the tip of my nose. His eyes are close, too close, drawing me in. I open my mouth, to let his fingers out and his tongue in. When he kisses me, his hand slides down, following my dress, just like all those years ago – first to squeeze my knee, as if putting a full stop at the first hurdle, and then up my thigh, before stopping again, as if the skin he finds there is too hot, burning, impossible to touch.

And then we are on the floor – we don't have the time or strength to get to the bed; those three extra steps are too much for our bodies – and the rug bites back as his body is on top of me. As he rocks, I stick my tongue under his armpit to taste his salty, sweaty desire. We roll over, and now I am pinning him down, hurting him as my nails dig into his shoulders, with the full intention never to let him go.

Not a word, not a sound, just the screeching of my teeth, our breathing in unison and Phil Collins outside: '. . . in too deep . . .'

It can't be over, but it is over, as abruptly as it started, and we sit next to each other in silence, and I have no strength left to fight, to talk, to understand what has just happened.

When he finally speaks, it is not about us. It is about the next step of the game. He sounds slightly out of focus, as if the encounter on the rug with me was a diversion from his plans. It was just that, I realise, as he gives me further instructions – what I should do and how and where. Somebody at the wedding below must really love this Phil Collins song, because I hear it for the third time in a row.

I need him to listen to me. There are so many questions

I would like to ask him – starting with why he is here, how did he know *I* was here – but I don't want to interrupt him, to make him move his hand away from mine. At last he stops talking and frees his hand, then slips away and gets dressed, not looking at me.

'What if they want to check the saxophone at customs?' I ask him.

'They won't find anything unless they try to play it.' He makes this sound light, nonchalant, easy – and before heading to the door, he leans over me again and touches my forehead with his lips. It is not a kiss, it is a blessing, wishing me good luck with the safe delivery. I am a courier, that's all I am.

He moves the doorknob and turns to me for the last time. 'Are you sure you are up for it? Will you be OK?' he asks.

'Don't worry, Tony,' I hear myself saying. 'I am OK.'

The door closes as silently as it opened, and he is gone.

This time I make it to the bed. I lie there thinking that it was all a dream, that it's still a dream . . . until the sun wakes me up, and the phone rings: 'Mrs Robinson? Your taxi for the airport is here.'

Only when I reach the neon corridors of Heathrow and walk back into my familiar world does the tiredness kick in.

Joyce is waiting patiently in the arrivals hall, holding a printed piece of paper with my name on. Despite my protests, she still insists on this – she claims that it's her professional habit. But boy, am I pleased to see that it's my real, maiden name she is clutching – when will I finish the paperwork to change it officially?

I am used to being the only adult in the house by now, though sometimes I miss the simple, everyday togetherness of the early days of our marriage: sentences you don't need to finish, comfortable silences that don't break into the thunder of an argument, of small choices – sushi or Indian?

At this rate, I'll start missing a future sport wandering hand in hand round National Trust car parks. My mother gave me family membership – the female equivalent of a reindeer sweater – for Christmas.

We live in a safe-ish area (where is totally safe in London?) and I am not scared of being alone (Christina hardly counts as an adult), or rather, I never thought I would be scared – until that incident last month, when I heard the alarm and ran outside just as a boy in a yob uniform – hoodie and tracksuit bottoms, was about to take my satnav out. 'What do you think you are . . .' I stopped, my swear words in mid air. He looked at me blankly, as if I was invisible, and carried on, concentrating fully on what he was doing – getting the screen out, jumping on a bike, riding away. That was the first time I was afraid of being a nobody. The blank look on the boy's face was exactly the same as Simon's – my ex-husband used to look at me like that when I tried to reason with him, and then just got on with his destruction.

'Take care when you get into the house,' Joyce says. Do I look that tired? 'I have no calls for now, so I'll wait outside in case you need me,' she adds.

Why would I need her? I think. I know Joyce by now, she'll refuse a cup of tea – that's her way of not growing too close to the customers, as she has explained to me more than once.

I could murder a cup of tea, though, so I go straight to the kitchen to put the kettle on. I wonder if Christina is already asleep or just in a huff in her room – this is her evening off, and I am late, too late for her to go out.

'Hello, Alexandra.'

There is only one person I know who uses my full name – he started doing it during the divorce proceedings. He is sitting in an armchair, comfortable, relaxed, reading some geek computer magazine.

'I came to check on Luke and Emma, because Christina said you were abroad – just wanted to make sure that they were OK,' he says. 'When you got custody, you assured the judge that you were committed to . . .' And Simon is off.

Five minutes into his torrent I say: 'Shh . . . you'll wake the kids,' just to stop the flow. But I only make it worse.

'You didn't think twice about waking them up when you returned home so late, did you? Where were you? Odessa, Christina said . . . Getting more exotic with our travels now, are we?'

'It was only for two days,' I say. 'It was a jazz festival, they awarded Max's memorial prize.' I am still holding Max's saxophone in my hands. Amazing how I still have to justify myself to Simon even though we have been divorced for two years now. A five-year habit, hard to break.

I turn and walk out of the room, back into the kitchen, with Simon following me.

'For this? You left the kids for this?' He pulls the case from my hands and shakes it vigorously.

The locks click open and Max's saxophone falls on to the floor with a sad, long sound. The anger is palpable, both his and mine, the silence interrupted by the kettle whistling.

I pick up the kettle, hold it high and turn to Simon, who is about to lash out at me.

He stops, his fist mid air, and I register the fear in his eyes as he looks at the only barrier between us now: the kettle full of boiling water.

I think what fantastic headlines we could make: *Abused wife slowly pours her anger out . . . Her patience finally boiled over.*

Or it could be a great slow-motion film scene: Simon stands there shaking, while I pour the water, looking straight into his eyes . . . Camera zooms on his shirt getting soaked, his silent scream . . . (mustn't wake the kids!), a close-up of his mouth, eyes in agony . . .

Only in real life it is not a film, it is a cartoon.

Suddenly I see Simon for what he has become – with his beer belly and flabby cheeks, shaking in anger, he looks remarkably like Homer Simpson holding Lisa's saxophone case. Does that mean that I should look like Marge?

It's hard not to laugh, and I stretch my lips into a smile, still brandishing the kettle.

'Would you like a cup of tea before you go, Simon?' I say. 'To thank you for checking on the kids.'

This throws him – boy, it throws him. He backs off, opens the door and disappears – from my house and from my fears.

When he has left, I take a mug of tea out into the street. I knock on the window of the waiting cab and hand the mug to Joyce, who accepts it without comment. I stand watching her while she drinks it.

'How did you know?' I ask her.

'I dropped him off, didn't I? But I refused to take the bastard back!' She laughs, then adds, handing me back the mug: 'You were right to kick him out as soon as you came in. You did yourself proud, girl . . . You did me proud.'

When Joyce has driven off, I lock the front door and wander about the hall for a while, collecting trophies from the floor. Max's saxophone case, Luke's trainer, Emma's school cardigan – not much to show for a victory. A leaflet advertising a new computer game, which fell out of Simon's magazine. I read it, amazed how appropriate the rules of this new game are: *There is no better way to conquer the world than customising your own monster and then destroying it . . .*

I have to go into the bedrooms to check that my kids are still the same – I have changed so much in these three days.

I open the door to Luke's room and negotiate an obstacle course of Action Men and dinosaurs to get to his bed. I cover my son and stand over him for a while, inhaling the comforting smell of shortbread.

How well I remember that smell, and the day. I was sitting in a coffee shop outside the Marie Stopes clinic, watching the world rushing by, laughing and kissing, thinking how alone I was in this decision. I had persuaded myself that abortion was the only option, that I didn't want any connection with that night in Las Vegas with the man I was so terrified of, when an elderly waitress suddenly said, placing my third cup of coffee with a shortbread biscuits on the table: 'Don't go, you'll regret it.'

'What do you mean?' I asked.

'We're opposite the clinic entrance, lovey. I've seen lots of women with your expression. You're about to go in, aren't you?'

'I'm already late,' I whispered.

'Good, so you've decided then,' and she turned and left her words hanging in the air, and I caught them and carried them with me in my pocket, in my tight fist, to the tube station, away from the clinic. I was afraid to open my hand to get my tube pass out, in case I let those words escape.

But they stayed with me for the next seven months, for the next seven years, and when I lean over to stroke Luke's hair, which always smells of shortbread, I wonder how I could ever have lived without those freckles and that toothless smile, and his grumpy 'Stop sniffing me, Mum! You are waking me up!'

I tiptoe into Emma's tiny, tidy bedroom – neat piles of books, rows of stuffed animals sitting by the wall, as though they are waiting for the exciting night performance. Yes, this is my daughter – the child who asked me if she could work in a supermarket when she grows up as her dream is to stack the shelves!

I was never romantic enough to become a Jane Austen fan, but my daughter's name came straight from the page of one of Jane Austen's novels. I was hoping my Emma would be just like that Emma – with *the power of having rather too much her own way, and a disposition to think a little too well of herself* . . . Great qualities for a modern woman, I thought. By then Simon had already started his campaign to stop me from thinking too well of myself.

Even in her sleep, Emma is orderly: curled into a neat ball, her duvet tucked around her. Where does she gets this streak from? Is it an attempt to sort out her disrupted life somehow? I am about to leave this kingdom of tidiness when I notice the only sign of disarray – a notebook that has slipped off the bed and is now resting on her slippers, open to me and the night. I pick it up – she was writing something before falling asleep.

*What I Want to Be When I Grow Up*
*A poem by Emma Robinson, age: nine years, three months and eleven days*

*I want to be a book. A fairy tale*
*With pictures bright and never pale.*

# The Game

*The kids will take me off the shelves*
*To look at unicorns and elves*
*And the story will be so fan-tas-tic,*
*With lots of brave heroes, lots of laughter*
*But never happy ever after.*
*I don't want my fairy tale to have a happy ending,*
*As I don't want it to end at all!*
*My fairy tale will last FOR EVER!!!*

I turn the page slowly, to discover other poems, some with letters underlined: *My life is <u>rainy</u> and gr<u>ey</u> on a dismal d<u>ay</u>* – that was when she was learning her vowels; others with capital letters brightly coloured, with the wrong spelling but the same enchantment:

*New Year's poem*

**N** *ecklases*
**E** *vening*
**W** *ine*
**Y** *ellow dresses*
**E***leganse*
*c***A***napeys*
**R** *eselution*

I look at the poems, then at my meticulous, orderly girl, wondering when and how I have missed this. I have no time to find an answer, as our perversely loud kitchen clock, a considerate present from my mother, starts its midnight bird-song. It is only meant to make a noise from six a.m. to nine p.m., unless you set it wrongly – which of course I did. Every hour it sings as a different bird, but I still don't understand why the midnight wren's song is the longest and the loudest. Our tawny owl woos us at seven a.m, when really we could do with the wren. Luke adores the greater spotted woodpecker at six – he says it sounds like morning drums – and Emma thinks that the nightingale at eight is really sweet. Looking at her romantic poems, I begin to understand why.

I rush out of the room, closing the door behind me, losing one slipper and still clutching Emma's notebook. I prop myself at the breakfast bar in the kitchen and laugh – what a scene! A middle-aged Cinderella in a blue velvet slipper under the midnight song of a wren!

No ugly sisters, no pumpkin, just the gift of my daughter's fantasies in my hand and a Phil Collins song melting into the Odessa night. Did it really happen?

I think it did. I even had documents to prove it, though I handed them to Jonty at Brussels airport, having escorted them with honour and secrecy, as instructed, inside Max's saxophone. It is my second delivery of documents to him; I am a dab hand at secure transfer now. As instructed by Tony, I handed Jonty the UN documents after our second Waterloo meeting. They had arrived from the US tucked into a big *Adventures of Huckleberry Finn* illustrated book my father sent for Luke and Emma.

'Do you think these Russian documents are copies of the same protocols?' I asked Jonty at the airport. He nodded and told me what his final task was; about the question he has to ask at the European parliament, showing one of the protocols.

'Which one are you going to talk about?' I asked.

'The one that will change the future,' he replied.

Good luck to him, is all I can say. Hope he has the guts to do it.

# JONTY'S WAR

*Brussels – Strasbourg*

I reread my task, though I know it by heart, have known it for years – it is exactly the same task as in the last game twenty-five years ago:

*You are to address the whole assembly and make a speech . . .*

That's what Tony expects me to do again – only it can't be a long speech, whatever the task states. It is only one minute at the plenary, during the debates – that's the parliament's rule N150.

I can't back out, I am deep in the task already – I have the documents in my hands and my lobbying worked: Xavier has used all the zeal and ardour pent up during his years of doing nothing, and as a result, the Governor of Crimea has been invited to the debate, together with the Turkish president and the Bulgarian prime minister. It is set for the afternoon of the plenary on the twenty-fourth of October. And now that I know the contents of the documents, I understand why the date is so important.

'They are in Russian,' Alex said when I met her at Brussels airport, unlocking the saxophone case and taking the rolled pieces of paper out of the tube. Just like that, at the coffee shop. Changing the world in front of a broken espresso machine and loud Moroccan teenagers speaking the clipped guttural French only they understand.

Judging by the ease with which she unclasped the case, she had no idea how important the documents were. 'Do you know what they are, Jonty?' she confirmed. 'I couldn't read them, but I suspect these are the same documents my dad sent from New York, only in Russian.'

'Couldn't Levi translate them for you?' I asked. I haven't seen Levi's task, but as he went to Crimea again, it's only logical that they met there.

Alex looked at me, surprised, and yawned. 'Sorry, had a sleepless night, quite tired . . . So, what's your task, Jonty?

Why doesn't she talk about her meeting with Levi? I wonder. Did they have an argument? Levi is the most laid-back guy, he would never start a fight, but Alex is constantly on edge.

'What are you supposed to do with those?' she asked with genuine interest, pointing at the rolled papers. 'Leak them to the press?'

'No,' I say. 'Just show one of the documents during the parliamentary session and speak about it for one minute.'

'Which one are you going to talk about?' asked Alex.

'The one that will change the future,' I replied.

'Good luck.' Alex smiled wearily. 'I am sure you have the guts to do it.'

I should be writing my speech now, not roaming the streets of Brussels trying to persuade myself that it will help me to think. How can I put the enormity of those lines into just one minute? I think, turning from Rue Lombard to Anspach.

I prefer Brussels to Strasbourg, I must admit. I quite like Strasbourg, in a detached, touristy way – the medieval film-set quarter of Petite France, cafés under sycamore trees, ice cream made to look and taste like flower petals in the parlours around the cathedral, the echo of young voices interrupted by the rumble of mopeds at Place Gayot . . . For me it is the city of Riesling and Goethe, of the Rhine and *choucroute* . . . and the empty glass circle of the European Parliament.

I enjoy Brussels, even though I try to walk everywhere to avoid the metro – it has a sinister bunker feel to it, with its black walls, piped music and neon lights.

My Brussels is not the world of the concrete buildings and less concrete decisions of the European quarter, not the world of the chocolate box of Grand Place and the hundreds of bronze peeing boys in the shop windows.

Another Brussels, my own, starts at Anspach as I enter the world of old vinyl and rare recordings. I love browsing here, looking for nothing in particular, going to the top floor or to the back of the shops to make an unexpected discovery. Soul or rock, new wave or disco – it doesn't matter, as long as it is the music I love but cannot play.

I hasten my pace past the homeless and the drunkards to St Catherine, taking my tie off, unbuttoning my shirt collar as I get closer to the familiar smell of grilled seafood. It is the best restaurant in town, this street-corner open-air café. Lucy wouldn't like it – she prefers a more orchestrated meal – and Magda wouldn't be seen dead here, so this is my time, my spot.

I am waiting for my prawns in chilli sauce when my phone rings. '*Ça va*, Jonathan?' asks somebody French, male and unknown.

'Who is this?' I ask.

'It is me, Xavier, *ça va*?'

Xavier? He hardly acknowledges me when he sits next to me at the meetings; he has never called me.

'Are you all right, Xavier?' I start carefully.

'No, I am not all right!' he shouts in my ear. 'The Governor of Crimea, whom I invited, is not coming next week – we just had an email from his office. It is a disaster, Jonathan!'

'Yes, it is a disaster.' I agree with him, but for very different reasons. 'Do you know why?'

'Something about the local elections, he has to go to a remote constituency. He is lying. I checked the map – the most remote constituency in Crimea would only be a couple of hours' drive from his office! You said your friend was his adviser; can he talk to the governor and persuade him to come? It is really important! Can you call him now?'

Ah, I think. It is not a disaster, it is a catastrophe. 'I'll try, Xavier,' I manage, getting up and walking down the street.

'Monsieur!' Somebody is running after me. 'You forgot your prawns!' I settle on a bench, next to a sleeping drunkard, munching my lunch and thinking what to do.

My old rugby trick would be to run around the block three times, or practise a dump tackle on somebody, but that will not change this situation. I need to think logically, analyse, add two and two together . . .

Levi! The most logical person I know – my last resort and my only hope. We are not supposed to communicate between meetings, but I have no option. Besides, he went to Crimea twice this month; he might have some friends there.

I am not as fit as I used to be, but I manage to run back to the apartment. I check the computer – Levi Freiman, GP, north London – and dial the number.

'Is it an emergency?' asks the receptionist.

'Very much so', I say.

Levi comes to the phone in a couple of minutes. I can hear the nurses laughing in the background.

'Levi, we don't have much in common, I know,' I start. (Is it the right way to start?)

'At least we both have abbreviated jobs,' says Levi. 'I am a GP, you are an MEP.'

Yes, Levi's jokes don't change. I fear that there will be more, and explain my request about the governor quickly.

Levi thinks for a moment, processing the information, then says: 'I have a friend who works as a guide at the Livadiya Palace in Criméa. He is a very influential man. I don't know his name, but I'll call the museum and find out. Leave it with me for two hours.'

Nothing of what Levi has just said makes any sense, but my choices are quite limited now: to wait for two hours or . . . That's it, actually.

So I have an excuse to escape for two hours to another place that I call mine. Even Magda, who knows about my passion for records and street food, doesn't know about this hideaway.

I feel at home here, and not only because of the giant letters – *OLD ENGLAND* – that loom above the ornate art nouveau entrance. I never looked up, never noticed those letters, though I had gone past this building a hundred times, until two years ago, when I stumbled over the billboard outside: *The Museum of Musical Instruments is pleased to announce the exhibition 'A hundred years of saxophone: from Adolf Sax's invention to the Belgian jazz rebellion'.* And below:

*In 2002, the Museum of Musical Instruments in Brussels was entrusted with an impressive collection devoted entirely to the history of the saxophone in Belgium. The collection contains over ten thousand books, magazines and files, and thousands of photographs and recordings. Facing a challenge to display all the unique archive items of this enormous collection, the museum decided to hold two exhibitions: 'A hundred years of saxophone' (open to visitors today) and 'The saxophone – from the post-war years to the present day' (to be opened next year).*

*The curators wish to express their gratitude to the Royal Museums of Art and History for their support of the exhibition, to the Centre Européen de Saxophone in Bordeaux and to the King Baudouin Foundation for all its support in printing and translating the catalogues.*

How could such a standard text deliver such a shockwave reaction? Of course, I had been working in the city where the saxophone was invented for years and had never thought about it! I just had to go in.

Three giant pieces of wood were stuck to the brass plate at the entrance, with the caption: *He chose wood for softness and brass for sonority*, and a photograph of a bearded young man next to it.

It can only get better, I thought, and walked in, scanning the exhibits.

The programme of the second Brussels Industrial Exhibition of August 1841, introducing an extraordinary new instrument, '*saxophone basse en cuivre*'.

A photograph of the Royal Belgian military band with saxophones, dated 1901.

An entire stand dedicated to the US 'saxophone epidemic' of the 1920s.

And then the last display: 'Jazz as a protest'.

A man in the photograph looks more like a star than a hero: an impeccable Hollywood smile under a groomed moustache, huge feral eyes, well-cut suit, expensive cufflinks. He looks strong and assured. He is not just successful, he *is* a success. Just another jazz player, I thought – until I read his post-war interview about the jam session in 1942. Then my old journalist's instinct kicked in (do I still have a journalist's instinct?): there is enough here for a book, never mind an article . . .

It takes me fifteen minutes to walk from the Place de Luxembourg; I know all the short cuts. It takes thirty minutes by taxi or forty if the driver is a total crook. I am glad that I have two hours to spare today.

I greet the cloakroom attendant, a former jazz player himself. ('He was quite good,' whispers the ticket lady, looking at him admiringly – I wonder if she works here just to be closer to him.)

Usually I start with a coffee on the roof terrace, where the geometry of rectangular Brussels is softened by the pyramids of the Palais Royal, round windows and oddly shaped rooftops, and then go to the first or the second floor, choosing a different hall each time. I put earphones on and stand on a numbered part of the floor, where an instrument will play just for me: Mozart's light touch on a harpsichord, the deep soul sound of New Orleans in a bass saxophone, the piercing octave of the Peruvian charango.

I might go into the Hall of Mirrors, where the music is reflected from walls and ceiling, look at the dark carved stories on the street organs, or try an unusual African horn. This is all about the anticipation for me.

But today, as I get into the old lift, carefully closing the grille door, I press the button for the third floor. The lift moves more slowly than I would walk, but I savour the moment before I get to the library, which is never library quiet; more concert quiet – somebody trying the strings, somebody coughing, waiting for a great performance, for a new musical discovery . . .

It is here that I come to do my research. I am writing an article that will probably never be published, but I am doing it anyway: *Belgian jazz as a protest.*

I have several ways to start it now:

*Verboten. A word common in occupied Belgium. Verboten for crowds to gather, for young people to dance . . . and verboten to play jazz.*

*The word 'jazz' in the eyes of the Führer is a synonym for Jewish, black, barbaric, and therefore is forbidden.*

*All the discs with English names are eliminated. Jazz goes underground, American discs are passed secretly from fan to fan, sold and resold on the black market. Still, despite being forbidden, jazz lives on: the number of discs recorded by Belgian artists during the war is the highest ever.*

*Verboten jazz becomes a political protest in Belgium. One Belgian saxophone player crosses the border to participate in a concert in Paris. And not just participate . . .*

Or maybe I can begin with something more generic and highbrow:

*Jazz made a spectacular mark on the twentieth century. From being music for pleasure and dance, it became an art form, an inspiration for the new cinema trends; it gave foundations to the pop culture, rock and rap . . .*

Or I'll begin with a historical note:

*The word 'jazz' first appeared in Belgium at the end of the First World War, and meant, primarily, a drum kit, introduced by American jazz bands. The drummer was the showman of the band and stood out as such . . .*

No, I'll start with a provocative question:

*Jazz in Belgium during the war – was it an escape or a protest?*

*Despite 'Swing Tanzen Verboten', orchestras still played in private clubs, changing the English song titles to French, sometimes with comic effect ('Lady Be Good' to the French 'Bigoudis', for example).*

*Belgian 'zazous', jazz fans, defied the Nazi regime by dancing, listening to their zaz zuh zaz music and wearing pompadour hairstyles. But was their light attitude to war and their mocking of Greta Gestapo really a protest? Especially if you compare it with the rest of Europe: the Swing Youths thrown into prison and sent to concentration camps for resisting the Nazis' rigid control over social culture in Germany; the horror of the Czech Terezin concentration camp band Ghetto Swing, whose musicians were forced to play in front of the cameras for a propaganda film about the ideal ghetto in 1944, only to be sent to the Auschwitz gas chambers straight afterwards.*

I am writing this article because of one man, writing about him after just one caption: *He was arrested by the Parisian Gestapo office in 1942 after he played the 'St Louis Blues' under a fake title following a harmless announcement during a concert in Paris.*

That's what started me, really. I know so much about this man with the feral eyes now.

That he taught himself to play the saxophone and clarinet, for example, after being a violin player . . .

That when asked what profession he would have chosen if he hadn't become a professional musician, he replied: 'I would have been an amateur musician, but still a musician' . . .

That the woman of his dreams had auburn hair – not red, not brown, but the rich colour of frescoes . . .

That he hated playing the 'melody of the day' when it was requested for the fifth time during a session.

But even though I know it all, I am rewriting the article for the tenth time now, because I cannot express . . . because I cannot feel what he felt during that jam session in 1942, the one he called his 'best, most ecstatic memory'.

I still cannot find the answer – why, but why did he do it? He was warned that Gestapo officers were in the concert hall; one of his compositions was already banned.

Why, knowing that 'St Louis Blues' would be recognised, did he choose to play it, under the fake title 'Lausanne Bleu', knowing that this five-minute number might cost him his career, his freedom, even his life? What did he feel besides fear; what sort of bravery was that?

Why did he say that he would never forget this concert, and the jam session with the genius gypsy guitarist straight after it – in a basement club in Paris, heavy with the smoke of Gauloises?

Did he think that good music was above politics?

Or did he, as I really hope he did, play the American blues as an act of defiance?

I have imagined him playing so many times now, his eyes closed. He starts with a rich, dark Louisiana sound, tapping the ragtime rhythm, but then unexpectedly goes higher, lighter, carefree, throwing several strands in.

My phone rings, I look at the number and rush out of the library, into the corridor. It's Lucy. Something must have happened; she stopped calling me for a chat a long time ago. In fact, we hardly talk at all these days. Our airy farmhouse gets more and more stifling, the bridges we built between our self-created worlds are cracking... It must be something urgent.

'Jonty, just a quick one.' She gets straight to the point. 'Somebody called Levi was trying to reach you – you didn't leave him your mobile number, apparently, but he found us through the constituency office somehow. He asked me to pass on a message that "Crimea is all sorted for next week". Does this make sense?'

I don't know if I am relieved or not. The governor is coming, which means that I have to leave the library and instead of the article concentrate on my speech now. And, what's even worse, deliver it.

Jonty the Brave... Whatever happened to my nickname? As if my courage disappeared, flash-flooded by events in my life.

They are quite common natural phenomena, apparently, flash floods. We went for a riverbank picnic in France three years ago – I planned it all, carried Minnie all the way to the river, with Lucy leading us, reading the map, only to discover when we got there that the river had disappeared a month ago, washed away by flash floods, leaving the crusty bed. Perhaps my spirit was flushed out the same way, and only a dry, crusty man now remains...

God, what am I fretting about? Sixty seconds is all the time I get!

Mr Smith, my childhood teddy, is propped on my standard desk in a faceless serviced apartment in Brussels, watching history spread in front of him. He surveys all three sets, studies them with me: the documents Alex brought from New York, the Russian originals, which arrived in Max's saxophone, and the Foreign Office ones. (I really should ask Tony how he got those – the name must have helped . . .)

'What do you think, Mr Smith? Are we ready to carry the weight of those three signatures, those decisions?' I ask him.

I think he nods, looking at me with his shiny new eyes, knowing that carrying those decisions to the Hemicycle will mean a long, slow journey – first to the Gare du Midi, then a change of trains and stations in Paris, before arrival in Strasbourg.

Slow, but not uncomfortable – the only dodgy bit is this walk between Gare du Nord and Gare de l'Est in Paris. I zigzag through the back streets between groups of young-sters loitering outside the shops which sell more than just phone cards. Luckily they are too busy to look at me, and I am already on my final descent – the fifty steps down to the Gare de l'Est.

And this is where my bag is snatched away from me – from the back, so I don't see who my assailant is. My body has a good memory, it turns out – my dump tackle comes in handy, and now I have the head of my attacker firmly pressed against my ribcage.

Suddenly I hear whimpering – *'Juste vous aider, monsieur . . .'* – and look down. My enemy is about twelve, and I notice there are three more street kids dotted around the flights of stairs – they work here, helping travellers shuttling between the stations to carry their bags up and down the one hundred steps.

You are paranoid, Jonty, I try to reason with myself, letting the boy go. You are safe – well, at least until you get to the plenary sitting at the Hemicycle . . .

I have always imagined our Hemicycle as the setting for a *Star Trek* film – dozens of neon lights on the concave cupola, the white sputniks of the loudspeakers, probing for the landing pad of the auditorium below . . .

My futuristic tram of a spaceship launches me next morning with an enthusiastic announcement of my final destination: 'Parlément Européen . . .' I have quite a landing today. One small step to the microphone, that's all I have to do.

The big hall is buzzing as I walk in.

I look up at the rows of press – why are there so many of them here today? Why all this sudden interest in the Black Sea? Or maybe it is interest in one of the speakers, judging by today's *L'Echo* in front of me: *The prime minister of Bulgaria, under investigation for corruption in his own country, will take part in the open house debate on the Black Sea in the European Parliament today . . .*

I am so glad that I won't need to go to the lectern – the MEP questions are asked from the seats, otherwise I would feel like a witness in a courtroom. Or maybe even like the defendant.

I look at the rows reserved for visitors, all full already: students, pensioners rights group from Slovakia, local MPs from Bavaria. Why are they all here?

The hall below is filling up too.

The stewards in white ties with chains and medallions are handing out the agenda of the meeting in five languages. I scan it when I get to my seat – there is nothing really debatable in our Black Sea debate: *Maritime cooperation and the development of Bulgarian cargo ports . . . Joint education initiative . . . Multilateral programmes on the environment . . .*

Franz Liebenz, our Tyrolean hunter, is already doing a crossword, his gold-framed glasses on, but secretly (at least that's what he thinks) he is scanning the 'end-of-row decorations' – the seats allocated to the MEPs' assistants.

Stephanie is talking to the girl from the secretariat, cutting the air with her tiny palm. She will speak, no doubt.

Xavier is directing the traffic, of course – this debate is his baby, and as the proud father, he will be standing in the centre of the hall for a while: greeting the MEPs, nodding to the secretariat, making sure that they know that inviting the Governor of Crimea and setting up this debate was his idea. '*Merci*, Jonathan,' he said to me this morning, in the tone he normally uses to thank me for a coffee. 'When I become a vice chair, I'll make sure that I recommend you as a rapporteur.' Which reminds me – I must thank Levi when we have our final Waterloo meeting. I still have no idea how he performed this 'Crimea all sorted' stunt . . . He has become an action man after all.

Monique, my charming assistant, is back from her Italian wedding unscathed, prettier than ever. She is my not-so-secret weapon today.

'Monique,' I say, 'this is important – could you please check if my speech is registered in the agenda under the one-minute speeches?'

'Is this very important for you?' she asks, teasing me with her smile and her French-accented 'thees'.

I think about the explosive revelations in the speech I am not sure I will make.

'No, Monique, not just for me,' I reply. 'Far from it.'

I have already seen Magda, my secret weapon, this morning. 'Listen,' I said, handing her a copy of my speech, 'if I don't have time to speak, will you add this to the press release somehow?'

She scanned the text and looked at me as if she was seeing me for the first time. As if the pages I had showed her had a headline shouting: *New Jonty To Be Admired*.

'Are you sure you can do this, *hlopak*?' she said.

I thought of Mr Smith's shining eyes, the comment of the toy doctor about my type only saying what others expected of me, and replied: 'Yes, Magda, I am sure.'

But that was two hours ago, I am not so sure now, looking around the crowded room.

The President of Turkey and the Prime Minister of Bulgaria are already seated on opposite sides of the table, not looking at each other, as the Governor of Crimea enters the hall. He is accompanied by two pretty assistants in skirts too tight and too short for such a formal occasion – a feast for Franz Leibenz's eyes.

Finally the chairman sails in, followed by a school of smaller fish: interns, *fonctionnaires*, organisers. He waves them off with a majestic gesture, and as he mounts the podium, I notice for the first time that the Hemicycle is more than a *Star Trek* film set.

I see it now as the architect might have seen it – as a sleek cruise liner, with porthole windows, an upper deck for panoramic views, and the captain's bridge. The flags behind the captain and the palm trees on either sides of the table signal our departure for tropical shores.

'Welcome to the debate: "The Black Sea – what's next?"' announces the chairman. 'We are going to start with the opening remarks by our guest speakers. They will be followed by the open house debate and a question and answer session.

'All political groups are represented here today – I am not

going to go through the list, it is attached to the agenda. There is only one slight change – the Czech MEP is not joining the Black Sea debate today. Maybe the fact that his country is landlocked has something to do with it . . .' He pauses, waiting for polite laughter. 'Now, let me introduce our guests . . .'

And off we sail, the words floating, the flags waving, in a ship steered expertly by the captain: avoiding the dangerous waters of human rights and border tensions, he leads us through the calm seas of cooperation initiatives and partnership building measures . . .

There is the occasional choppiness –

'Twenty-five years ago, central Europeans would have seen joining the EU as impossible, but now . . . When can Turkey join? Shall we propose a date?'

'We should do something about Transdnistria, a painful wound on the body of Europe . . .'

– but the captain always steers us to safety.

The debate is successful, the questions are mild and benevolent – nothing about Bulgarian corruption – the nosy journalists will be waiting on shore when the passengers disembark from the Hemicycle.

The winds are warm, the beaches are close, and nobody will ask any questions now to rock the boat. My seat is at the end of the row, upstairs, easy to slip in and out, easy to escape, not many people will notice . . .

Except the captain is already saying: 'We have a one-minute

speech registered here from . . .' He has to check his notes. Of course he doesn't even remember my name!

I switch my microphone on, aware that they are all looking at me, thinking: this guy is just a 'don't give a fuck any more' voiceless backbencher, an invisible cell . . .

And they are right, because I can't speak. I look at the papers in front of me, shuffle my notes . . . Ten more seconds and the chairman will switch his attention to somebody on the front row – somebody outspoken or used to expressing their opinions naturally, like Stephanie, or Xavier, whose questions will be all about making sure that everybody knows he was the mastermind here.

I can't do it. Then suddenly I hear music. Nobody turns or looks at where it comes from, so I must be the only one hearing this melody.

And I see him – my Belgian saxophone player, in the smoke-filled cave of the Parisian Hot Club, playing in total oblivion, his eyes closed . . . And I know how he felt when he played 'St Louis Blues'.

That melody is slowly seeping into me, travelling to all my nerve endings, bringing me to life – as if I am a victim of encephalitis lethargica, that strange disease which allows some of its victims, frozen for most of the time in a statue-like state, to move to music.

'I have a question for the Governor of Crimea,' I begin. Is it really me? The red light of the mike is flashing; they are all looking at me.

'You represent a fascinating region, Governor, a place that is connected to all continents through sea and land, a place where many historic decisions were made. Your peninsula, covered in steppes, with a narrow strip of paradise climate between the sea and the mountains, has been a focus of attention for centuries.

'At the end of the eighteenth century, the Russian empress agreed to allow a number of British convicts to move to Crimea. The idea was so popular that people wanted to become prisoners in order to be sent to new lands, to warm Crimea . . . Only the efforts of the Russian ambassador Vorontsov stopped that project. If he hadn't, just think where Australia would be now.'

I can hear laughter. Are they laughing at my joke?

The governor is nodding, the captain is smiling – a perfect end to the cruise, praise from a harmless passenger.

'Crimea has always attracted projects that could change destinies. Just take the 1920s idea of creating California in Crimea: millions were spent to make it happen. Or the idea of establishing an autonomous Jewish republic there after the Second World War.'

The chairman is now studying my face – a captain assessing the strength of a quiet sailor: is he really the one to start the mutiny?

I am about to confirm his suspicions. 'The details, the names in those projects, if made public, might be formidable,' I continue, 'but they will not change the course of history. They belong to the past.

'There is one document, however, that looks into the future, one protocol from the Yalta Conference that is still valid. And what day would be more appropriate to remind ourselves of its existence than today: the twenty-fourth of October, the International Day of the UN.'

I lift my hand, waving the papers, looking at the captain. I can see that he is about to blow his whistle. I have seconds to say what I need to.

'You all know about the historic if controversial agreements of the Yalta Conference of 1945. There is one particular agreement that the world still remembers with gratitude – the agreement on the creation of the United Nations. One thing the world does not know, however: this agreement had a codicil.'

I read from the proceedings of the Yalta Conference, read quickly, aware that my precious seconds are ticking away.

'When Churchill asked, "How would you feel, Marshal Stalin, if the international organisation proposed to hand Crimea over to international control?", Stalin answered that Crimea was already under the international control of three countries for the period of the Yalta Conference, as the security was provided by the representatives of the armed forces of the Soviet Union, USA and Great Britain, working together.

'I would like to draw your attention to the document which states that Crimea should have been under international control for *longer* than eight days in February 1945.

*The Game*

'According to the Crimea Conference protocol, "the five nations which have permanent seats on the Security Council should consult each other on, among other issues, any . . . territory which might voluntarily be placed under the trusteeship of the UN".

'I have here in my hand three originals of the Codicil to the Protocol of Proceedings of 11 February 1945, signed by all three leaders during the conference: one on loan from the Yalta Conference Museum in Crimea' (God knows how Levi managed to do it); 'the British original' (thank you, Tony) 'and the American one' (Max and Alex – thank you, guys), 'which explain the territory the protocol refers to. They all state the same thing clearly: the territory voluntarily placed under UN trusteeship is . . . Crimea. Agreed term of trusteeship – one hundred years.

'That historical agreement, forgotten but still valid' (thank you, Alex, for checking with your father), 'could change the way we look at the Black Sea today.

'The Black Sea region is not stable, due to various military bases, tensions, loss of influence by some countries and new influence gained by others – this jostling for power could cause a dangerous chain reaction.

'While there is no clear answer to the question of why the Yalta commitments failed to be honoured, though many reasons can be cited and offered, one thing is clear – this agreement is still alive today, and it is our duty to make sure that this small peninsula, with connections to all continents, by sea and by land, becomes the route of peace, rather than the route of spreading war.

'President Roosevelt expressed this point of view in his message to Congress on the first of March 1945, after the Yalta Conference: "The structure of world peace cannot be the work of one man, or one party or one nation. It cannot be just an American peace, or a British peace, or a Russian, French or a Chinese peace. It cannot be a peace of large nations – or of small nations. It must be a peace which rests on the co-operative effort of the whole world . . ."

'At the Yalta Conference dinner, Winston Churchill made a toast: "The whole world has its eyes on this Conference, and if it were successful, there would be peace for a hundred years . . ." We still have thirty-five years to go. Crimea might have failed as Australia, as California and as an autonomous Jewish republic, but it is a place where great battles were fought and important lessons learned . . .

'I will leave the details to the international lawyers. But I am strongly convinced that Crimea as a neutral international zone managed by the UN should become the door to the new world, and that this agreement, long forgotten, will be the key.

'So my question to the Governor of Crimea is: do you agree?'

The silence is all-absorbing. There is always some background noise in the Hemicycle: shuffling of papers, coughs, muted whispers, an occasional phone call, but not this time.

Finally the chairman breaks the silence: 'Your speech was slightly longer than one minute, but well worth it.' He turns to the governor. 'Would you like to reply?'

We had all forgotten he was there. I had, for sure.

'I agree . . .' is all the governor says. It sounds like a doomed 'I do' at a rather public wedding. What else can he say?

And then I hear another sound. Lone, remote – a woman by the door has her hands up in the air, clapping. Magda. It does not last long, this lone applause, because then the chairman stands up and claps. And then everybody does. The journalists, the Eurosceptics, the pensioners from Slovakia, students from Italy, Franz, Stephanie . . .

And I know that the applause is not just for the governor. In fact, it is not for him at all. They are all looking at me, turning to me . . .

The only person who does not applaud is Xavier.

I have made my speech; I should sit down now, but I dash to the door instead. As I run past Magda, she leans over to whisper:

'I am very proud of you, *hlopak*.'

I nod to her, but carry on – I need to thank him before he disappears. At the end of the hall by the porthole windows there is a tall man in an old-fashioned suit, his hair shining with brilliantine, his smile beaming from under a neat moustache. He is giving me a thumbs-up. He is grateful to me, my saxophone player – not just for the speech, but because he can leave me now. I know how to finish the article about him; I know how he felt when he played that 'St Louis Blues' in the concert hall in Paris in 1942 . . .

*'If I'm feelin' tomorrow like I feel today . . .'*

I rush out into the corridor, but he is not there. Of course he is not there, why should he be – he was created by the adrenalin rush and my imagination.

I push the heavy door to the toilets, splash my face with cold water and look out of the window – it is a bright, sunny day, so rare in grey Strasbourg. A pensioner shuffles along, walking a dog so small that I can only see a lead from here. I lean over the windowsill to check out the details of everyday life, which suddenly interest me intensely.

I need to unwind now, to join the pensioner on the path outside, by the canal. Will I recognise him down there? What sort of dog has he got?

I didn't hear the door open at all, didn't hear the steps. I only switch on, tune into the place where I am now, when I hear the heavy breathing in my ear. I look into the mirror, and see the reflection of him standing behind me, hands gathered in fists. He is watching me, silent, waiting for me to turn, and I know what is going to happen next.

I look to the right, at the A4 sheet pinned to the door – *Evacuation plan: when the alarm sounds, please leave the building immediately* – and know that no evacuation plan in the world can save me now. So I turn to face him.

I try to explain, but I haven't got the time. Xavier might be a mediocre politician, but I forgot that he used to be a champion boxer when he was younger. The blows are instantaneous, well aimed, blinding.

Blue tiles are the last thing I see as the light closes in. There is the metallic taste of blood in my mouth, and I feel my tongue touching the gap . . . I've lost my tooth. Not that it matters any more.

# PART 3

## *Full Stop*

*I want to be a full stop*
*Not a comma*
*Not a hyphen*
*Or not even a dash*
*But a full stop is the one*
*I want to be*
*Because*
*It is completer in itself*
*Beginning and end being within*
*That insignificant dot*
*Which is lost in the sea of text*
*Yes I want to be a full stop.*

Athar Mohd, 'Full stop'

*We shall not cease from exploration*
*And the end of all our exploring*
*Will be to arrive where we started*
*And know the place for the first time.*
    T. S. Eliot, 'Little Gidding' (*No.4* of *Four Quartets*)

# FULL STOP

**Levi**

'I know what it's like to be beaten up when you least expect it, Jonty.'

I called Jonty last week, when I found out from Tony why our last meeting had been postponed. 'I have been through this myself quite recently – you see, another thing we have in common!'

'Sorry, Levi, I can't laugh – my cracked ribs hurt,' replied Jonty. 'But thank you and thank you for making sure the Governor of Crimea turned up at the debate! How did you manage to do it? You are a real hero! You must tell me all about it next Sunday, at our Waterloo meeting.'

I am looking forward to the last Sunday meeting, and, surprisingly, to seeing Jonty, too. But before that, there is one crucial announcement I need to make . . .

Shabat is an evening of good food rather than religious ceremony for me – my parents left Odessa at the time when

Soviet slogans replaced the Torah, and never really arrived at any religion.

Just another reason for my mother-in-law not to accept me, constantly repeated with many others: 'My lovely daughter didn't marry well . . . No money, first-generation immigrant, no respect for . . .' Off she goes, talking to anybody who will listen, but not to me. She refuses to notice me most of the time, not realising that this is a situation any son-in-law would really dream of.

But I like Shabbat – the only time my wife gives in to my mother, letting her, the eldest woman, light the candles. It is also the only time when my mother and my wife only throw daggers of glances across the table, when all other sharp exchanges are left for the kitchen.

Dana insists that I bless the children, and I like that as well: Friday night is when I see my children together for the first time in days – not that they take much notice of me.

Tonight is my chance not just to see my whole family in one place, but to make an announcement to all of them. I have to get the timing right, probably when we are having chicken soup, rather than fish – the hazard of choking will be much higher then, with what I am about to say.

'I have taken a sabbatical,' I say to nobody in particular, studying my soup plate. 'I am going to Odessa to set up a hospital that will be run by an international charity to help HIV victims. I applied and was accepted, am leaving in a fortnight.'

'For how long?' asks Dana.

'Three months.'

I wish the Veteran, my old chemistry teacher, could watch this spontaneous chemical reaction, when two elements – A (my mother) and B (my wife) – that cannot usually combine form an unexpected bond to make an explosion as soon as the catalyst (element C – me) is provided.

The activation energy, the raising of the temperature, the hastening of the reaction are spectacular.

'Just look at him, Rimma,' says my wife, turning to her arch-enemy for support. 'I wish *I* could go wherever I like whenever I like. He decides to save the world when I have a bar mitzvah to plan, he . . .' She is boiling fast, lost for words. 'Is this a midlife crisis? What's next – a motorbike and a candy girl?'

'You are forty-three years old, Levi, not a gap student. If you wanted to travel and do things on your own, you should have thought about it before you had the family.' My mother's energy adds to the collision. The explosion is inevitable.

The kids continue with their food, with bored expressions, not in the least bit interested in the chemical experiment. They can easily describe it, analyse it, predict the result and write the one-line conclusion: 'You are not letting yourself down, Levi, you are letting all of us down.'

The thud is so loud that the whole table shakes, the glasses tremble. My father's heavy working hand is resting from the blow on the tablecloth.

It is the first time he has interfered, I think. First time in years. No, first time ever . . .

'Leave Levi alone, *perestante*, both of you,' he says, mixing Russian and English words. 'He is not a boy any more, he is a man. This is his decision and you are going to respect it. If you want to express your opinions about it, go and do it in the kitchen and not in front of the kids.'

The silence is crashing, louder than the thud. Nobody raises their head from their plate; only my father looks up and winks at me. He actually smiles and winks! I am in shock, so I do what I always do when I am nervous, upset or happy – I eat.

'Dad,' I say, walking into his office after dinner, 'thank you for your support.'

He doesn't answer, just stares at my photographs of Odessa, laid out neatly on the table, as if he is playing a game of patience – which he has been doing for many years, come to think of it.

'Dad,' I say, pointing at the photograph of the fragile old woman in the pink gown. 'Do you know who that is? It's Klava, our neighbour in Moldavanka. Do you remember her?'

'Of course I remember her – glad she is still alive,' he says.

This is the right time to ask him, I think. I have nothing to lose. 'Dad, why did we change our last name? I know we were Shapiro . . . Klava told me. Why are we Freiman now?'

I'm starting with this, and maybe, just maybe, I will

dare to ask him the question about the reason for leaving Odessa . . .

He doesn't look at me when he answers – as always, he looks out of the window, rocking slightly, as if he is praying, his fingers stroking the photograph of our courtyard.

'It is a long story, Levi. I was working at the Odessa shipyard, and there was a significant theft of metal. I mean, big – thousands and thousands of roubles' worth. Several people were involved – the accountant was fiddling the numbers, the head of maintenance was fiddling the weights . . . I didn't know anything about it, I was just a simple foreman. One evening, Lora's mother – do you remember Lora? – came to see me. "Misha," she said, "you have to run, all of you – you are being investigated." She was a secretary in the prosecutor's office, you see. "Your bosses were investigated too," she said, "but they have already bought off their freedom with bribes – they had all that money from the stolen steel, didn't they? So they decided to dump the blame on you. You'll be arrested on Thursday, I have seen the papers. Ten years in prison, Misha! You have to run. Go and speak to Nyuma . . ." Uncle Nyuma – do you remember him? He really liked you, Levi, he never had a son himself, just daughter after daughter.

'Nyuma was a docker, and he agreed to hide us in a tangerine container on a truck going to Romania. You don't remember *how* we left, Levi, but I always will. It was dawn, when everybody was still asleep. It was pitch dark, cold, and we had to squeeze between the crates in that Romanian fruit truck. You were so scared, Levi, you started to whimper, and I had to hold you tight, really tight, and tell you how happy we would be when we got across the border. Only I did not know myself what to expect when the truck stopped in Bucharest.

'I remember everything, Levi – how we walked in Bucharest, heads down, to the American Embassy, and Rimma kept glancing back, convinced that we were being chased . . . How you were sick, physically sick with fear, just as we reached the embassy gates. When I breathed "Sovetsky . . . Odessa . . ." to the guard at the embassy, he did not understand, so I said one of the few words I knew in Yiddish: "Freiman!" – free man at last. That's the name they put in our passports, that's the name we've had since then.

'We became political refugees – stateless, displaced – and as such, we could choose where to live. And I thought: I don't speak English, I can't even talk to the guards, but at least my son will be able to . . . and we came to London. That's how we became Freiman, son . . . But am I really free? Just look around.' He nods at the walls of his tiny office. 'I was a shipyard foreman, a hundred people were reporting to me . . . And what do I do here? Spend all day putting food on to plates and counting coins.

'I don't understand them here, you know, Levi – the food, the humour . . . I was at the dentist last week, asked him if he had any anaesthetic with the smell of cognac – and preferably the taste as well, like in Odessa. And you know what? He was so surprised that he asked the nurse to investigate, asked if this was a new development and for the name of my Odessa dentist. I mean, how sad is that?'

He pauses and looks out of the window, his back to me, at the garden behind our café, junked with boxes and black bin bags.

'You know what I really miss about Odessa, Levi?' he says. 'I miss the horizon. Where is the horizon in Golders Green? I miss the feeling you get as you look at the sea, wondering what worlds are out there. Sometimes, when I can't sleep, I stare at the ceiling and wonder – did it really happen to me? Is this really my life?

'We had a customer in the café last week, Levi – an old woman, born here. I was returning with the shopping when she called out to me:

'"Dear Misha," she said. "I did not come here to eat, though your wife's cooking is not bad, thank you. I came here to ask you a question, just one question. You are from Odessa, aren't you? What sort of place is it, this place that never lets you go? My mother was from Odessa, and when I was little, she would put me on the windowsill and we would both stand and look out of the window, and she would whisper into my ear: 'Remember you are from Odessa . . .' Why, Misha? We had a good house and good money here – what was it about Odessa that she could not forget?" And what could I tell her, Levi?'

My father slides the photographs away with his finger, as if rejecting them.

'Could I tell her that I was pushed back into life as a five-year-old boy, only to be pushed out of Odessa at the age of thirty-three?'

'Dad,' I say, 'you could tell her the same thing you told that barman, remember? On the Thames boat trip three years ago, when there were ten of you old Odessites, and the barman got stroppy because you brought your own booze. You said something to him, but he got really angry, and for a while I could not decide whether it would be brave or silly to have a word with him.

'Finally I said: "I know this is against the rules, but I would not have a go at those men, sir. Though they are all in their seventies, they are still strong. If you try to stop them from enjoying the party, they will throw you overboard; that's going to be much more hassle. Why don't we make a deal: you let them have their own vodka, and they will be happy, but I'll pay and you can keep your booze for the next trip, so you'll be happy too."

'The barman liked the plan – who wouldn't, but do you remember what he said to you when he found out where you were all from?

'"Odessa? I was in the merchant navy," he said. "I know there is a port called Odessa . . . on the Black Sea . . ."

'And you told him: "Young man, Odessa is not a port. It

is a passport. Odessa is a nationality . . ." Dad, how I understand you now.'

'So, it looks like you are in love with Odessa.' My father points at my photographs and then turns to me.

Wrong preposition, I want to say. I am in love *in* Odessa . . .

I think of Zoya, and suddenly I can see clearly what this mad, brave girl, who is half my age, means to me. She is just like the Odessa of my childhood: brash and chaotic, reckless and cheeky, always ready for adventure, smelling of sun and sea . . .

And I smile at my father and say: 'Yes, Dad, I am in love with Odessa. I always was, I just never knew it.'

I will be glad to get out of the house on Sunday. I'll go early – to brace myself for the perennial weekend engineering works.

What envelopes is Tony going to give us? I've thought it through – the only thing that remains for him to do is to hand us our old notes from twenty-five years ago. 'Put your fears into the envelopes, gentlemen, and we'll come back to them when you are ready . . .' I am ready to see my note now. But for the sake of it I don't remember what I wrote.

# FULL STOP

**Alex**

Not that I envy women like Janice. I am just wondering how she does it, that's all. Her life is so regimented – I don't even know if she *has* a life outside the office. But even if she slept here, on a rug behind the pot with some office creeper (a plant, not a man!), she would still emerge in the morning with not a hair out of place, her shirt ironed and in full make-up.

'Ian was wondering if you could pop by, Alex.' She is hovering over me, and the firmness of her tone leaves me in no doubt that the popping by needs to be immediate. Why didn't she just call? I wonder. Did she want to exercise her power? She clicks her heels and totters away, nailing every step into the brown carpet.

No, I don't envy her at all, I just don't understand how it is physically possible to have the whole look in order, like Janice does. I admire her ability to achieve this 'comprehensive image', as my boss would say.

I have tried to get this immaculate look for years, but there is always something, a little something that spoils it for me: a coffee stain on a silk blouse is my trademark, and I remember the key meetings by whatever I had to hide – a ladder or two, mud on my shoes, belt buckle snapping as I stood up to do a presentation, or the blue nail varnish Emma decided to try on two of my nails the previous night. Just another zap of confidence I never had but successfully play-acted for years. Creativity is the key here – a scarf is a great prop to hide stains, and a jacket with a shift dress works well in warm climates – you can always take the jacket off when you spill something on it, or lose a button.

Even now, as I walk into Ian's office, I look down at my blouse and realise with horror that when I washed my hands, checking my 'comprehensive image' in the mirror, water splashed on all the strategic places, so I have to sit with my arms crossed, covering my chest.

Maybe that's why Ian is looking at my arms, not at me now.

'Alex,' he begins, 'you have been through a lot lately. We have been very understanding, as you know, but unfortunately . . .'

He pauses, looks at me, smiles and I shift to the edge of the chair, like a schoolgirl caught smoking by the headmaster. I know this smile, I have seen it many times before. I need to wipe it off his face, change it back to the look of concern and fatherly care he had when I came in.

'I am pulling myself back together,' I say, 'and work certainly helps. I couldn't have coped without it.'

His Cheshire cat smile is still there, though. It exists on its own, it floats over me like a cloud and I am stuck in the heavy stickiness of it. My mouth is stuffed and I am coughing, trying to get it out, trying to say something else, trying to, trying . . .

Boy, I know this smile. I know what's coming before he says it.

'Alex, we have discussed your situation at board level and decided that you are obviously under too much pressure.' (This is another one of his tactics – hiding behind the shield of 'we' when he is afraid to make a decision himself.)

'These sudden disappearances during key stages of the current project,' he continues, 'first New York, then Odessa . . .' (How does he know where I have been? I have taken time off for 'family circumstances', that's what everybody was told.) 'We cannot go on like this,' floats the smile. 'Next time you might decide to take time off to fly to Zanzibar on a day when you need to sign a contract. We can't keep chasing you when your key customers need you.'

He stretches his mouth; his smile is going for the kill.

'We would like to suggest that you take some time off . . . on a more permanent basis, perhaps. You will have more time to spend with Emma and Luke, and maybe you can come back as a consultant, doing some of the most interesting projects? George at HR would be the best person to talk you through the details – actually, he is expecting you now. We all care about you here, Alex, and the terms are as generous as possible.'

He knows that to fire a single mother in distress can be dangerous – cub protection instinct kicks in. And at my level, it can be expensive, very expensive. Unless I have done something which is deemed to be gross misconduct, which I haven't; unless there is some confidential information about me to discourage me from suing the bastards, which there isn't.

But before I have a chance to pounce back, he totally smothers me with his best firing-people smile.

'I also wanted to bring it to your attention, Alex, that we never took action on the letter we received about you three years ago. Though your erratic travelling now leaves me in no doubt that we should have let you go . . . go and spend time with your children sooner.'

'What letter?'

He is looking at my water stains, as my hands are on my knees now, nails dug in. Not that I care.

He puts a copy of the letter in front of me, not saying another word. I scan the lines.

*. . . I am writing because I am seriously concerned for the well-being of my wife . . .*

*Her recent behaviour is worrying . . .*

*. . . forgetting to pick the children up from school, regularly losing keys and money . . . crying a lot, not sleeping . . .*

*I have tried to persuade her to get treatment for her depression, but she refuses . . .*

*. . . only writing because . . . affect her performance at work . . . cloud her judgement . . . mistakes that will cost the company thousands if not millions . . .*

Ian is looking at me, not hiding his curiosity. How will I react?

How *can* I react? Where do I start – with the airport argument, my broken arm, the Las Vegas trip?

'Well prepared' is an understatement. Aimed and fired well. Literally.

Even wounded, I give my last desperate growl: 'But the project . . . I have been working on it for months. Who is going to lead it?'

'Oh, don't worry about that.' The smile has already settled back on Ian's face, quite comfortably. 'You have built an excellent team. Robbie did you proud last week when you were away on your . . . escapade. Brilliant presentation, clear understanding of the project, fresh ideas . . . We think he will be quite capable of . . .'

I realise that Robbie was the only one who knew about Odessa and New York . . . the only one who saw my presentation, my notes . . .

Good shot. All I can do now is crawl away and lick my wounds. My bruised ego carries me to my desk to get my bag, to get out of here – past Robbie's desk, I can't miss it.

'Well done, Robbie,' I say. 'I hear you made a great impression last week.'

He already knows, I am sure; Ian would have discussed this with him before enveloping me in his firing smile.

'I'm sorry, Alex,' he says. 'This is my only chance, you understand . . . with my father in the care home.'

'Hey, don't worry about it. Of course I understand,' I say without stopping, on my way out. 'What is one betrayal among friends, after all?'

This is not my phrase, about betrayal, I have heard it somewhere before. Isn't that what Norman said to Max? 'You know what Norman told me, Alex,' said my brother, sobbing. 'When he asked me if I knew where his bag was and I said "no idea", he said, "Hey, what's one betrayal among friends?" He died knowing that it was me who betrayed him.'

As I step out on to the pavement, the crowds carry me. I am not going to see George at HR, not ready yet. It will be a generous package, I am sure, but I am fuming. I'll start my own agency, take my clients with me, my team. Only I can't – Robbie will be doing my job now, he knows how to stop me.

I call Joyce: 'Could you collect me, please, pleeease . . . Where am I? No, not at work. I'll be in the coffee shop opposite the office, waiting for you.'

I clamber on to a bar stool (it gets harder and harder – am I getting too old for perching on a bar stool?) and think:

why am I always in the coffee shop for the most vital decisions of my life? And always alone?

Of course I have friends to talk to – and they will listen, only I am not sure whether they will hear what I say.

This is going to be my third period of emptiness.

The first was during the court proceedings, just after the divorce, when everybody listened, relishing with quiet relief the fact that it hadn't happened to them. The invitations trickled away – the 'Robinsons' invitations – and gradually the vacuum filled – parents' meetings, single mothers at the school gates, drinks with colleagues . . . After the divorce, I wasn't really lonely; there is a big difference between being alone and free, and being with somebody but at your lowest and loneliest.

The second time was worse. It is weird how there is a 'don't step in' circle around somebody in grief. Is it because people don't know what to say to you, or because they are afraid that your grief is contagious?

I learned to exaggerate my social life. 'I went to see a new play last night,' I would tell Robbie at lunchtime, though it wasn't strictly true – the script for the school nativity play hardly changes every year.

Emma's screams in the middle of the lake – 'Mum, I hate this thing, take me off this stupid pedalo' – translated into 'What a fun boat trip we all had this weekend.'

I decided to make more of an effort – my theatre and boating scenarios were wearing thin.

There are websites in London with interest groups, apparently – you can invite some stranger with a similar interest to join you in whatever you are doing.

Seemed a great idea: to start with a clean slate, to have a laugh with a stranger who shared my passion. Maybe go to the BFI to watch some independent film. I used to love those French films, where subtitles were obsolete – the action was all in gestures, glances, awkward silences. They defied everything I was about – logic and logistics. Those uncertainties had to be shared and discussed with somebody.

The reality hit hard when I looked at the interest groups: postgraduates in first employment . . . new to London . . . twenty- to thirty-year-olds . . . newly unemployed . . . Perhaps the last group should be mine now – I am newly unemployed after all.

My first step, or rather drive, to my new life is here: Joyce is waving at me from the cab.

'I've just been fired, Joyce,' I blurt out. 'I don't know where to go.'

Joyce offers me great words of consolation, as always: 'Will Richmond do?'

I am silent all the way home, and Joyce is too.

'Could you take me to Waterloo on Sunday, Joyce?' I ask as she parks the cab.

'Why don't you catch a bus this time? Or a direct train from Richmond?' Joyce asks through the mike.

'Are you abandoning me too?' I ask, shocked. I can't cope with another blow now.

Joyce switches off the engine and turns to me from a bright day, blinking, into the darkness of the cab. I am so used to talking to her grey feathers that I am not ready to meet her stare. For the first time I notice that her eyes are baby blue.

'Nobody's abandoing you,' she chuckles. 'Of course not. I just think it's time you went it alone, gal. You're ready.'

She has aged, my Joyce, I notice. With her round glasses and droopy cheeks, and feathers of greying hair sticking up above her ears, she resembles our six a.m. tawny owl.

'Listen, Alex,' she says. 'When I started, there were only a handful of women cabbies. I did my yellow badge suburbs exam first, then the green badge one for the whole of London. It took me over a year to do my first cab exams, but I tried and tried – wanted to escape from my first job, see. I was a debt collector, charging around in my minivan. And the people I dealt with were nasty to me, all of them – because who would be nice to a debt collector?'

Joyce has never told me her story. Maybe because I never asked. I look at her and a childhood memory supplies a verse: 'A wise old owl sat on an oak. The more she heard, the less she spoke. The less she spoke, . . .'

You have listened to me all these years, Joyce! I think, horrified. It was all about me!

I open my mouth to apologise, but Joyce just waves at me to shut up, and continues:

'The first time I drove my cab to the station rank, I was petrified, you know. I forgot everything I'd learned for the exams. All the maps, all the street names just left me, flew out as the first passenger opened the door. I was lucky that that ride was straight . . . I mean, straight all the way, down Wimbledon Park Road.

'But in those first months there were times when I had no clue about where to go. And the male cabbies, who didn't even notice me at first, came out of their cabs to help me: "Orright, love? I'll check the map for ya . . ." Or the passengers would tell me, "Never mind, girl, let me guide you." See what I'm getting at, Alex?'

'You want me to become a cab driver?' I start hesitantly.

Joyce's familiar contagious burst fills the cab. That's how she laughs when she notices something funny in the street – often pointing to me when it is already too late. I've learned to look out of the window the moment I hear her start, so as not to miss the fun.

'Alex,' she starts again, wiping tears of laughter off her owl cheeks, looking at me with her baby-blue eyes. 'I am trying to say that in all those years on the job, I discovered that not all people are nasty. I had more nice people crossing my path and showing me directions. They are out there, Alex. I have driven quite a few, so I know. And one more thing.

In all those years of driving, my eyes welled up more than
once – I am quite chicken-hearted, as you know – but I was
in fits of laughter more often.

'You remember that old gentleman who tried to chase my
cab when you got out at the station once, because I didn't
see him and nearly drove off? How I said to him: "I am so
sorry . . ." and he replied angrily: "So you should be" – and
tried to reach me through the window with his stick? Do
you remember his face and how we were both laughing?
Well then, go out and laugh, stop being a bitter nutcase.
Wait for a bit, like in a cab queue, and somebody will give
you directions.'

I listen to Joyce and remember all the times she was there
waiting to take me to Heathrow at five a.m., her huffs and
puffs going up Richmond Hill as if she was pushing the cab
herself, her war cry when somebody tried to cut her up or
block her: 'Clear off, you nutcase!'

And her listening. Years of it.

Today is the first time she has given me advice, so I'd
better take it.

'I'll miss you, Joyce,' I say.

'Hey, I'm not going anywhere – just to pick somebody
up from Gatwick. Better fares than getting it off you
Richmond lot! I'll still drive you when I get the mood on
me . . .'

. . . I hear the phone ring before I open the door.

'How are you, Alex?'

'Fine, Mum.'

'I went to Stow-on-the-Wold yesterday, was invited to the antique bookshop presentation on their new acquisitions,' she starts, to fill the silence.

I wonder what she does when she's not invited to book presentations – does she have an appointment to visit another room in the house? It is too big for her. There is nothing cottagey about Orchard Cottage, with its grand piano nobody plays in the hall, its huge conservatory windows overlooking the orchard with the trees nobody climbs.

'It is such a sweet place, Stow-on-the-Wold,' she continues, 'so quaint and so close, amazing that I've never been before . . .'

I imagine her looking at her hands as she talks to me, checking her immaculate manicure, and think how her life resembles the name of this Cotswolds tourist magnet: she lives as a stowaway in the world without the 'r', without 'we are' – no Max, no Dad, and a distant me . . .

'There are some wonderful bookshops there,' she continues.

'Did you buy anything?' I ask.

'Not really, I was just browsing.'

'Are you reading anything interesting now?' I am about to ask, but stop.

It might tip the balance; the fragility of peace is obvious now. She will start by describing the books she reads, then she'll turn to the sleepless nights when she reads them, then to Max . . .

'I'm calling about the kids – you are dropping them off on Sunday as agreed, aren't you?' She sounds insistent. 'And could you collect them around five?'

I have completely forgotten about this. Maybe I would have surrendered to wandering around Oxford, even going to the Ashmolean – if only to keep the truce. But not this week.

'You know, Mum,' I say, 'I am really busy this Sunday. Would you like to come to us instead? You could stay the night on Saturday, then take the kids to the cinema on Sunday, maybe have a pizza somewhere (does my mother eat pizza?).'

There is no protest or comment, so I add a full stop instead of a question mark. 'We'll be expecting you after six tomorrow, but don't come too late, so we can have supper together.'

It takes my mother so long to answer that I wonder whether we've been cut off. And then she says something that is not in our armistice treaty, the thing I least expect her to say and feel: 'I would absolutely love to do that,' she says. 'Thank you for inviting me.'

I am so relieved that she has agreed to come here. Relieved because it might be a first step to peace rather than just a ceasefire, and because I absolutely have to make that meeting on Sunday.

I will take my time. There is a direct train from Richmond to Waterloo, only twenty minutes, but I will take a different route – a slow 419 bus to Hammersmith, then the tube. I'll take coffee and a croissant and climb on to the top deck – one thinks clearer above the crowds, I find.

It will be our last game meeting, my last chance to get the answers to all those questions I am dying to ask.

Not Jonty; my key question to him – 'Which document are you going to talk about?' – was answered by a Radio 4 newsreader last week:

'A British MEP has made an explosive announcement about the discovery of the forgotten agreement signed at the Yalta Conference in February 1945.' And then Jonty's voice: '. . . I am strongly convinced that Crimea as a neutral international zone managed by the UN should become the door to the new world, and that this agreement, long forgotten, will be the key . . .'

All my questions are for Tony.

Does he know anything about the anonymous Australian sponsor of the Max Chandler memorial prize, for example? 'Came out of the blue,' the organisers of the Odessa jazz festival told me – the suggestion to set up a prize and the money. 'Must be a jazz lover from the Odessa World Club – Odessites are everywhere . . .'

Will he call me when he is next in London?

Is he going to kiss me when he says goodbye?

I'll drink my coffee, bite into my croissant and smile to the world and to Sunday. It is not going to be Ian's smile;

it will be Alexandra smiling. Because it's not just my name that I share with a young violin teacher from Odessa.

As I see her going down Prymorsky Boulevard, a skinny half-angel, half-teenager with short curly hair, hand in hand with a broad-shouldered pilot in tattered uniform – my Grandpa Jack – I know what else we have in common: the comforting smell of freshly baked bread and this new-found freedom. I'll take another bite and close my eyes. So what if I am going to see Tony for the last time, that I was just a courier for his game . . . My war is over. I am not a prisoner any more; I am free. And in love.

# FULL STOP

**Jonty**

'We need to talk . . .' usually this is Lucy's opening gambit, not mine. This is what she says before something crucial, that leads to 'That's settled, then'.

So how come I find myself saying now: 'Lucy, we need to talk'?

I have become a chameleon; my face is changing colour daily – from red to purple to orangey-yellow. Lucy has looked after me since I was discharged from hospital – who could do it better? She was a professional nurse well before becoming a professional wife and mother.

For the first time in a week, I can see her with both eyes – Xavier's hook, aimed at my right eye, left it swollen and closed.

Lucy is looking at me, hands locked on her lap, her back too straight, her face blank. She has got the message. 'We need to talk' means something life-changing. Her cosy world changing.

There is no easy way of saying this, so I blurt it out in one breath, wincing (my ribs still hurt when I exhale): 'I have decided to resign from the parliament, Lucy, and try freelance journalism again. It might mean downsizing, but I'll be at home more . . . maybe even working from home.' There, I have said it; there is no way back. I can't face the consequences, so I turn my head to the window, to watch Minnie jumping on the trampoline outside, squealing with delight.

I know what will happen now – there will be a long discussion about Minnie's future, about the house and the pony club.

But Lucy says nothing. Then I hear an odd sound – between a gasp and a muted sob – and when I turn and look at her, she is fighting tears, her hand covering her mouth. And it hits me – I have never seen Lucy cry. She is a nurse through and through – her care for the family is her professional duty, her emotions are always controlled, just like mine.

Her care and control – that's what pulled me through when my world was smashed to pieces ten years ago.

It was Lucy who sat me down, handed me a mug of tea and calmly explained to me that it was not my mother who was aggressive and angry with me; that the tumour, pressing on her brain had changed her personality.

It was Lucy who persuaded me to go in and say goodbye.

# The Game

I heard my mother before I saw her.

'The hospital food is rubbish, I should write about that,' she said in her husky, brisk voice, and I was so relieved to hear that she sounded like my mother – strong, forthright, opinionated.

But when I walked into the room, the woman I saw there was pale and gaunt, the remains of her grey hair in clumps, and worst of all, she was looking through me.

'And who are you?' she demanded. 'They send me these new doctors every day, the young ones. I bet you haven't got a clue what to do. Go away,' she shouted. 'I want my consultant.'

I stood there clinging to the only thing left of my mother – her husky voice, its familiar rich undertones . . .

'Shoo, go away,' she shouted again, getting more and more agitated.

And as I turned to leave – what else could I do? – she shouted at my back: 'You can make yourself useful – call my son, tell him to come and see me.' The last words I heard before closing the door were: '. . . and tell him to bring Mr Smith . . .'

It was Lucy who suggested that we go out for a cup of coffee to talk about it . . . and then another cup, and another . . . and it was Lucy, my mother's nurse, who was there with her at the end. Lucy and Mr Smith, not me.

Lucy is still cupping her hand over her mouth, stifling her sobs.

I don't know what to say, but the irony does not escape me – a professional speaker, lost for words.

Then suddenly she smiles. There is so much in this smile – love, patience, forgiveness – and I am surprised that I can finally relate to all those emotions, as if the curtain has lifted and I can feel as well as think what I should feel.

'Welcome back,' is all she says. 'I have been waiting for you to come back for a long time. Almost too long.'

I wonder if she knows about Magda . . .

'It's for you – from the press office,' said Lucy last week, handing me the phone.

'How are you, *hlopak*?' I heard Magda's voice. 'I wish I could see you now.'

No, you don't, I thought. My face is swollen and mostly a definite violet colour.

'I wanted to tell you in person,' she continued. 'I am going to Krakow.'

'For how long?' I asked.

'No, I am leaving for all time.' She probably didn't know the English word 'forever', but the message was there.

'When, Magda, why?' I was firing questions at her.

'Next Wednesday. I have decided to retire.'

Retire? She must be much older than I thought . . .

'My mother is getting old,' continued Magda. 'She finds it difficult to look after the house and the orchard now. So I have decided to go home. I'll teach history at Krakow University and look after the goat.'

'What goat?'

'My mother's goat, Malgosia.'

The idea of our powerful head of press office running after a goat called Malgosia across her mother's vegetable patch was hilarious – I laughed, forgetting my bruised ribs for a moment.

'I am glad you can see the funny side of it,' said Magda. 'Glad you are laughing – haven't heard you laugh for a while.'

'Why didn't you tell me?'

'I am telling you now, Jonty. You have grown up, *hlopak*,' she added. 'You don't need me now.'

'I'll miss you, Magda,' I said.

'Well, I'll be coming to Brussels once in a while,' she replied. 'There are many friends I am leaving here . . .'

The way she said it left me wondering whether I was the only 'friend' she was comforting.

'I hear you have been invited to stand for vice chair of your committee now that Xavier is not there any more,' continued Magda. 'Congratulations! Let's celebrate next time I am in Brussels . . .'

Lucy is tapping me on the shoulder, forgetting all her nursing skills – that shoulder hurts even without her tapping on it.

'Jonty, I was saying – shame we can't go and celebrate now, but when you're better, why don't we go to London together? We haven't been for ages.

'There is this little street just off Charing Cross Road . . . You turn into it, and you are in another world: antique maps, children's books, old shop windows – it is totally oblivious to time, to noise . . . I used to go there a lot when I worked at the Royal Marsden, that was my place to unwind . . . and then we can take Minnie to a dim sum place in Chinatown – not a posh one, somewhere with plastic tables and a lot of choice . . . Next Sunday? Can you hear me, Jonty? *Are you with me?'*

She jumps off the sofa with the same agility as Minnie, and I suddenly remember that she is still young, ten years younger than me. I think how her strength, her get-on-with-it attitude has been my support all along, and how I never knew she liked old books and dim sum.

I look at this girl, whose smile is shining at me now – no wonder her name means 'light' – and realise that there is a lot about Lucy that I still don't know.

'I have a meeting in London next Sunday', I say gently, trying not to extinguish this new light in her eyes, 'but I am here this Sunday' (of course I am here – where could I go looking like this?) 'and all week during half term, so maybe we could drive to Paris then? We always said we would like a house within driving distance of Paris, but we never actually drove there.' (Since when have I included myself in Lucy and Minnie's 'we'?) 'And to answer your question – *yes, I am still with you* . . .

'Just give me next Sunday – it is important. And it is going to be the last one.' I can't tell her that I need to go to tell Tony that it was all my fault, that last game – that I started it.

It began at our summer jazz concert, when Max was sitting in front of me, ready to go on stage. Norman tapped me on the shoulder and asked me to pass Max a note. That fatal note. A good luck one, I thought, what else.

But then Max turned and smiled at Norman through me, as if I was invisible. Smiled at the boy whose name sounded like a history lesson, whose nickname was '*ma chérie*', who wandered the dorms wearing a silk gown with paisley print – how could anybody take him seriously? And yet Max's smile was for that invader of our friendship. And it was a different smile, too.

It was then that I stretched my neck and managed to read what the note said. It was simple and final: *I. Love. You.*

Max was already getting up to go on stage, putting the note in his pocket, leaving me with the consequences, with the knowledge. That's how our last game started.

I could still have stopped it three days later, after the English lesson. I still had a chance when Mr Brown asked us the question . . .

Mr Brown, our eccentric English teacher, co-owner of Brown Brothers Classic Cars, passionate about two things in life: cramming English literature into our ignorant heads, and Morris Minors, was standing by the open window, reciting: '. . . the day is hot, the Capulets, abroad . . .' He had already shared with us one of his Brown

Brothers stories ('. . . and when Mr Foreman got out of his car, I discovered that he was probably the same age as the car and should have been left sitting there . . .') and was into his favourite, final part of the lesson: 'Ten-minute dilemma'.

'Gentlemen,' he started, 'looking at your excited faces, I understand that you have all read *Romeo and Juliet* with great attention and are ready to talk about the drama of love.'

'The only drama we can think of is that we are not outside yet,' said Tony.

'All right.' Brown waited for the laughter to die down. 'Let's talk about fighting instead, maybe that would be of more interest.

'Act Three Scene One: Enter Tibault.

'"I pray you, good Mercutio, let's retire: The day is hot, the Capulets abroad . . ."

'Romeo enters and declares his love for Tybalt, trying to prevent him fighting with Mercutio. He begs Mercutio to stop, but his plea makes things worse. Why doesn't Mercutio listen to his best friend? Romeo was the heart and soul of their gang. You all know, gentlemen, the sad end to that scene, the death of Mercutio.

'I am sure you are all listening with great interest, but let me repeat the question just in case: why didn't Mercutio stop when Romeo begged him to, for the sake of their friendship?'

'Easy. It was a hot day and everybody was irritable,' said Levi.

'Thank you for the meteorological analysis of this scene, Mr Freiman.' Anybody else?'

'Maybe Romeo's friends are so surprised by his sudden change of attitude to Tybalt, they think he is joking, pushing Mercutio into fighting even more.' It was Tony, I think.

'Romeo's request is ignored because they don't consider him a friend any more – he is sleeping with the enemy,' I said, looking straight at Max. 'The betrayal of friendship kills by itself; fighting is secondary,' I continued. 'Don't you think, Max?'

He didn't answer, just looked away.

'What was all that about?' asked Levi at the Tepee Council the next day.

'I think Max has found himself a new friend,' I said. 'Have you noticed how Norman is always hanging around during Max's rehearsals? He is too much of a fan if you ask me.'

'I've noticed that as well,' said Levi. 'But I think he is after Max's sister. She has only been here two or three times, but when Max goes to collect her, Norman is always around, glued to the two of them from the moment she comes through the gate. It's as straightforward as a ninety-degree angle what's going to happen next.'

'Me and Norman . . . it's not like our friendship. The Tepee Council means everything to me,' said Max. He could express himself so well in music, but often struggled with words.

'Then you'll have to prove it,' Tony said. 'Why don't we call the next game "Norman"? Levi will remain on fact-finding alert, Jonty – it's time you tried some "do and distract", as you haven't done much distracting, have you? And Max . . . you will have the honour of the action.'

I will tell Tony about this next Sunday at Waterloo, before he takes our final envelopes out; will tell him, Jonty and Alex the whole story. I stood up and talked in front of a thousand people a fortnight ago, so to tell the truth to three old friends in an empty bar will not be *that* difficult, will it?

# FULL STOP

**Tony**

We are all immigrants, all displaced, if you think about it, not just me. Levi is still the same Levi, walking slightly sideways, stooping, as if he wants to disappear – always an outsider, always the underdog.

Jonty is permanently dissatisfied, shuttling between two worlds and two countries. Is he unhappy in both?

Alex is in emotional emigration, on the edge of her own country of despair. She is holding up after Max's death, but I feel there is something else there, something sinister she is hiding.

I think the game was different for all of us: it was a roller-coaster ride for Levi, with the vertigo and dizziness of new challenges, a make-believe jazz festival game for Alex, a chess game for Jonty.

I was playing a strategy game – that's what they think.

Yes, I planned it all carefully, thought it all through – the travel, the tasks, the whole game plan, the ending.

But it has been a game of chance for me all along; I was feeding the envelopes into the slot machine, thinking: what if they don't turn up at Waterloo, won't open the envelopes, decide not to go . . .

I had to change the game plan once, when I accidentally booked Levi and Alex into the same hotel in Odessa: I needed to persuade the girls at the reception of the Hotel Londonskaya to upgrade Levi to the hotel on the opposite side of the city.

Learning to live with your mistakes is much harder than not making them at all, and however different this game was for all of us, we have all relived our mistakes by playing it. I certainly have: how could I think then that power was everything, that control could replace friendship?

I remember the evening of Jonty's Birthday Bath, when I watched him being carried away by the multi-handed, multi-legged monster he had created with my power, with dozens of voices chanting in unison: 'The joke is on you today, Jonty . . .' I remember his look of despair when he turned to me. I was still smiling, but it was the first time I felt this coldness in my chest. If this is what power means, do I really want it? I thought.

And Levi, our clumsy Levi – how have you coped all these years without my support? Were you really strong enough to go through life on your own?

I remember watching as you drowned in brambles, suppressing the desire to give you a hand, to get you out – you had to learn to find your way out of trouble by yourself, you couldn't rely on me all the time. When I saw you next morning at breakfast, covered in cuts but still finding the strength to smile at me, I thought: how much loyalty and love can one give before feeling betrayed? Because I should have pulled you out, I shouldn't have left you in pain.

Max, our golden boy, our soul . . . What would we be without you? How proud we were of your music, of your talent; we were your fans, the groupies basking in your limelight. Did you ever forgive me, Max? Did you ever understand that I only planned that last game because of my fear of losing Alex?

When Levi said: 'I think Norman is after Max's sister . . . When Max goes to collect her, Norman is always around, glued to the two of them,' I should have left it, should have dismissed it as lazy afternoon banter, but I could not delete from my head the picture of Norman, our Prince Charming, luring Alex in with his suave, graceful movements, whispering: *'Ma chérie . . .'* And the more I thought about it, the clearer that picture became. I remember that English lesson, when Jonty said: 'Romeo is sleeping with the enemy', and I cringed, thinking of Norman taking off his paisley gown, leaning over Juliet, over my Alex . . .

How could I have missed that it wasn't Alex he was after? That when Jonty said, 'Romeo is sleeping with the enemy' and you blushed, Max, it was because you were in love with Norman?

Only years later, reading about you, revisiting those school days, putting two and two together, did I understand why Norman was always around you and Alex, why he was your number one fan, leading you out of our group into temptation . . . Why didn't I pick it up? Maybe because I was blinded by power, always power. Because I felt it on my face, this northern wind, blowing away our group, our friendship, our Tepee Councils. Because I was afraid of losing my grip over you. Because I was a coward.

So when Mr Brown said: 'Often in Shakespeare's dramas, unknown forces are pushing people into the scene, not letting them escape, even if they are too scared to act,' I decided that I had to be that force, to push you back into our group however frightened you were.

I should have stopped our game when you shouted: 'Run, Norman, this is an ambush!' I should have stopped the moment I saw how humiliated and ashamed you looked.

I thought that tasking you with distracting Norman when we hid his bag would seal it, lock you back into our friendship. It seemed the most innocent of jokes.

It was an easy operation. We all sat together at lunchtime – so what, we always did. Max talked to Norman (to distract him), apologised for the dress joke, while Levi passed Norman's bag under the table to me. I passed it to Jonty, whose blazer fell on the floor – by chance, surely, to all the casual observers. Then Jonty picked the blazer up – with the bag inside – and took it out. And the fact that Jonty was sitting so close to the door was pure coincidence, of course.

I didn't expect Norman to keep quiet for three days about the bag's disappearance. He was waiting, hoping all that time that Max would return it. Hoping to salvage their love and our friendship. He was more generous than the rest of us.

After three days, we heard the headmaster's assembly plea: 'We have had an unpleasant incident at school: Norman's bag is missing. It is imperative that whoever took it returns it immediately. Norman is a diabetic, and the bag contains his emergency medication. This is not a joke, gentlemen.'

'What are we going to do, Tony?' asked Levi after the assembly. 'We're up to our necks in trouble!' He was sweating profusely, his eyes scanning the corners of the hall as if looking for escape. 'Three days without insulin – I calculated: he is going to slip into a coma very soon.'

'An emergency council meeting today at lunchtime,' I said, trying to keep calm. 'We need to discuss how to get the bag to Norman so that it just appears by magic – and game over!' I managed to smile reassuringly.

But at the emergency council Levi said: 'By the way, there is nothing to retrieve – the bag is not in the bushes where we left it, I checked.'

'What do you mean, it's not there?' asked Jonty.

'I don't know.' Levi shrugged. 'Somebody must have found it already and returned it to Norman. They'll all think we did it, I am telling you.'

'Norman does already, for sure,' said Max. 'We were together . . . we were talking – fuck, I mean I was distracting him when the bag disappeared, so he worked out that I was involved.'

'How do you know?' I asked. The day had suddenly become cold and endless. 'Because he asked me.' Max was not looking at us. 'He said: "Max, do you know where my bag is? I really need it."'

'Ah, assumptions,' I said. 'He just wanted you to help, that's all.'

'No, when I said that I had no idea, he was silent for a moment before saying: "Never mind, what's one betrayal among friends?"'

Max was almost crying. I had to act quickly, so I said:

'Change of game plan, then. Max – you've got to say your bag's been nicked too. Talk to Norman, to your band and to whoever is listening.'

'Why me?' asked Max.

'Everybody loves you and people will feel sorry for you. Nobody suspects a victim . . . or the victim's friends,' I explained.

'What should I do?' asked Levi.

'Oh, don't worry, nobody will suspect you, Levi. It's not like you usually do anything cheeky; you're no action man!

Use your powers of observation to find out who returned the bag.

'Now, Jonty, you've got to tell the world about it. Why don't you stand up at assembly and make a jokey speech about those indecent, insensitive bastards who stole Norman and Max's bags? Not even a speech, a couple of minutes only.'

'By the way,' said Levi, 'did you know – a guy at Cheltenham yesterday bet on six races and got five wins! It defies any theory of . . .' We were back to normal.

We left the Tepee Council calm and confident again – the bag had found its way back to Norman by itself, he was saved. I had worked out a plan to save our necks too – what was there to fret about? It was a great game! Only we never finished it . . .

How was I to know when I devised our final tasks ('Max – your bag is missing too; Levi – find out who returned Norman's bag; Jonty – you let the world know that Max's bag has been nicked as well') that nobody had found the bag yet?

We heard later that the gardener had discovered it in the bushes. He thought that younger boys had been smoking there and had run away, abandoning the bag, when they saw the Veteran approaching. So he locked it in his shed, planning to take it to the school office later, and carried on with his work. And that's where it stayed for the whole day. A day that would have saved Norman.

I was the lone spectator of the whole show, doing my maths revision during the cross-country run. The classroom was on the second floor, with huge bay windows, and I could see the route clearly. They started at the far end of the rugby field, disappeared behind the bushes, and emerged again five minutes later, by then stretched out into a thin line of sports hierarchy – leaders, followers and outsiders, with a few nerds lost at the end. I saw Jonty running back to encourage the weaklings who were losing points for his house, then speeding forward again to the front of the line.

A couple of minutes later, I saw Norman emerging from the bushes. He was stumbling, shouting something, and then I saw him falling sideways, waving his hands comically. I felt like laughing, but I didn't – I knew straight away. I couldn't see his face, but I could imagine his lips already turning blue, the same shade of blue as the dress we used to lure him to the girl called Max. I couldn't stop thinking about his eyes, I remember – were they closed, or were they wide open, slate grey, reflecting the low clouds above him?

And then I saw Mr Brown, literature buff, classic car fanatic, our bow-tied oversized penguin, shuffling across the rugby field.

But the Veteran was there first. He was leaning over Norman, saying something. 'Get up, stop being a wimp', no doubt. Then he shouted something at Mr Brown, who turned and hurried back towards the school.

The Veteran was kneeling next to Norman, frowning,

touching his neck . . . And then I saw him – our impassive Veteran, who let Levi lie unconscious so that he could finish his experiment – put his face into his hands. His shoulders were moving, and I guessed that he was crying.

He knew before everybody else, just as I did; he had seen young men dead before . . .

I felt that our Tepee Council was somehow connected to that scene, but I still didn't understand how. At that moment it was just the knowledge that nothing could be changed now that it had happened, that this moment, framed by the bay window, would stay with me for ever, just like the photograph I took of Max, Levi and Jonty that day.

It was the last day of term, and by the time we came back for our final year, the school had returned to normal: the Birthday Bath tradition lived on, the youngest boys were still pushed off the armchairs on the landing by the sixth-formers, Mr Brown was still torturing us with his ten-minute dilemmas as if nothing had happened. Only Norman was not there.

We never talked about what had happened, but then hasn't some clever professor worked out that eighty per cent of male communication is silent? We never played the game again, persuading ourselves that we had grown out of it, were too busy with A levels and chasing girls . . . Until now.

'Put your fears into the envelopes, gentlemen, and we'll come back to them when you are ready' was all I said on the last day of school. Then we sealed the envelopes and got on with our lives.

'We are the only ones in the know zone,' I told them then. I wonder if they remember that I still have the evidence.

I thought I was the only one affected by that last game, that the others had deleted Norman's bag from their memories, until I opened the *Sydney Morning Herald* six months ago:

*Sydney Was His Favourite City*

*The famous musician, 'Golden Saxophone' Max Chandler has been found dead in his flat in Kensington, London. The police a recovered brief suicide note: 'Don't forget. I couldn't.' It is not clear what Max Chandler was referring to.*

Could he have meant our game?

It was then that I realised that I might not be the only one tormented by our childhood tragedy; that we needed to close the past.

And I thought of the second photograph, of my last year's summer trip with Jane, of Peter Bodrov's 'The war is imminent', and decided – what a perfect game that would be.

I never planned Levi's border arrest, or Jonty's beating – although if you watch the news, there are more MPs fist-fighting in various parliaments around the world than you would expect.

And there was another thing I didn't plan. I sent the letter about the meeting to Max as well as to Jonty and Levi to cover my tracks, just in case they asked: 'Have you sent the letter to Max too? You don't know then . . .' I didn't expect to see Alex again. It was her scent that caught me by surprise, the fact that I still remembered it all those years after our first kiss by the lake . . .

I was never relaxed with girls or women. I knew they would leave me eventually: my annually renewed nannies; Nadine, my French eco-warrior at university; Ruth, my straight-talking hardcore Australian . . . But it was Alex, my dreamcatcher, that I found it most difficult to communicate with. As if she could see through me completely, as if she could guess the grand goals, could read what I thought.

Everything about her was so strong: her willpower when she wanted to join us at the Tepee Councils, her voice when she sang, her hand . . . It was stronger than mine, her hand – holding me, guiding me that Easter when she came with Max to stay at our house. Max wandered off to the lake, and I was one stroke away from the line of her knickers, I could almost touch the cotton with my finger, when she whispered: 'Tell me something nice . . . something I will remember from this moment . . .'

I wanted to tell her that I loved her wildness and strength, that her beauty was so natural, that she smelled of freshness . . . But I had never paid any girl a compliment before, and I certainly couldn't think of one when she was guiding my hand up her thigh . . .

So I tried to think of something fresh and alluring, something breathtaking . . .

'You are . . . you are like Canada,' I said, feeling the heat of her thigh under my hand. 'I was in the Rockies last year, and that's a place where you understand that the people and the cities are just an addendum to nature.'

'What?' Alex opened her eyes and looked at me in disbelief. 'You idiot!' Then she started laughing, her head thrown back, the vein on her neck pulsing, her whole body trembling.

And that was it. Even though I really, really wanted to lean over and kiss her open, laughing mouth, to explore her more, I knew that the moment was gone. I had made a complete fool of myself.

Why, after that incident by the lake, did I think about the words I should have chosen for Alex countless times? Play in my mind dozens of word combinations, metaphors, phrases?

Was it just the failure I could not forgive myself for, or something else, something I couldn't explain?

In Odessa I stood close, too close to her. She had changed, become a tired woman with blue circles under her sad eyes, her briskness turned to edginess, but the scent was still the same, that sweet scent of a boy's first desire, and no soap, no perfume could overpower it.

Amazing how when I saw the boys, when I saw Alex, it

all came back – the pain, the guilt, the desire, nothing was in the past any more.

I am glad Alex came in to the game; thank God I had the envelope for Max with me at the first meeting, just in case the boys asked.

I don't know if they are going to be there today, whether they will talk to me again after Levi's road trip, Jonty's beating, Alex's night in Odessa.

We have arranged to meet upstairs, and I cannot see them when I come in, but I stop by the entrance. 'What the . . .'

Giant paper sunflowers hang from the ceiling, interspersed with balloons with the number 30 on; oilcloths in primary colours cover the tables. And the music, this familiar melody, this progression of chords: 'St Louis Blues . . .' Have they brought the CD with them?

'We have a retro evening tonight, to celebrate thirty years since our opening,' explains the waitress. 'The band is rehearsing – I hope you don't mind.'

I go upstairs and there they all are, in the same place where we started, the same table. We had to postpone the meeting for two weeks, to let Jonty recover – his massive bruise is yellow now, as if he has one-sided hepatitis B. But he is smiling at me, Jonty's proper old goofy smile, parading his newly crowned tooth.

'Do you remember the bubbles in the fountain?' he says by way of greeting. 'When we kept putting Fairy Liquid into the fountain every night and the air was filled with multicoloured bubbles . . .'

'And my stuff on the roof,' adds Levi. 'Do you remember that? When Jonty laid out all my clothes and books in perfect order. It was Parents Day, and my mother looked up and said to my father, "Misha, look, some idiot is drying his stripy underpants on the roof! How has he got them there? They look just like the blue underpants I packed for Levi."

'You were quite daring, Jonty, looking back. And as the parliament session shows, you are still quite fearless,' says Levi.

'You've done pretty well yourself,' replies Jonty. 'Let's go out for a drink to discuss your recent adventures, shall we?'

'And the "sax with the socks" performance,' I add, surprising myself. 'Do you remember that? When Jonty put his rugby socks into Max's saxophone, and Max was concerned that the sound was muted . . .'

'Even I remember that,' laughs Alex. 'It was before the Christmas charity concert, when I sang the "St Louis Blues". Amazing they are playing it now – I bet you've arranged this!'

'And that day when I decided to try the peanutting technique Jonty had taught me, yanking the long bit of his tie,' says Levi. 'I pulled with all my strength, but on the wrong end, and nearly killed him.' Then he adds, switching the subject suddenly, following his own Levi logic: 'It wasn't us.'

We all stop laughing and look at him, trying not to guess what he means.

'There was another reason for Norman's death,' continues Levi. 'He wouldn't have survived without insulin injections for four days; he would have slipped into a coma much earlier, within twenty-four hours – any first-year medical student will tell you that. The school must have been looking after him and he was injected by the matrons regularly but kept it secret, ashamed to admit that he had diabetes. The insulin and the needles in the bag were his safety blanket, as if he knew that he would never die as long as he had this medicine with him. It wasn't a lack of insulin, guys, it wasn't us – he must have died from sudden arrhythmic death syndrome. It's common in boys of seventeen, eighteen, when the heart's pacing during exercise causes it to stop. The diabetes didn't help, but it wasn't us,' he repeats for the third time. Then he adds: 'I did a paper in medical school on insulin deficiency, and another one on the risks and reasons for sudden deaths in teenage boys.'

I look at Levi, wondering why our maths genius decided to apply to medical school in the first place.

Music saves us for now as the invisible voice sings to us. We are still sitting together, but looking after our own separate silences: a silence of relief, a 'why didn't you tell us that earlier?' silence and the silence of 'what were my own reasons for playing to the end, really?'

In a minute, when the music stops, they'll ask me what's

next. But as I have nothing to tell them, I have to ask instead – anything to stop that silence.

'So, guys,' I say. 'What are your plans now?'

'I am going back to Odessa,' says Levi. 'They are about to open an HIV treatment centre – I'll go for three months, to set it up. No, the family is not going with me. Not for the moment, anyway.'

'I'll be moving house,' says Jonty. 'I've had enough of being a politician.

'I'll go back to journalism, write a political column, maybe for the *Guardian* . . . I have a lot to say.'

And that's when I know that I don't need to give them the envelopes with their notes written twenty-five years ago. 'Put your fears into the envelopes, gentlemen, and we'll come back to them when you are ready . . .'

*I am afraid that I'll be sent back to Odessa when they find out what I've done* – Levi's note, in neat, diligent handwriting.

*I am afraid that I'll have to speak in front of everybody at the assembly. Afraid that I'll be punished if I tell the truth* – Jonty's marching letters.

The notes will be shredded, just like their fears were. Game over. They will never know that I played on those fears all along: the fear of not belonging, of being laughed at for being different, of being punished for telling the truth. The usual schoolboy fears of grown-up men.

'It's such a shame that you're busy, guys,' I say. 'But Alex could come and visit me in Australia with the kids, stay for a couple of weeks or so – say, for the Christmas holidays?' I say, looking at Alex. 'It's waterside living at its best where I am, and my garden is a jungle for the kids to explore. I've got a mango tree, and even an old mulberry they could climb.

'Come and stay,' I say, trying not to think that to accommodate anybody in my house means a major clear-out operation.

Alex is looking up for some reason, at the brick arches above us. What has she seen there?

'My bank is going through restructuring,' she mutters. 'There are some voluntary redundancies flying around. I suppose I could take the redundancy money and think what to do next . . .' She still doesn't look at me. Is it a yes? I hope so.

I am not afraid that when she comes to Australia, she will discover that I am not a venture capitalist, but the headmaster of a busy school. That my house in Sydney doesn't have a view of the bay, and that a lot of my savings went into the game.

She probably doesn't know that I read history at university – my family has been always involved in making it, so I thought my father would be pleased if I decided to study it . . . but he wasn't.

I didn't do well at university – the whole course was blurred by substances, drowned in toxic fumes, lit by glittering disco balls. So I decided to escape from myself in

Australia for a year, to teach history at a school. That was twenty years ago . . . I have been a headmaster for nine years now.

One day I'll tell my pupils how different countries have dealt with history: how one brought together a whole committee to classify it as secret, the second locked it away in the glass sarcophagus of a museum display cabinet as the past not to be touched, while the third quietly hid it among millions of library volumes, following the principle that if they don't know about it, they won't find it . . .

Because that's where the British copy is from – the second floor of the British Library, Social Sciences reading room, Foreign Office treaties, third row . . .

I'll never let Alex, Jonty or Levi know – they might ask me why I sent them to Odessa and New York; wasn't the British copy enough for Jonty's speech?

But if they were to ask me, I've got the answer:

'When I said I wanted us to change the world, I didn't mean the whole world, I meant our own – that's where changes start, don't they?'

I hope Alex will come to Australia, I really do, because I am not ready yet to give her the one note I cannot shred – in Max's jumpy writing, the letters chasing one another: *I am afraid that when my sister finds out, she will turn away from me and forget me.*

And at the end of her stay, I might show her another

letter. The letter offering me the post of headmaster at our old school.

When they invited me for an interview in February, I was mildly surprised, even though my school in Australia is consistently in the top rankings, winning Distinguished Achiever awards, science and maths prizes.

I am confident I can do it, though, I know so much about adolescent boys now: about their need for a large audience when they defy authority, about safety in numbers, and about jealousy.

Amazing how fast news travels through the old boys' telegraph.

My father called me before I got the final offer: 'Well done, Antony. Glad to see you made it,' he said. 'We can have lunch more often during the school holidays' (I am not a schoolboy any more, Father!) 'now that I am retired (you still can't say 'now that you are coming back, Antony?' can you, Dad?).'

The job offer is sitting on my desk in Sydney, unanswered, tucked underneath other papers, under the photograph of the three leaders waiting for me to play the game. I am ready to come back to our school now, even though I'll have to walk past the bay windows of the maths class and past our mulberry, where other boys might be holding their Tepee Councils now. 'Mulberries are just like humans,' I'll tell those boys. 'If you touch them carelessly, the berries will collapse and the juice will seep out . . . Please remember that and take care.'

I have to give it another try with Alex; this is my only chance. 'The kids would love Australia,' I say to her. 'Probably as much as I love Canada.'

'Why Canada?' asks Levi. 'What's the connection?'

'Canada is an amazing country – strong, wild and natural – and I . . . I love it,' I say, looking straight at Alex.

She is now looking at me too, and her eyes are dark, moist, as if she has been drinking. Or crying, though I cannot imagine Alex crying.

She is sitting opposite me, squeezing one of my legs between her knees under the table. We are locked in a silent embrace of eyes and legs, her hands clutching the edge of the table, until Levi asks:

'So, what's next? Have you brought our old envelopes – you know, the ones we gave you at school?'

In the background, the singer echoes my thoughts about making my getaway.

'Let's have a break and then do this bit again,' says the singer on the balcony to the invisible saxophone player.

The music stops and so does time. I could tell Levi that I lost the envelopes with our old notes, that they were destroyed a long time ago, but there is another option I have just thought of.

'I'd better be going,' I say. 'I'll send you an email, Alex.'

She gives me one long look and I realise that she expects more, much more. So do I, but not here. We have a long way to go yet.

## The Game

We are leaving the place where we started, crowned (only the teeth) and unbeaten (well, I didn't mean it literally). And as I get up, I know that among the envelopes in my pocket is my own note too:

*I am afraid that my friends will not play the game any more and I'll have to let them go their own ways, without me.*

There is not much more to say – except one thing. We all know it's not going to happen, but I'll say it anyway. I nod to Alex, Jonty and Levi, trying to look cool and carefree: 'See you, guys . . .' I stop to compose myself, as my voice breaks treacherously and my eyes tingle, before adding the words they are all waiting for: 'Until the next game.'

# ACKNOWLEDGEMENTS

This book would have never happened without the journeys I had to make and people I was lucky to meet.

David and Shirley Rollitt, the Woollett boys of all ages, my son and stepson – thank you for guiding me through the country of teenage boys.

Valya Shvedova, Tanya Bukharina and Sergey Yurchenko – Crimea became brighter thanks to your help.

Valya Nizova, a guide extraordinaire, Mikhail Pozner, the connoisseur of vintage and modern Odessa life and true Odessites Inna and Jasha Mikhalevich – I was privileged to discover your Odessa.

Adrian Adlam, a wonderful musician – Sasha plays the violin concerto so well thanks to you.

I am grateful to those, who gave me shelter during this book's journey – Sarah Hosking, Fiona Coulter, Helen Butler, Quentin and Maggie Edwards.

A special heartfelt 'thank you' goes to Ina Reeves, one of the first female cab drivers in London, who helped me to create Joyce.

My intrepid readers, who braved the first draft – Judi Legon and Andrew Woollett – thank you for all your suggestions and comments.

And finally, I am truly grateful to my editor, Flora Rees, for all her help and patience.